Best in Show

Books by Laurien Berenson

A PEDIGREE TO DIE FOR

UNDERDOG

DOG EAT DOG

HAIR OF THE DOG

WATCHDOG

HUSH PUPPY

UNLEASHED

ONCE BITTEN

HOT DOG

BEST IN SHOW

Published by Kensington Publishing Corporation

Best in Show

A Melanie Travis Mystery

Laurien Berenson

KENSINGTON BOOKS
http://www.kensingtonbooks.com

This book is dedicated to the wonderful, hard-working members of the Poodle Club of America, whose efforts safeguard the Poodle breed and who, once a year in June, put on the greatest dog show there is.

Best in Show

1

There are those who say that life is a game of chance, and considering some of the things that have happened to me, I'd probably be inclined to agree. It wasn't serendipity, however, that took me to Maryland in mid-June to participate in the Poodle Club of America National Specialty dog show. Nor was it chance that volunteered me to work on the raffle committee. It was my Aunt Peg.

Margaret Turnbull is a formidable woman. Anyone who is involved in the dog show world will tell you that. Her Cedar Crest kennels have produced top winning Standard Poodles for three decades, nearly all of them owner-handled by Peg herself. Now in her sixties, she had cut down on the number of dogs she kept and recently added a judge's license to her already impressive arsenal of accomplishments. No one in the Poodle community would dare underestimate my Aunt Peg. Least of all me.

So when she told me that I'd been assigned to spend my week at the specialty show helping out Betty Jean and Edith Jean Boone, the cochairs of the raffle committee, I didn't argue. I didn't mention this was the first time that Sam Driver, my almost-fiancé, and I had had the opportunity to go away together and that we'd been hoping to carve out some time for just the two of us. I didn't point out that my seven-year-old son, Davey, love of my life, chaperone par excellence, had stayed behind with his father in Connecticut, leaving me free to do just as I wished for the first time since I'd become a single parent years earlier. I didn't even bring up the fact that I had my own Standard Poodle to show, which would certainly keep me busy.

No, I simply showed up at my appointed day and time, Monday morning, nine A.M., and waited to be put to work.

PCA is a huge undertaking, one of the largest specialty, or single breed, dog shows held in the country each year. All three varieties of Poodles—Standards, Miniatures, and Toys—are in competition. More than a thousand dogs and several times that many Poodle fanciers travel from all over the world to enjoy and take part in the spectacle.

Originally the national specialty was simply a conformation show, but over time it had grown to embrace and celebrate all the varied talents of the Poodle breed. The activities began on Saturday with a club sponsored field event, where Miniature and Standard Poodles could earn Working Certificates. On Monday, there was an agility trial. Tuesday, the Poodle Club of America Foundation hosted a morning of seminars and symposiums on topics of interest to serious breeders and exhibitors. In the afternoon, there was an obedience trial.

Wednesday, Thursday, and Friday, the arena was given over to the conformation classes. Even with three judges working almost continuously (one for each variety) it took that long for the enormous entry to be sorted through. Also included were a Parade of Champions and a veterans sweepstakes. Everything built toward Friday afternoon, when a fourth judge would choose among those Poodles that had been named top in their variety to find Best of Breed. The festivities concluded that evening with the PCA banquet.

It was an exhilarating, and often exhausting schedule. Not wanting to be away from Davey for too long, I'd skipped the field trial on Saturday, loaded my Poodle puppy in the car, and driven down to Maryland on Sunday afternoon. Aunt Peg was, of course, already in residence at the host hotel when I arrived. Sam would be coming down sometime Tuesday.

Monday morning, I presented myself at the equestrian center where the show was to take place. The enormous indoor arena was covered with turf; two big rings were landscaped with potted flowers and trees. One end of the ground-floor arena was reserved for grooming and preparation. The other two thirds contained the show rings and the tables devoted to the various show committees.

The trophy table had the best location, of course. Silver bowls and challenge trophies, several of them in competition for decades, glowed in the aura of the spotlights from above. When I had time, I loved to stop and look at those old trophies, tangible reminders of the history of the breed. I would run my fingers over their soft, shiny sides and trace the names of the past winners. Many were breed greats, dogs that I, a relative newcomer to the sport, knew only as pictures in the Poodle books.

That morning, however, time was something I didn't have. I'd brought a Standard Poodle to the specialty with me, a puppy named Eve whom I'd be showing later in the week. For the time being, until I'd found out what my duties were going to be, I'd left her resting in a crate in the grooming area. Unloading and getting the puppy settled had taken longer than I'd anticipated.

The raffle table was situated about halfway down the arena. I was almost there when someone stepped back out of the throng already congregating at ringside to watch the agility classes and blocked my path. Aunt Peg.

"You're late," she said.

"No, I'm not."

I had to look up to argue. Peg stands nearly six feet tall to my own five-six. It wasn't the height difference, however, that often made me feel like a recalcitrant child when

I was in her presence. It was Aunt Peg's unwavering belief that she was right in her opinions. That, and the fact that she usually was.

A black Standard Poodle bitch stood at Peg's side. Hope, litter sister to Eve's dam, was at the show to compete in agility. I reached down and gave her chin a scratch, hoping to buy some goodwill. It didn't work.

"Betty Jean and Edith Jean have already been here for nearly an hour," Aunt Peg said. I supposed that meant she'd been there for that long, too. "They've got the table all set up for the day."

"I checked the schedule. It said the agility trial started at nine."

"It does. But everything has to be in place and ready to go before the show opens. You'd better hurry up. I recommended you to the sisters, you know. I wouldn't want you to make a bad first impression." Her hands were already shooing me away. "The two of them are quite a couple of old characters. I'm sure you'll enjoy working with them."

Presumably because of my prior experience working with old characters. Wisely, I didn't voice the thought aloud.

The raffle table, as I saw when I reached it, was eight feet long, four feet wide, and stocked with all sorts of Poodle-related items. Donations received from various sponsors and club members ranged from gold and diamond jewelry to grooming supplies and a print of a *New Yorker* magazine cover from the fifties that featured a Miniature Poodle. There was a money tree covered in two-dollar bills, as well as such diverse articles as a lamp shade, a Christmas stocking, and tea towels, all decorated in a Poodle motif.

What, I thought, no Poodle skirt? I probably just hadn't seen it yet.

"You must be Melanie." A compact older woman with a lined face, tightly waved gray hair, and a ready smile, stepped out from behind the table and held out her hand. Her voice was softened by the lilting cadence of a southern drawl. "I'm Edith Jean. Sister and I have been waiting for you."

"Sorry I'm late." I grasped her hand. Her fingers, long and thin, felt surprisingly fragile. "I didn't realize things got started so early."

"Not to worry, you haven't missed a thing." Edith Jean turned and swatted at the colorful tablecloth that covered the table and fell to the floor. "Betty Jean, haul your butt out here and say hello to Melanie."

"Hold your horses," a voice grumbled from beneath the table. "I'm trying to find the tickets. They're not in the box you said they were in."

"Are, too," Edith Jean snapped, then sent me an apologetic smile. "You'll have to excuse Sister. Her eyes aren't what they used to be."

"I heard that. There's nothing wrong with my eyes, *or* my ears."

I leaned down and lifted the hem of the floor-length cloth. Half a dozen boxes were piled haphazardly beneath the table. I caught a glimpse of more gray curls, then Betty Jean lifted her head and looked in my direction. She had the same sharp blue eyes, narrow nose, and thin, pursed lips as her sister. In fact, they looked remarkably alike. Maybe it was a trick of the dim lighting. Or maybe Aunt Peg had neglected to mention that the sisters were twins.

"Anything I can do to help?" I asked.

"Not a damn thing." On her knees, Betty Jean began to inch backward. "Hold on a minute. Let me get out from under here so I can say hello properly."

"Didn't I just tell you to do that?" Edith Jean asked.

"Maybe you did, but I don't know who you think died and left you in charge." Betty Jean braced her hands heavily on her knees, pushed herself up, and gave me a smile. Like her sister, she was small and angular; bony, as though over time her skin had slowly deflated over the structure of her skeleton.

"I'm pleased to meet you. Peg says you're a worker, and if Peg Turnbull says you're okay, that's good enough for us. I'm Betty Jean. You can probably tell we're not from around here. North Georgia born and bred, Sister and I are. Our mama's name was Jean, and she wanted to make sure neither of her children ever forgot about her—"

"Now, Sister, we just met Melanie. She doesn't need to hear about all that."

"But you didn't even know our mama," Betty Jean continued, ignoring the interruption. "So if Betty Jean and Edith Jean seems like too much of a mouthful, you can just call us B.J and E.J. We'll answer to that right enough. Hell, we'll answer to just about anything."

"Speak for yourself," Edith Jean said. "You don't want to give Melanie the wrong impression. Not on the first day anyways."

The two women were like a pair of bickering bookends, bracketing the raffle table. As if their physical resemblance wasn't enough, they'd added to it by wearing the same hair-style and dressing similarly. Both had on denim skirts, red sweaters, and sturdy shoes.

"Are you twins?" I asked.

Betty Jean cackled in reply. "Did you hear that, Sister? She wants to know if you're as old as I am."

"Of course I heard her. I'm standing right here, aren't I?"

"Can't tell us apart, can you?" Betty Jean sounded pleased. "Happens all the time. I'm the older, though, by eleven months. Nearly a year. I guess I must look pretty good for my age."

"You do," I said quickly. The threat of hot coals wouldn't induce me to ask what that age was. On my other side, Edith Jean snorted loudly. I took that as my cue. "And you look great, too."

"Little late now to go sucking up, don't you think?"

"That depends," I said. "Is sucking up going to be required?"

Edith Jean laughed, a dry rasping cackle that sounded as though it might have been influenced by years of smoking. "Peg was right about you, Melanie. She said you'd fit right in."

E.J. and B.J. spent the next few minutes describing my duties. They didn't sound too arduous, especially as all the advance work had already been done. The sisters had contacted past patrons and secured this year's donations. Now all that remained was to keep a watchful eye on the bounty on the table, sell lots of tickets, and hold the drawing late Friday afternoon right before the judging for Best in Show. Simple.

"You're going to be what we call our roving raffle lady," Edith Jean explained. "Sister and I take our places here at the table. If anyone wants to buy tickets or see what the prizes are, they can come and talk to us."

"But that still leaves a whole bunch of potential sales unmined," Betty Jean said when her sister paused to draw a breath. "What about the people who are busy grooming in the handlers' area? Or the spectators who'd be happy to support the club and take a chance on winning something fabulous but they're watching the action in the ring and never bother to make their way over here?"

"That's where you come in." This was E.J. again. Their tag-team style of conversation was beginning to make me dizzy. "Not everyone takes the time to come to us, so you're going to go to them. Sister and I will outfit you with a basket to carry around. You'll have tickets to sell and money to make change. All you have to do to make the raffle a success is convince every single person at the show to take a dozen tickets."

All I had to do . . . ?

"Now, Sister." B.J. reached over and poked the other

woman in the shoulder. "Don't go scaring her off already. Talk like that and we may never see Melanie again. She'll grab that basket and go running for the hills."

"No, I—"

"Don't worry, you'll do just fine." Edith Jean's voice dropped to a whisper. "Last year, there was one morning when Betty Jean managed to misplace a whole hunk of money and some raffle tickets too, and we still ended up coming out ahead."

"I did not!" B.J. squawked.

"Did too!"

"Umm, ladies?" I was beginning to get the impression that the sisters' squabbling was going to form the backdrop for my entire PCA experience. "Don't worry about a thing. I'm sure I'll be able to sell plenty of tickets." Even if I had to coerce Aunt Peg into taking them by the roll for getting me into this.

"See? I told you—"

"What are you talking about? I'm the one who said . . ."

Tuning them out, I let my gaze wander over the spectators around the ring. Even this early in the week, the agility trial had drawn a good sized crowd. By the time the conformation classes started on Wednesday, the arena would be filled with hundreds of potential ticket buyers, all of them fans of Poodles and friend of PCA. With any luck, getting them to lend their support to the raffle would be a breeze.

As I waited for the sisters to stop arguing and remember that they had yet to show me where the basket was, my skin began to tingle with the sudden awareness that I was being watched. Slowly I rescanned the crowd. Most people were facing the other way, intent on the Novice Class taking place in the ring.

One man wasn't. Hands jammed in his pockets, a pugnacious scowl on his face, he was staring. Not at me, I realized abruptly, but past me at Betty Jean and Edith Jean.

With his sturdy build and shiny black hair, he reminded me of a Rottweiler. A very unhappy Rottweiler. I didn't know who he was, and yet there was something familiar about him. The dog show world is not a large one; the Poodle community, smaller still. Perhaps I'd seen him at other shows, or past PCAs, or maybe in one of the dog magazines.

I leaned over and gave the closest sister a nudge. "Who's that man? The one who's standing over there, glaring at us?"

As one, the sisters turned and had a look. "Oh, that's just Harry Gandolf," said Betty Jean.

As soon as she said the name, I was able to place him. Harry was a prominent Midwest professional handler. I'd seen his picture in dozens of ads in *Dog Scene* and *Dogs in Review.*

"He looks fit to be tied, doesn't he?" Edith Jean lifted a hand and sent a jaunty wave in Harry's direction. "Don't you mind him at all. He's not mad at you. Betty Jean's the person he wants to kill."

2

"**W**hy?"

So help me, the question just popped out. A reflex response. It's not as if I needed to know. Over the past several years, I seem to have developed a reputation as a solver of mysteries. I'm not quite sure how this came about. I don't go looking for problems, and, yet, somehow they have a way of inevitably finding me.

Looking at those two little old ladies, however, it was hard to take talk of death threats seriously. I couldn't imagine someone actually wanting to do them harm. On the other hand, even on such short acquaintance, I could easily imagine them coming up with some sort of diabolical tall tale. No doubt they'd argue over every single detail, too.

"Can't tell you," B.J. whispered. "It's a secret."

"A really big secret," E.J. echoed.

Yeah, right. If I thought somebody wanted to kill me, I'd be telling everyone about it. You know, just in case.

Betty Jean leaned down and retrieved something from behind the raffle table. "Much as we love talking to you, dear, it's time to get to work. Here's your basket, all ready to go. I think you'll find it has everything you need."

The wicker container she handed me looked like something Little Red Riding Hood might have carried to visit

Grandma. Or the Brady Bunch might have taken on a family picnic. With the ribbon-bedecked handle slipped over my arm, the body of the basket bumped against my knees.

I did a quick inventory and found several rolls of tickets, fifty dollars in various bills for making change, half a dozen pens, and a list of the more than forty prizes the raffle offered.

"Don't forget," E.J. said. "It's very important to make sure everyone fills out the back of their tickets with name and telephone number. That way, they don't have to be present to win."

"You'll sell more tickets if you remind people of that," B.J. chimed in. "It helps if they know they don't have to hang around all week until the very end."

Judging by the PCAs I'd been to in the past, hanging around until the very end seemed to be the whole point. Although perhaps the agility and obedience people whose trials took place early in the week wouldn't feel that way.

"Got it," I said. "See you later."

My first stop was the grooming area where I checked on my puppy. Though I actually owned two Standard Poodles, I'd only brought one to Maryland with me. Faith, Eve's dam, was the older of the pair and the one I'd regretfully left behind. On a trip such as this where she wasn't entered in the show, she would have ended up spending most of her time in a crate. Not only would she be happier in Connecticut with Davey, but she could also keep an eye on him for me. I never doubted for a minute that she would be up to the task.

Standard Poodles are the largest of the three varieties. Faith was big, and black, and beautiful, and possessed a vibrant personality. Eve, who was waiting for me in the grooming area, shared many of her dam's characteristics, among them, intelligence, exuberance, and a sense of humor guaranteed to keep her owner on her toes.

Eve was the more thoughtful of the two, however, and

the more sensitive. Whereas Faith rushed headlong into any situation, her daughter was more likely to hang back and to consider the options. That streak of maturity had stood her in good stead in the show ring. Registered as Elysian Eve with the American Kennel Club, the puppy was eleven months old and already in possession of seven of the fifteen points required to attain her championship. I planned to show her in the 9 to 12 Month Puppy Bitch class that would be held Thursday morning.

With competition as fierce as this would be—thirty-six puppies from all over the country were entered in Eve's class—I wasn't planning on winning. All I wanted was for my puppy to show well and make a good impression on the knowledgeable spectators standing ringside. With luck, we might even make the cut.

As I'd expected, my puppy was fine. Accustomed to the bustle of a busy show, Eve was snoozing happily in her crate. I left her and headed back to the agility ring where I found that Aunt Peg had barely moved since I'd seen her last.

She was keeping one eye on the action in the Novice class and the other on the wide grassy aisle that ran along the ring. PCA was a great gathering place. Breeders from various parts of the country who only saw each other once a year, spent the entire week catching up. Though the Poodles were, of course, paramount to the PCA experience, socializing ran a close second.

"I see the sisters put you right to work," Peg said as I drew near. "Made much money for the club yet?"

My aunt has been a member of the PCA for decades. More recently, she'd also been one of the founders of the Poodle Club of America Foundation, a philanthropic organization whose purpose was to raise money for dog related research and charities. Peg was all in favor of anything that supported her favorite cause.

"I'm just getting started. You're my first victim." I lifted out the heavy roll of tickets and began to unspool a long stream. "They're a dollar apiece or twelve for ten dollars. How many would you like?"

"One dozen ought to do for a start."

I handed her a pen and lowered the basket to the floor between my feet. Aunt Peg counted out and ripped off the tickets. She started at one end and I took the other, writing her name and phone number on the back of each stub.

"What do you think of the Boone sisters?" she asked as we wrote. "Aren't they a hoot?"

"A hoot and a holler." I resisted the temptation to drawl. "Please tell me they don't always dress alike."

Aunt Peg scribbled away busily. "To tell the truth, I haven't any idea. The only time I ever see them is here at PCA. I'm not sure anyone from the club knows them really well. They live in some remote, rural area of the Georgia mountains. And of course, Georgia doesn't even have its own affiliate club."

Affiliate clubs were local Poodle clubs, serving states and major metropolitan areas. They were satellites to PCA's hub, and the fact that Georgia lacked one was a major omission in Aunt Peg's eyes.

"The sisters have had Toy Poodles for nearly as long as I've been in Standards, though they haven't done any showing to speak of in years. I didn't even realize they were still breeding until Edith Jean e-mailed me looking for volunteers and mentioned they had a new puppy who would be making his debut this spring. I saw him on one of the southern circuits and he was cleaning up. Roger Carew handles the puppy for them."

"Funny, they didn't mention him to me." Dog people usually lead with news about their canines, a subject that they find endlessly fascinating, and are quite certain everyone else does too.

"I'm sure they will when they get a chance." Peg finished the last of the tickets, balled up the long strand, and shoved it in her pocket. "The sisters probably wanted to start things off right by getting straight to work. Considering how little interaction they have with the rest of the club during the rest of the year, the board is very grateful that the two of them take the time to run the raffle for us every spring. It's not a small undertaking, you know."

"I'm beginning to get that impression."

Peg searched my face for signs of sarcasm. That she found none was testimony to the fact that my acting skills are improving. I picked up my basket and prepared to move on. "Any tips for telling them apart?"

"Just do what I do. If you're talking to one and you're not sure which, just call her Sister. In case you haven't noticed, they'll both answer to it."

As soon as I stepped away from my aunt, another spectator saw my basket and motioned me over. "Whatever you're selling, I'll take some," she said.

"Raffle tickets," I replied brightly. "Would you like to hear about our terrific prizes?"

"Not really."

Monday morning, opening hour of the greatest Poodle show on earth, most of the participants were giddy with excitement and enthusiasm. This spectator, an attractive woman who looked about my age—early thirties—but sported a much better haircut and manicure, already seemed bored. I hated to think how she'd be feeling by week's end.

She fished around in a Kate Spade bag and came up with a twenty-dollar bill. "What do I need to do?"

"Just fill out your name and phone number on the back of the stubs. The raffle will be held Friday afternoon before Best in Show. Will you still be here then?"

"I expect so." She took the pen I offered and began to sign her name in an elegant script. Nina Gold, I read as she tore the first one off and handed it to me.

"Are you showing a Poodle or just here to enjoy the show?"

"My husband has some dogs entered. Christian Gold?" She said the name as though she expected me to be familiar with it. One perfectly plucked eyebrow lifted. "Golden-Dune kennel?"

"Sorry, I haven't been showing all that long. I don't know everybody yet."

"That's all right." She smiled briefly as she ripped off the last stub and tossed it in the basket. "I imagine I wouldn't recognize your name either."

The offhand comment sounded vaguely insulting. I decided to overlook it. "Melanie Travis," I said. "I have Standards. I'll be showing in the breed classes."

Nina looked just as bored by that information as she had by the agility trial taking place in the ring. "Christian has Minis. With any luck, he'll win the variety. Dale Atherton handles for us."

That name I recognized. Like Harry Gandolf, Dale Atherton was a well-known professional handler. Ads featuring his winning Poodles graced the covers and pages of all the dog magazines.

"You must be from the West Coast."

"Marin. We flew in last night. Christian was anxious to get right over here and see how his dogs were doing, but it doesn't look as though Dale's arrived yet."

"Exhibitors and handlers aren't allowed to come in and set up today," I said. "There's a rather strict protocol, and the grooming area doesn't officially open until tomorrow morning."

"I could have sworn Dale said—" A small frown creased Nina's brow, then she stopped and shook her head. "Never mind. It isn't important. I'm sure we'll see him back at the hotel."

I thanked her for her business and prepared to move on, but a group of breeders from Maryland flagged me

down before I'd gone two steps. Six women who'd partici-
pated in the raffle in previous years, knew the quality of
the prizes offered, and were all eager to lend their support
to the club. I passed out tickets and pens, and made
change. Selling raffle tickets in this crowd was easier than
giving away beads at Mardi Gras.

By eleven o'clock, I'd only covered half the arena, but
I'd already sold all the tickets the sisters had supplied me
with. My basket was jammed with stubs and cash. I headed
back to the raffle table to restock.

The sisters, standing side by side behind the table,
beamed at me as I approached. "We're doing a bang-up
business," one said. "How about you?"

"The same." I held out the basket for their inspection.
"I need more tickets. I sold all the ones you gave me."

"Well done!" The sister nearest me—Betty Jean, I
thought—reached beneath the table and withdrew a cash
box. It was, I saw when she opened it, much fuller than it
had been when I'd left. "Let me help you unpack."

"Thanks, B . . . er, E . . . J?" I felt myself flush.

"B.J.," she corrected with a smile. "Had it right the first
time. Not to worry, Sister and I are used to that. Let me
give you a little tip." She leaned forward and a small gold
locket, worn tucked inside her sweater, caught the light
briefly before disappearing again. "Sister and I always
stand behind the table the same way. She'll be on your left
as you approach, I'll be to the right. We never switch
sides."

"How come?"

Betty Jean shot a quick glance up at her sister who was
busy showing off the money tree to a potential customer.
"I'm left-handed, you see. Sister is right-handed. If we
both put our good sides in the middle, we'd just keep
bumping into one another. So this way works out better."

B.J. grinned wickedly. "Whatever you do, don't let on
that I told you. I think she likes all the confusion."

I'd be willing to bet they both enjoyed the confusion. Why did they dress so similarly otherwise?

"What are you two whispering about over there?" Edith Jean came up behind us. "Not planning to take the money and run, are you?"

"Not today." There were new rolls of tickets in the lock box. I got out another and added it to my supplies in the basket. "Maybe tomorrow when there's more here."

"Can't leave before Wednesday," E.J. said. "That's when our boy is showing. Puppy Dogs, 9 to 12. You'll be guarding the table." Her index finger poked me between the shoulder blades. "Sister and I will be hiding somewhere over by the ring, cheering like a couple of silly old fools."

"Tell me about your puppy," I invited. "I've heard he's a good one."

"Bubba's going to win his puppy class," Betty Jean confided. "He'll be the best one there."

"At least *we* think he is. Others"—Edith Jean scowled briefly—"may have another opinion."

"As if that matters a fig. The only opinion that counts belongs to the judge. He loved Bubba's sire, and our puppy's his father's spitting image. When Roger walks into the ring, Mr. Mancini will think he's seeing a ghost."

"That judge loves a good silver. You can mark your catalog right now. Look for BoonesFarm Bubba-licious and put a one right next to his name. Roger thinks Bubba might even have a shot at Winners Dog."

Edith Jean ducked down briefly beneath the table and came up with pictures. Eight-by-ten color glossies in a familiar white cardboard envelope, they were win photos from the puppy's successes on the Cherry Blossom circuit. I thumbed through them, while both sisters supplied commentary on each win. The little Toy had done his owners proud. Not only had he been Winner Dog five times, he'd even racked up two Best of Variety wins and a group placement.

"How many points does he have?" I asked.

"Shhh!" Edith Jean held a finger up to her lips. "We don't talk about that."

"Fourteen," Betty Jean said firmly. Her voice was loud enough to override her sister's and her tone allowed for no argument.

"I see." It sounded as though the sisters had run into a common problem. Judging by their demeanor, someone—probably their handler, Roger Carew—had gotten over-zealous in planning little Bubba's career. The silver Toy had done extremely well on the spring circuit, perhaps too well.

In order to achieve a championship, a dog must accumulate a total of fifteen points under at least three different judges. Points are earned by beating same-sex competition in the classes. At a specialty show like this one, those classes would be Puppy, 6 to 9 Months old, Puppy 9 to 12 Months old, Dog (or Bitch) 12 to 18 Months, Novice, Bred by Exhibitor, American-Bred, and Open. Once the individual classes have been judged, the class winners return to the ring to compete for the award of Winners Dog or Winners Bitch.

These are the only two who receive points, and the number of points awarded varies from one to five, based on the amount of competition. A win of three, four, or five points is referred to as a major win, and two are required (under two different judges) before a dog can secure the title of champion. Some dogs chase the points needed to attain their championships for a year or two. Others, like Bubba, race through a serendipitous circuit of shows and seem to fulfill the requirements almost overnight.

Under normal circumstances such success, especially with a young puppy, would be considered a blessing. However, when exhibitors are calculating the chances of their dogs securing a coveted BIG WIN at the national specialty, normal is a concept that flies right out the window.

At PCA a puppy like Bubba would be a standout in his age-restricted class. He'd have a good shot at taking the prestigious blue and perhaps even, as the sisters hoped, going on to Winners Dog or maybe Best Toy Puppy. If, however, he had already finished his championship, Bubba would have to be entered not in the classes, but in the much more rigorous Best of Variety competition.

There he'd be up against more than forty of the top Toy Poodle champions from all over the world. There, a cute silver puppy like Bubba would, most likely, get lost in the shuffle.

Hence the confusion regarding Bubba's point total. My guess was that Roger Carew had forgotten to keep count and that the puppy had finished several weeks earlier. No doubt Bubba had been keeping a low profile ever since, biding his time and awaiting his chance to sparkle in the puppy class at PCA.

Other exhibitors might grumble but there wasn't much that could be done to prevent such subterfuge. Truth be told, many had done such a thing themselves. Those who hadn't had probably been guilty of other, similar white lies, such as fudging a puppy's birth date to keep it eligible for the puppy classes beyond a year of age, or dyeing a Poodle's coat to enhance its color.

When the stakes were high enough, anything could happen. And for Poodle lovers, PCA was the biggest game around.

3

After lunch I got Eve out of her crate and took her for a walk around the equestrian center. The area surrounding the outdoor riding rings was beginning to fill up with big rigs: handlers, and exhibitors from around the country who had found that the easiest way to transport large numbers of dogs in comfort was to pack them into a motor home. Eve tugged at the end of her leash, eager to go exploring. At home, I would have turned her loose to run a little, but PCA had very strict rules about dog control at the specialty. Exercising off-lead at the equestrian center was grounds for expulsion from the show.

"Well, well, well, look who's here."

I turned at the sound of the familiar voice. Terry Denunzio, one of my favorite dog show people, was reclining in a lounge chair set up beside one of the motor homes. The words "Bedford Kennels" were stenciled discreetly on the cab's door, identifying the rig as belonging to Crawford Langley, the top professional handler in the Northeast. Terry was his partner and assistant.

Many of the handlers who came to PCA, I saw just once or twice a year. I knew them only by reputation, or from their pictures in the magazines. But Crawford and Terry, who lived half an hour away from my home in Connecticut and showed at most of the same shows I did, were friends.

Terry, by virtue of being one of the best-looking men I had ever seen, was, of course, gay. His hair, newly darkened to follow some fashion trend that I was oblivious to, was crisply styled. His face bore the beginning of a spring tan. He wore a brightly colored Hawaiian shirt, open at the throat, and a pair of khaki shorts brief enough to make most men blush.

Not Terry, though. He was charmingly incorrigible, both the bane and the blessing of Crawford's much more dignified existence. Terry folded away a piece of cardboard he'd been holding and patted the recliner beside him.

"Come, sit," he said. "Tell me the news."

The motor home's awning was unfurled to shade two, now empty, exercise pens. Both held bowls of water. Eve helped herself to a drink and lay down in the shade. I joined Terry in the sun, perching on the edge of the chaise.

"What news?"

"I don't know, anything. " His grin was cheeky. Terry loved gossip. "Whatever's new and exciting."

"For starters, you're going to give yourself skin cancer." I reached over his legs and retrieved the board he'd dropped. Unfolding it, I found what I'd suspected. "A sun reflector? Don't you know these things went out in the seventies?"

"Oh, please. Don't tell me you actually thought that horrid, pallid, stringy-haired, heroin chic look was going to last? Golden is good. Do I have to teach you *everything*?"

"Maybe." A woman could do worse than to get her beauty tips from Terry. As it was, the man already cut my hair. And did a great job of it, too. "What are you guys doing here so early in the week? Has Crawford developed an interest in agility?"

"Hardly. The PCA board met yesterday. Crawford's a member, so he had to be here. It didn't make sense for us to drive down separately, so we just packed up the dogs a couple of days early and came on down. Which means that I have two days off to loll around and have fun in the sun." He stretched back out on the lounge chair and turned his young, unlined face back up into the warm rays.

"I have to admit, Terry, you're one of the best lollers I've ever met."

"If you're trying to insult me, doll, you'll have to try harder than that." He opened one eye. "However, I think you got that sentence slightly wrong. What you actually meant to say is that I'm one of the best-*looking* lollers you've ever met."

The man had absolutely no shame.

"So what about you and the canine companion?" His hand waved carelessly in Eve's general direction. "Bitches don't show until Thursday. What brought you down to Maryland so early in the week? Here's an educated guess. I'll bet your aunt roped you into helping out on some god-forsaken committee."

"Am I that predictable?"

"Not you, Peg. That woman would have the queen of England breeding Poodles instead of those ridiculous Dorgis if only she could get her on the phone. So what does she have you doing? Banquet? Trophies? Hospitality?"

"Raffle," I admitted. "I spent the morning selling tickets."

"Ahhh. You're working for the Doublemint twins."

"Yes, except they're not twins."

"Could have fooled me. Maybe it's a southern thing. You know, after so many generations of marrying their own cousins, everyone begins to look alike?"

I swatted him on his flat stomach. Terry barely flinched. "You're terrible!"

"Of course I'm terrible. It's one of the things you like

best about me. That and the fact that every time you get yourself into a jam, I wheedle some sort of information out of Crawford and ride to your rescue."

"You have *never* rescued me."

"In my dreams, doll. In my dreams."

Yeah, right.

"Flirting with me does you no good," I pointed out. "In case you haven't noticed, I'm the wrong sex."

"My God!" Terry lifted a hand to his mouth and feigned shock. "Is that what it is? I knew there was something—"

"Oh, shut up." I was sorely tempted to hit him again.

"I'd be delighted to, except that would leave you doing all the talking and so far you haven't said much of anything. Come on, the show's been open a whole half a day. So what have we learned? What's new and delicious?"

Well, now that he mentioned it, not a whole lot. I thought for a minute. "Betty Jean and Edith Jean have a silver Toy puppy that they're very excited about—"

"Betty Jean and Edith Jean?" Terry sat up. "Tell me those aren't their names."

"Don't make fun. Their mother's name was Jean."

"I would never have guessed." Sarcasm 101. "I guess we should be glad she wasn't called Maybelline or Magnolia—"

"Nobody—I don't care where they're from—names a child Magnolia."

"I think you need to get out more."

Quite possibly. "Back to the puppy. Bubba—"

"No!" Terry snorted in disbelief. Obviously I was nothing more than a continuing source of amusement.

"*Bubba?*" Laughing, he rolled back and forth on the chaise. In a minute, he was going to roll right off. In a minute, I might be tempted to help him. "This is too good to be true. They actually have a Toy named Bubba?"

"That's what I'm trying to tell you. He's very cute, I saw

his pictures. He's supposed to win his class. Maybe even Winners Dog."

"Possibly." Terry stopped laughing and began to pay attention. "Though not if Harry Gandolf has anything to say about it. Scuttlebutt I've heard is that his Toy dog is the one to beat."

Making preshow predictions was a long-standing tradition among knowledgeable exhibitors. They were usually based half on good PR—make everyone think your dog is going to be the winner, and he's that much closer to being there—and half on an educated guess that took into account the judge's preferences as well as the dog's record and his strengths and weaknesses. Throw in a dash of intuition to round things out, and it was amazing how often the scuttlebutt turned out to be right.

"I guess Wednesday's judging will be interesting, then. I can't help rooting for the sisters, though. They seem like nice ladies."

"When they're not sniping at one another," said Terry. "Either one alone could just about talk your ear off. Together, they're enough to drive you half mad. Besides, they had the bad taste to name that poor innocent puppy Bubba. No, I think I'll put my money on Harry."

The sound of a horn, loud and shrill, made us both turn around and look. The noise was coming from the far end of the arena building, where a wide ramp led down to the unloading area. The exhibitors who were showing in agility had long since finished setting up and moved their cars over to the parking lot. A few who had gotten done early were leaving, but there hadn't been a line on the ramp when Eve and I came out.

The horn blared again.

"What do you suppose that's about?" I asked.

Terry was already getting up. "Let's go see."

Eve was on her feet as well, anxious to get moving. I

snagged her leash and hurried after Terry who was striding toward the arena. Meanwhile, the horn continued to
honk. Even from the other side of the building, the sound
made my head pound. Eve had her ears flattened to her
head. Inside, the noise must have been deafening.

Terry walked around the arena, but I went directly into
one of the side doors that led to the upper seating levels.
From there, I walked Eve down the stairs and out into the
turf-covered ground floor. Some sort of fracas was going
on in the grooming area. Though the agility trial was still
in progress, most of the spectators around the ring were
looking instead at the end of the arena where a big garage
door opened out onto the unloading ramp.

Thankfully, the honking had stopped. As I took Eve
back to her crate, the cluster of people who'd been standing in the doorway, arguing, began to disperse. I recognized most of them at a glance as they included several
PCA board members and an equal number of committee
heads. Not surprisingly, Aunt Peg was among them.

One person I didn't recognize was the man who went
stamping out of the building. He climbed into a truck that
was parked at the base of the ramp and gunned the engine several times, leaving a thick cloud of exhaust behind
as he drove away. I tucked the puppy back in her crate and
flagged down Aunt Peg as she came by.

"What was that all about?"

Peg rolled her eyes toward the heavens. "Damien Bradley,"
she intoned as though the name alone should have been
explanation enough.

It wasn't, at least not for me. Aunt Peg kept on walking.
Since I didn't have anywhere I needed to be in the imme-
diate future, I tagged along after her. "Who's he?"

"A professional handler, and I use the term loosely, from
Ohio. You've heard me talk about him."

Had I? I didn't remember.

"In what context?"

Aunt Peg stopped abruptly, "Melanie, don't you pay the slightest bit of attention when I talk to you?"

"Usually." Whatever had caused Aunt Peg's snit, I was pretty sure it wasn't me. After all, with the number of tickets I'd sold that morning, I was the fair-haired girl of the raffle committee. Quickly I sorted through other options.

"How did Hope do in agility?" I asked.

"That's not a subject we're currently discussing."

Bingo.

"Miss an obstacle?"

"Missing it would have been preferable." For a moment, I thought she wasn't going to continue. Finally Aunt Peg said, "Hope went in one end of the tunnel and didn't come out the other. Sat down somewhere in the middle, I expect. Heaven knows what she thought she was doing. Taking a nap, while the clock continued to tick away. I nearly had to crawl in and retrieve her."

Hope, like her litter sister, Faith, had a wicked sense of humor. I could well imagine the Poodle having a little fun at Peg's expense. Most dogs liked to get through the tunnel as quickly as possible. On the other hand, few are as adept at playing jokes as Poodles are. My aunt is not a small woman; the thought of her six-foot body trying to fold itself down and fit into the tunnel entrance was enough to bring a smile.

"Don't," Aunt Peg warned.

The smile vanished. "Damien Bradley?" I said instead.

"Yet another annoyance in an already trying day."

"Oh, pish." It's one of Aunt Peg's favorite expressions. Somehow I seem to have started using it myself. "You love PCA. You *always* love PCA. You look forward to it for months. You're sorry when it's over."

"And while it's going on I work like a slave for a week straight to make absolutely sure that nothing goes wrong," she grumbled.

"But still . . ."

Aunt Peg sighed. "You're right, I love it. I love every blessed minute. Even the impossible ones, which would be any that include Damien Bradley."

"What was his problem?"

"His problem is, was, and always will be that he thinks he's the most important person on the face of the earth. The club makes rules for a reason, usually to make everyone's life a little easier. But Damien thinks they shouldn't apply to him."

"He wanted to unload his dogs," I guessed.

"Of course, he wanted to unload his dogs. When he knows full well that the setup time for breed exhibitors doesn't start until tomorrow morning, eleven A.M. Numbers are preassigned through the mail, and members of the grounds committee are on hand to make sure that all the handlers, big and small, get the space they need. It's the only way to ensure that everything goes smoothly."

"And yet Damien thought the club would make an exception for him?"

"Apparently so. Which is nothing short of astounding when you realize that he was the cause of our being kicked out of our last headquarters hotel."

Finding hotels that will allow large numbers of dog fanciers to use their facilities has become a nightmare for show-giving clubs everywhere. It's not the hotels' fault. Over the years, dog owners have earned themselves an often justified reputation as slobs and miscreants, leaving soiled rugs, chewed furniture, and flea infestations in their wake. No wonder that most hotels, faced with the prospect of housing such problem guests, simply refuse to take dogs at all.

Bearing this in mind, PCA's hotel coordinator works year round to ensure that hosting our large contingent of Poodle owners is a pleasant experience for all concerned. Participants are warned not to let their dogs bark excessively. No grooming is permitted in the hotel rooms; instead, the club rents a conference room within the hotel where exhibitors can work on their dogs. Areas where Poodles may be exercised outside are very strictly marked. Pooper-scoopers and garbage cans are lined up in readiness and all owners are expected to pick up after their dogs. Club members patrol all common areas—inside and out—cleaning and straightening as needed to make sure that our week-long stay is a happy one.

Even with all those precautions, I knew that the club had switched host hotels recently. What I didn't know was why. "What did Damien do?"

"What didn't he do? There were complaints from other guests from the moment he arrived. Crates jammed cheek by jowl into his room, dogs barking at all hours of the night. I gather he took it upon himself to dye several Poodles black in his bathtub. At least part of the resulting mess was apparently wiped up with a bedspread.

"But the final straw was when it came time to leave. In order to facilitate loading up, he backed his truck across the hotel lawn and parked it outside the door to his room. As for the door itself, he removed that from its hinges and set it aside. Somehow it was either lost or broken in the process. Who knows, maybe he took it home with him for a souvenir. Somewhat understandably, the hotel asked us not to return. We, in turn, were tempted to ask Damien not to return, but of course we have no control over who makes entries and who doesn't."

"So here he is again," I said. "Even a day early, wouldn't you rather have his dogs unloaded here than back at the hotel?"

"If we make an exception for Damien," Aunt Peg replied, "what will we tell the next person who asks us to do the same? Besides, Damien can't take his dogs back to the hotel. We tipped off the management. Heaven knows where he's staying, but it's not with the rest of the club. We can't afford to let one bad apple ruin things for us again. That's why he was so anxious to bring the dogs in here. He said he had no other place to put them until tomorrow."

"Why did he come a day early then?"

"Why, indeed? I've long since stopped trying to figure out how his mind works."

"I guess he'll think of something."

"Either that, or he'll circle around and try to bully his way inside again later." Aunt Peg sighed. "Where Damien Bradley is concerned, I'm sorry to say I wouldn't put anything past him."

4

I devoted the remainder of the afternoon to watching the agility trial and selling more raffle tickets. At times it seemed as though I could hardly hand them out fast enough. Of course, I reminded myself, it was easy to be successful on day one when everyone had just arrived, was eager to join in the club sponsored activities, and had money to spend. Later in the week, my job was going to become much tougher.

The sisters expressed no such qualms, however, when I turned in my basket late that afternoon. They were delighted with the first day's total, highest in the raffle's history, B.J. announced.

"Wait until the board hears," she said. "They'll be thrilled."

"It's a good omen," Edith Jean added happily. "This is going to be our show."

As the agility trial drew to a close, the sisters began to pack up for the night. The most valuable items would go back to their hotel room with them. Other things were placed in boxes beneath the table. The remainder would simply stay where they were, covered by a sheet. They assured me that they had the job well in hand, so I retrieved Eve from her crate and she and I headed back to the headquarters hotel.

There, I found nearly as much activity going on as there

had been at the show site. Dozens of PCA participants were arriving each hour. Some were entered in the obedience trial on Tuesday. Others were planning to attend the PCA Foundation Seminar to be held the next day at the hotel.

The seminar was a PCA tradition, consisting of a daylong program of panels and symposiums on topics of interest to serious Poodle fanciers. Past programs had discussed such diverse issues as genetic research, strategies for better breeding, and Poodle rescue. The seminar was always widely attended and I had no doubt that its success was at least partly due to the fact that Aunt Peg was the person in charge of selecting the speakers.

Before going up to my room, I took Eve around the back of the hotel to the wide grassy area that had been designated for the club's use. After a day of virtual confinement, I could finally take off the puppy's leash and let her run free. I'd already stuffed several Baggies in my pocket, prepared to clean up, should the need arise.

Some lucky exhibitors had ground-floor rooms that opened out directly onto the exercise area. Many had set up portable pens around the perimeter. Everywhere I looked I saw Poodles playing in the grass: big ones, little ones, Poodles of all ages and colors. The meadow was a Poodle lover's dream come true.

I would have been happy to hang around outside and socialize except that now that I'd been gone for a day I wanted to call and check on Davey. This was the first time in his seven and half years that he and I had been separated for any length of time. Considering that I'd spent the majority of his life acting as a single parent, this unaccustomed freedom took some getting used to.

Oh, let's be honest. I wasn't sure I liked it at all.

When I'd originally made arrangements to come to PCA, I'd planned to bring Davey with me as I had in previous years. The difference this time was that in the interim,

Davey's father, Bob, had relocated back to Connecticut. Had moved, in fact, to a house no more than a mile or two from our own.

Both Bob and Davey were enjoying the opportunity to spend time with one another. To my delight, Bob was turning into the father I'd always hoped he would be. Not that there hadn't been some missteps along the way—the purchase of a pony in the spring being notable among them. But Willow had since moved on to greener pastures, while Bob was trying his damnedest to live up to the responsibility he hadn't been sure for years that he wanted.

It had been Bob's idea that Davey and Faith stay with him for the week while I came down to Maryland. He'd started by convincing our son of the wisdom of his plan. I'm not saying that bribery was involved, but let me just mention that Bob's idea of a nutritious dinner runs to chocolate-chip pancakes and French fries. Still, when the two of them approached me as a united front, I'd found it hard to say no.

Which didn't mean I had any intention of allowing the two of them to run wild all week long without someone checking in. Up in my room, I sat down on the bed and dialed the phone. I'd thought calling at dinnertime would be a good idea. Still, the phone rang half a dozen times before Davey picked up.

"Hi, it's Mom," I said. "How are you doing?"

"Great!" Davey yelped.

There was something in the background. A siren, perhaps? "What's that noise?"

"Dad's smoke alarm. Hold on."

My son dropped the phone. I spent the thirty seconds he was gone plotting out how long it would take me, if I left right that minute, to get home to Connecticut.

"Okay," said Davey, coming back on the line. He sounded breathless. "Dad wanted me to be sure and tell you that everything's fine."

Like P.T. Barnum, Bob believes there's a sucker born every minute. Unfortunately for him, I'm not quite that gullible.

"If everything's fine, why did the smoke alarm go off?"

"We were making s'mores."

As if that explained everything. I sighed. Prayed for patience. Toyed briefly with the idea of dialing 911.

"Did your father singe his eyebrows again?"

"Not yet." Davey giggled.

"How about you? Eyebrows intact?"

"Moo-om!"

When did my name become a three octave epithet? That's what I would like to know. Under the circumstances, it was a fair question.

"Does Dad have a fire extinguisher?"

"Yup," Davey confirmed proudly. "He's using it now. Hey, wait! I want to see! Sorry, Mom, gotta go. Talk to you later. Bye!"

Just like that, he was gone. The child of my heart, the son I adored, the infant I'd nursed through colic and ear infections. Gone fire fighting, three hundred miles away. Isn't that what every mother hopes her little boy will do when she takes that first step and relinquishes a modicum of control?

And I hadn't even had a chance to ask about Faith. I wondered if I should call back.

Before I could decide, there was a knock at the door. "Who is it?" I called.

"Surprise!"

Like I needed another one. But I recognized that voice and was already smiling when I threw open the door. "Bertie! What on earth are you doing here?"

"Come to watch the dog show," said the redhead. "Isn't that why everyone in this whole freakin' hotel is here? And I do mean, everyone. I've never seen so many Poodles in my life. But what the hell, I'll deal. I'm on vacation."

"Vacation?" I reached out and pulled her inside. She was, I noted, carrying a tall, dark bottle and two wineglasses. "I didn't think professional handlers got those."

"Huh," said Bertie. I took that as agreement. She plunked the bottle down on the nearest table and gave me a hug.

Bertie Kennedy had been a friend for several years; as of the previous Christmas, she was now my sister-in-law. So far, her six-month-old marriage to my younger brother, Frank, was progressing splendidly. Frank had matured, seemingly overnight. Falling in love and making the decision to take a wife had rearranged my brother's priorities and firmed up his sense of responsibility. Speaking as the older sister who'd spent much of her life cleaning up after his scrapes and indiscretions, the metamorphosis was welcome and well overdue.

As for Bertie, she'd changed too. For years, she'd focused on her career, devoting endless amounts of time and energy to the task of making a name for herself in a difficult profession. By the time she met Frank, Bertie had a sizeable string of dogs to handle and a social life that was in shreds. This for a woman who was knockdown, drop-dead gorgeous. It was enough to make you wonder whether the rest of us even stood a chance.

When I first met Bertie, she'd flaunted her looks. She was the kind of woman that men stared at openly, the kind that other women envied even as they tried to dismiss her. Little by little, however, Bertie had lost her taste for being the center of attention.

She still glowed, but the neon sheen was gone and her radiance had dimmed to a fine luster. The hard edges she'd built for defense over the years had softened. She'd finally relaxed, taken a deep breath, and found what she truly wanted in life. And I couldn't have been happier with the way things had turned out.

"Don't tell me you brought wine," I said.

"Heaven forbid. In my condition? I don't think so."

Bertie was three and a half months pregnant, though she hadn't begun to show yet. There wasn't even a hint of a ripple in her slender outline. She picked up the bottle and squinted at the label.

"I thought we deserved a toast, so I picked this up. The guy behind the counter at the convenience store promised it was drinkable. It's some sort of sparkling, alcohol-free . . . crap." Bertie hooted with laughter and she pried off some foil and unscrewed the cap.

"What are we drinking to?" I asked, staring at the fizzy pink liquid that came pouring out of the dark green bottle. It looked like something you might bolt down to calm an upset stomach.

"To vacations, to taking a week off." Now Bertie was staring, too. "To freedom!"

"Freedom from indigestion looks more like it." I picked up my glass and took a sniff. The sparkling wine smelled like liquid sugar. Bubbles teased my nose.

"Go on," Bertie prodded. "How bad can it be? At least you're not in my shoes, throwing up everything you eat just for the hell of it."

"Still?" I took a cautious sip. The stuff wasn't awful. If you'd never outgrown your taste for Kool-Aid.

"Still." She chugged down a gulp. "But mostly only in the mornings these days. Hey, for something pink, this isn't bad."

"I think your hormones must be affecting your taste buds."

"Whatever." Bertie poured herself another glass, carried it over and sat down on the bed. Obligingly, Eve moved aside to give her room. "So tell me all about the schedule. This show has more stuff going on than the Macy's Thanksgiving Day parade. What's up for tomorrow?"

"Two things." I settled in a chair by the window. "There's an obedience trial—"

Bertie waved a hand, urging me to move on. The dogs she handled showed in the conformation classes. Though obedience attracted just as many die-hard fanatics, it was a different taste entirely.

"Plus the PCA Foundation Seminar."

"That sounds interesting. Did Peg put the roster together?"

"Of course. Dr. Arthur Law is doing the main program. He's some sort of DNA specialist, talking about gene mapping or genetic diversity or something like that."

Bertie cocked her head. "You going?"

"Are you kidding? Aunt Peg would kill me if I didn't at least put in an appearance. Although I'm also due to sell raffle tickets over at the arena, and at some point I have to give Eve a bath."

Bertie didn't show Poodles, but she'd handled enough longhaired dogs in her career to know that bathing a Standard Poodle was an arduous and time-consuming process. Just blowing the puppy's hair dry would take several hours.

"If you're looking to be helpful . . ." I said.

"No way! I'm on vacation, didn't I mention that?"

"You did. You just never quite explained how it came about. Who's taking care of your dogs?"

A not inconsiderable question. One thing about being a professional handler: you had to love your job because you never got time off. Even on those days when everyone was home with no shows to attend, the string still had to be fed, and exercised, and cleaned up after. Those who didn't truly enjoy the sport, and the dogs, simply burned out after a couple of years and went off to find regular means of employment. *Easier* means of employment—like digging ditches or painting bridges.

"Frank's in charge of the kennel." Bertie grinned. "Can you believe it?"

"Since you asked," I said truthfully. "No. Whose idea was that?"

"His, which makes it even more amazing. He volun-teered, told me I was looking tired. Asked if I felt like I needed some time off."

"I think impending fatherhood has sent my brother around the bend."

"Could be, but I wasn't about to argue. Of course, the problem was that we both couldn't go away at the same time. Plus Frank's been pretty busy at the coffeehouse. But then I remembered this was PCA week. I figured I might as well come down and pick up a few pointers. So I hopped in my car and here I am. Frank thought it was a great idea. He's under the impression that you and Peg are going to keep an eye on me."

My brow lifted. Bertie was one of the most self-sufficient women I'd ever met. "Do you need keeping an eye on?"

"No." Her hand drifted to her stomach. "But try telling your brother that."

"I wouldn't dream of it. Actually, I think his concern is rather sweet."

"For now. Check back with me in six months and see how I feel."

I thought back to my own pregnancy. "By December, you'll probably want to throttle him and anyone else who looks at you cross-eyed. By the way, are you hungry?"

"Are you kidding?"

That was what I'd figured.

"Let's go find some dinner," I said. "On the way, I just need to stop by the grooming room for a minute and check out the facilities, so I'll know how to set things up for Eve's bath."

"Grooming room? What grooming room?" Bertie waited at the door as I explained the situation to Eve, telling the puppy that she'd have to stay and be quiet, and that I'd be back soon. Several minutes later, we walked out into the hallway together.

"Here in the hotel. PCA books a conference room for

the exhibitors. The club lines the floor with plastic, makes sure the lighting's good and that there are plenty of outlets. Especially for this show, where everyone wants their Poodle to look perfect, there's a ton of grooming going on. This way we have a legitimate place to do it."

"Great idea," said Bertie. And how.

The grooming room was located on the basement level of the hotel, just off a hallway that led outside to the exercise area. Walking past, Bertie gazed out the door at the Poodle-filled field. She wrinkled her nose. "In a day or two, nobody will be able to set foot out there without stepping in something. How many of those people do you suppose are cleaning up after themselves?"

"Everyone."

"Dreamer."

"I'm serious. PCA mandates it and, believe me, it happens. Club members take it upon themselves to patrol with pooper-scoopers to clean up after scofflaws. Everybody pitches in. When we leave on Saturday, that field will be spotless."

"Really?" Bertie still sounded dubious. That was because she'd just arrived. PCA wasn't like all the other dog shows she'd been to. It was special, different. Bertie just hadn't figured that out yet.

"Really. You'll see."

The wide double doors that led to the grooming room were standing open. As we approached, we could hear the low, humming sound made by dozens of big, free-standing blow-dryers. Layered over that was the animated buzz of conversation. Bertie and I paused in the doorway and took in the scene.

The room was bright and spacious. Even so, it was mostly full. Rows of portable grooming tables held all three sizes of Poodles in various stages of preparation. Some were being brushed, others clipped or scissored. Still others, fresh from being bathed, were having their long hair blown dry.

"Yikes," said Bertie. "I thought I knew lots of dog show people. Hardly anyone here even looks familiar."

"That's because you're based in the Northeast and PCA draws breeders and exhibitors from all over the country. Lots of these people only come east once or twice a year. Don't worry, everyone is really friendly. Anyone who loves dogs will fit right in.

"Look over there," I said. The Boone sisters were standing beside a table that held a small silver Poodle. Rather than grooming, however, they seemed to be arguing with one another. Par for the course, based on my experience with them earlier. "Those two ladies are Betty Jean and Edith Jean Boone. They're the cochairs of the raffle committee. I'll be working for them all week."

"Which one is Betty Jean and which one is Edith Jean?" Bertie asked.

"Good question."

I gazed at them and frowned. Since I'd seen them last, one of the sisters had put a white grooming smock on over her clothing. The question was, which one? As I watched, she turned to say something to a person working on a Standard Poodle behind them. Light, from the bright, fluorescent bulb above, glinted off a small gold locket that peeked out from beneath her sweater. That helped.

"Betty Jean is the one in the smock," I said confidently. "Edith Jean is closer to us."

"If you say so." Bertie was scrutinizing the Toy puppy on the table. "That's a cute silver."

Dog people. They have no idea what color eyes you have; don't remember that freckle on your nose. But they can recount in the most minute detail, every attribute of every dog they've ever seen. And Bertie was no different than any of the rest of us.

"Very cute, I'm told. The sisters think he has a shot at Winners."

"Who's handling?" Bertie asked. Professional interest.

"Roger Carew." I'd seen his picture earlier that day in the win photos the sisters had shown me. "I'm pretty sure he's the guy working on the Standard behind them."

"Yup, that's him. We cross paths in Virginia and the Carolinas occasionally. He does a good job with a dog."

"I hope so, for their sake. I hear the competition's going to be pretty stiff."

"Are you kidding?" Bertie glanced over. "At a show this size, with everyone who's here, just getting a ribbon is going to be a big deal."

Tell me about it, I thought.

"There's another familiar face," Bertie said. I followed the direction of her gaze. A tall, well-built man was scissoring a brown Mini puppy on one of the grooming tables. The puppy fidgeted as he worked, but unlike some handlers, his touch remained gentle. One hand was propped beneath the Mini's chin; his fingers stroked the puppy's muzzle to quiet him. The man's other hand held a pair of long, curved scissors whose blades flashed open and shut swiftly as he perfected the dog's trim.

"Who is that?" I asked.

"Dale Atherton. From California."

I knew the name; it just took me a moment to remember where I'd heard it. California was the key. Nina Gold, the woman from Marin who'd purchased some raffle tickets, had told me that Dale Atherton was her handler.

"Not bad," Bertie said appreciatively.

Trust me, that was an understatement. Dale Atherton looked damn good. Like a California surfer boy all grown up, he had the sort of natural good looks that those of us in snowy New England our information supplied by the likes of *Baywatch* and the Beach Boys—think all Californians can boast of. His rich brown hair was shot through with golden highlights, his skin tanned to an even bronze. It wasn't a stretch to picture that body in a bathing suit. Maybe even a Speedo.

"Don't tell me," I said with a sigh. "He's probably gay, right?" It wasn't an uninformed guess; many of the Poodle handlers were.

"Dale? No way. He's as straight as they come. And from what I hear, there are hordes of happy women willing to testify to that fact."

"Hmmm." I had another look.

"Hmmm, nothing. When is Sam arriving?"

"Tomorrow," I said, grinning. "Late."

"Who's late?" asked Aunt Peg, coming down the hallway. She stopped beside us and stared into the grooming room. Her hands were on her hips; her face wore a frown. "Don't tell me someone else is missing."

"Someone else?"

As one, Bertie and I turned to see what she was talking about.

"My genetics expert for tomorrow's symposium. The esteemed Doctor Arthur Law. He seems to have disappeared."

5

"Disappeared? Aunt Peg, what happened?"

"I have no idea." My aunt sounded suitably miffed. "Isn't that what I just said?"

"You mean he's vanished?" asked Bertie.

"No, I mean he never arrived at all. Unlike you." Aunt Peg paused in her tirade to stare at her newest relative. "Am I always the last to know everything? Were we expecting you?"

"No." Bertie smiled. "It was a spur-of-the-moment trip."

"Good for you. Everyone should come to PCA at least once in her lifetime. How's my nephew?"

"Working hard."

"Best thing for him. After you, that is."

"Time out," I said. Family harmony was a rare and precious commodity among my relatives. However, that didn't stop me from trying to steer them both back on topic. "What about Doctor Law? What do you mean he disappeared?"

"Oh, good grief, Melanie. There's no call for melodrama. The man isn't dead, at least not as far as I know. He's simply not here. As he ought to be, as he *promised* to be, months ago when I first contacted him, and then again last week when I called to confirm.

"Everything was supposed to be all set. I had absolutely no notion that it wasn't until this afternoon when I got the message he'd left at the front desk canceling his appearance. As if genetics experts grow on trees and I could replace him at a moment's notice. Honestly, some people have no consideration at all. Which brings me to my next problem." My aunt was now glaring into the grooming room.

"There's another?" asked Bertie.

She was new to the family. She hadn't been around long enough to know that there was always another problem. Let her ask the questions, I thought. I was content to wait. We'd find out soon enough what Aunt Peg was raging about.

"Damien Bradley!" my aunt snorted.

There you go.

"Damien Bradley?" Bertie repeated on cue.

You see? My participation in the conversation would have been entirely superfluous.

"He's here."

So he was. I peered around the grooming room and saw the handler tucked away in a back corner.

"Is that a bad thing?" asked Bertie.

"It's not a good thing. We warned the hotel not to give him a room."

"His bad behavior got us kicked out of our last place," I told Bertie, forestalling what was sure to be her next question. "Maybe he's not staying here," I said to Peg. "Maybe he's just visiting."

"He shouldn't be on the premises at all."

"Okay, but . . . is there a reason that's *your* problem?" As if I had to ask. You'd think I'd have learned by now.

"It's the club's problem, which means that every single member should feel a responsibility. If Damien does something idiotic, which we all know he's perfectly capable of doing, then I'm the one who'll feel stupid for not preventing it."

I wasn't about to argue with her. I'd learned early on that the best way to defuse such a situation was to offer my full and unwavering support. I stepped aside, leaving the doorway clear. "I suppose you could march inside and tell him he shouldn't be here. In fact if you really wanted to, you might even be able to pick him up and throw him out."

"Me?" my aunt asked innocently. "Cause a scene?"

Like that had never happened before. Even Bertie looked as if she needed to bite back a smart remark.

"Or . . ." I had another look inside the room, just to check. "Since Mr. Bradley doesn't seem to be causing any trouble right at the moment, you could ignore his transgression and accompany Bertie and me to dinner. We can check back here afterward. He'll probably be gone by the time we're done."

Aunt Peg's expression brightened. The mention of food tends to have that effect on her.

"I haven't eaten all day," said Bertie, joining in the cause. "I'm starving."

"Starving?" Peg's gaze swung around. "My dear girl, what *are* you thinking? You're supposed to be taking care of yourself. Not to mention the baby."

It was easy to tell my aunt had never been pregnant. She meant well, but her advice tended to be a little over-zealous. I started walking away. As I'd hoped, the two women fell in step behind me. Peg slid an arm around Bertie's shoulders and ushered her, with all due haste, toward the hotel restaurant. Before we'd even been seated, she'd already ordered the mother-to-be a tall glass of milk.

"I don't like milk," Bertie grumbled under her breath as Aunt Peg conferred with the waitress about the evening's specials, probably hoping to find something suitably nutritious for germinating a fetus.

"Drink it anyway," I advised. "Damien Bradley will appreciate the sacrifice."

"Will he? From what I've heard about Damien, I don't think he appreciates much."

"What are you two whispering about over there?" Aunt Peg asked from across the table.

"Milk," I said quickly, before Bertie could say Bradley's name and get Aunt Peg going again.

"Would you like a glass too?" She turned to place another order with the waitress. Bertie stuck out her tongue. I was tempted to kick her under the table but decided that one of us regressing to her childhood was probably enough.

"They have salmon," Aunt Peg announced, looking meaningfully at Bertie. "And mahimahi. You know what they say about fish. Brain food."

As we ate, we discussed the next day's symposium. These seminars were Aunt Peg's pet project; she'd been in charge since their inception. Back then, the show itself was only three days long, and Poodle fanciers had had to extend their trips by a day if they wished to attend. That they had come by the hundreds was ample reward for Aunt Peg's dedication. Now, with this year's seminar a mere twelve hours away, she was minus her star speaker.

"I've thrown something together," Aunt Peg said. "Not a perfect solution, but the best I could do on such short notice. We're expecting a good turnout this year. People were intensely interested in hearing what Doctor Law had to say."

"What will you be offering them instead?" I asked curiously.

"In the morning, a talk on show-ring presentation. Mary Scott has agreed to step in and help out."

I whistled softly under my breath. Mary Ludlow Scott was a legend in the dog show world. She'd started out handling as a teenager, rising quickly to the pinnacle of that profession where she'd reigned for many years. For the last several decades, she'd been a highly esteemed judge, one of only a handful approved by the American Kennel Club to judge every recognized breed.

Though Mary Scott had bred and handled a number of

different breeds over the course of her career, Poodles had long been a favorite. Notoriously blunt, infamously sharp of wit, she didn't suffer fools gladly. Nor did she squander her skills on neophytes. A seminar on Poodle presentation with her at the helm was a rare offering and sure to be a popular choice.

"It sounds like you landed on your feet," said Bertie. "Surely no one will be disappointed by that change of schedule."

"I should hope not," Peg agreed. "Mary has long been a supporter of the seminar. It was gracious of her to offer to fill in."

"That takes care of the morning," I said. "What about the afternoon program? What are you planning to substitute for that?"

Aunt Peg stuck a piece of baked potato in her mouth and mumbled something unintelligible. My aunt has better manners than that. And I could recognize an evasion when I saw one.

"I'm sorry, I didn't hear what you said."

She swallowed and said, "I've booked Rosalind Romanescue."

"Who?" Bertie and I exchanged a glance. Her faint shrug said she was as much in the dark as I.

"Rosalind Romanescue," Aunt Peg repeated tartly. "The much esteemed . . . animal communicator."

Bertie's eyes widened. I stifled a laugh with a hasty sip of milk. Aunt Peg had to be kidding. She'd booked a clairvoyant to follow Mary Ludlow Scott? That was like hiring Abbott and Costello to follow Hank Aaron in the batting order.

"A psychic?" Bertie blurted. "What a great idea! Can she predict the future? Is she going to tell everyone who's going to win the show?"

"The woman is not a fortune-teller." Aunt Peg's tone was testy. "She's an animal communicator. She talks with dogs telepathically and lets their owners know what they're thinking."

"More biscuits, please," I said in a small voice. "And no more visits to the vet if you don't mind."

"Make fun if you must," said Peg, "but I've spoken to Rosalind over the phone—"

"Funny," Bertie mused. "You wouldn't think a psychic would need a telephone."

"*I* needed a telephone," Aunt Peg snapped. It was clear we were trying her patience. "And she's very serious about what she does. I'm told she's very good."

"So is David Copperfield," I pointed out. "But in the end, it's still all just sleight of hand. And how can anyone know whether she's good or not? Presumably, the dogs she talks to aren't the ones passing judgment."

"She has a number of satisfied customers," said Peg. "And besides . . . she was available."

Ah, yes, there was that. Under the circumstances, availability counted for a lot.

"Rosalind Romanescue." I let the name roll of my tongue. It had a certain ring.

"She sounds like a gypsy," Bertie mentioned.

"I'm sure she'll do fine," I said.

"Of course she'll be fine," said Peg. "Whoever decided that every single seminar topic had to be so all-fired serious? I'm sure people will appreciate the opportunity to view something lighter for a change."

"Too bad she can't predict the future." Bertie pushed her uneaten salmon around her plate. "I can think of a few questions I wouldn't mind asking."

"Boy or girl?"

"No, not that. Frank and I want to be surprised. Actually I was wondering about peace in the Middle East."

"Speaking of surprises," said Peg, "I wonder what Damien Bradley is up to downstairs."

And here I'd thought we'd managed to distract her.

Stomach full, Aunt Peg was once again in full problem-solving mode.

"There were plenty of other PCA members in the grooming room," I pointed out.

"Not to mention several strong men in case he needed to be handled." Bertie looked at me and winked. "Maybe Dale Atherton will take him in hand."

"If he's lucky," I said under my breath.

Aunt Peg glared at us across the table. "I may be getting older but my sense of hearing hasn't entirely vanished. Why is it I keep getting the impression that you two would rather be holding a private conversation?"

"Sorry. We were talking about Dale Atherton. Bertie pointed him out to me earlier."

"I gather women have been pointing at Dale his whole life," Aunt Peg replied. "Not to mention, throwing themselves in his path. You two wouldn't be the first. Nor, most likely, the last."

"Aunt Peg!" I protested, even as I felt my cheeks begin to grow warm. "Nobody was thinking of throwing anything at him. Bertie and I were just admiring—"

"—from afar," Bertie clarified.

"I met one of his clients earlier while I was selling raffle tickets, so naturally I was curious . . ."

"Naturally," Peg agreed. "Which client?"

"Nina Gold. From California?"

"Minis." Aunt Peg was a walking encyclopedia of Poodle lore. "GoldenDune kennel. Christian Gold's wife."

"That's the one. Blond, beautifully dressed. She looked like a woman who loves to shop. I sold her two dozen tickets."

"On the first day?" Aunt Peg was impressed. The waitress cleared our plates, offered coffee and dessert, which we all declined, and went to get our bill.

"I think Nina was bored," I said. "She was an easy touch."

"Bored?" The very idea made my aunt quiver with in-dignation. "At *PCA*?"

"I know it may be hard for you to believe," said Bertie, "but there *are* people in the world whose lives don't re-volve around dogs and dog shows."

"Fair enough," I agreed. "But then why is she here? Especially all the way from California?"

"I imagine she came with Christian," Aunt Peg said. "The GoldenDune kennel is his bailiwick. There are at least ten or twelve generations of champion GoldenDune Minis behind the ones he has in the ring now. It's a very solid breeding program. Christian's worked hard on it for years."

"Nina didn't look like the type of woman who worked too hard on anything," I said. "And unless she's had some great plastic surgery, she certainly isn't old enough to have been around the dog world for years."

Aunt Peg stopped and thought. "No, she's a good deal newer to the scene than Christian is. I'd say they've been married five years, give or take. Christian's a bit older. Not so much that people would snicker, but there's definitely an age difference.

"He's one of those men who concentrated on his career when he was younger, never had time to find himself a wife or have a family. His dedication to his dogs seemed to take up what little spare time he had. I heard that he made himself an enormous dot-com fortune in the nineties. He and Nina were married soon after that."

Aunt Peg seldom mentioned people's finances. Since she had a bit of a fortune herself, I knew we were talking about real money. "If that's the case, I ought to hit her up for even more tickets."

"Don't worry. I'm sure Christian will buy his share." Aunt Peg waved away Bertie's and my objections as she picked up the check and signed it to her room. "I dare say we've left Mr. Bradley to his own devices quite long

enough. Who would like to walk back down to the grooming room with me and see if he's still around?"

"I'll go," I volunteered. "But first I want stop in my
room and pick up Eve. While we're downstairs, she can
have her evening run."

Bertie begged off due to fatigue, and promised she'd
see us at the symposium the following morning. Aunt Peg
headed to her room to fetch Hope. Ten minutes later, we
met downstairs outside the grooming room. The two
Poodles scooted around the carpeted hallway, greeting
each other with joyous leaps and playful bows.

By now, the room was nearly empty. Later in the week,
the preparations and primping would continue until all
hours of the night. But this early, with only the obedience
trial on tap for the next day, most exhibitors had already
packed up and left. The Boone sisters were gone, as were
the handlers we'd seen earlier, including Damien Bradley.

"That's good news, right?" I said, staggering back slightly
as the two big black Poodles bounced off my legs in their
play.

"Let's hope so." Aunt Peg didn't sound convinced.

We headed out the door on the other side of the hall.
Even though it was June, the evening air still held a chill.
Following Aunt Peg outside, I was glad I'd thought to pick
up a sweater in my room.

By night, the field that had been designated as our exercise area was a sea of darkness and shadow. The hotel
had outdoor lights but their beams were meant to light
the walkways that ran beside the building. Aunt Peg and I
weren't the only ones outside with our dogs, but the ranks
of those looking to exercise their Poodles had thinned
considerably. For most exhibitors, the day's work was finished. The hotel bar was probably doing a booming business.

I'd been planning to let Eve loose to have another run
before going to bed but abruptly I realized how easy it

would be to lose sight of the black puppy in the shadows. The L-shaped hotel bordered two sides of the field. The third was edged by a stand of trees and the last ran along the parking lot. It wasn't the best situation.

Aunt Peg, whose older Poodle had had more training than Eve, didn't even hesitate. She unsnapped Hope's leash and let her go. After a moment, I followed suit. Immediately, the two Poodles dashed away.

"I hope that wasn't a mistake," I said, staring into the night. Eve and Hope were running flat out. Neither Poodle was accustomed to spending most of the day crated; now they worked off their excess energy by galloping side by side, dodging and feinting, each trying to bowl the other over with a playful shove.

"My Poodle comes when she's called." Aunt Peg slanted me a challenging look.

"So does mine," I muttered. "Usually."

Peg handed me Hope's leash to hold. "Since we're just standing here, I think I'll hunt up a poop-scoop and go patrol the field. With this much of it in darkness, I imagine people think they can get away with anything. Keep an eye on those two, will you?"

"Right."

Of course that task was easier said than done. My job was helped by the fact that the pair was staying together, but hindered by the speed with which they traversed the vast grassy area. Finally their mad dash slowed, then stopped. I watched both Poodles sniff the ground, then squat to pee.

I was about to call them back in when I saw Hope's head snap up. Her ears pricked, her attention caught by something I couldn't see. Suddenly she whipped around and took off toward the end of the building that bordered the parking lot. Eve was only a step or two behind.

"Hope, come!" I called out firmly. "Eve! Over here." Neither Poodle paid any attention to me. As they began to run, Aunt Peg materialized out of the shadows, poop scoop in hand.

"What's the matter?" she asked.

"I don't know. Something—"

I never got a chance to finish. A chill slithered up my spine as a piercing scream shattered the night.

6

Aunt Peg dropped the scoop and ran in the direction the scream had come from. She's a good person to have around in an emergency. Whatever was wrong, she'd know what to do or how to call for help.

That left me free to chase after the two Poodles. Fortunately Eve and Hope had run toward the building. They were much easier to see in the lights. The second time I called, Hope responded to her name. When she circled back toward me, the puppy came with her. I grabbed both big Poodles and snapped the leashes onto their collars.

Aunt Peg had ended up in the corner where the two wings of the hotel building met. Several other people were standing in the shadows with her. As I headed their way, doors to several of the guest rooms along the inner corridor began to open. People stuck their heads out and looked around curiously.

"What's going on?" Dale Atherton asked as I passed by. Standing in his doorway, he looked charmingly rumpled, his hair tousled, feet bare, shirt untucked. Briefly I wondered if he'd been asleep.

"I don't know yet. Someone screamed."

"I heard that. I wonder if someone needs help." He pulled his door shut and jogged past me toward the cluster of people in the corner.

Propelled by the two Poodles, I reached the small group only a moment after the handler did. Aunt Peg looked grim. Cliff Spellman, the club vice president, was speaking urgently on a cell phone. I looked past them and saw a body lying crumpled on the ground. A decorative planter, part of the hotel's landscaping, partially blocked my view. Taking care to keep the Poodles out of the way, I edged around the back of the group until I could see better.

The body in the shadows belonged to a woman. She looked so small that, for a moment, I thought it might be a child. Then the crimped gray hair registered in my shocked brain, followed by the red sweater and the white grooming smock. I gasped softly. Her face was turned away from me, but I still knew.

"It's Betty Jean," I whispered. Several people looked at me and nodded.

"Must have had a heart attack," I heard someone say.

"Maybe an aneurysm," voiced another.

Cliff snapped his phone shut. "Help is on the way. They said they'll be here in five minutes. We'll need someone out in the parking lot to direct them this way."

Hands shot up. People volunteered. The club pulled together, everyone eager to do what they could.

Dale had knelt down beside Betty Jean. He looked at her closely, but didn't touch. Aunt Peg, also standing nearby, kept a watchful eye on the proceedings. I sidled over to where she was standing.

"Is she alive?" I whispered.

Aunt Peg gave her head a small, negative shake.

"Are you sure?" I hated to think of Betty Jean lying there on the cold ground with none of us helping her, no one knowing what to do.

"I turned her over, I felt for a pulse. I thought maybe mouth-to-mouth . . ." Her voice, edged with unhappy resignation, trailed away. In the distance, I heard sirens. Too late now.

More people: club members, exhibitors, hotel guests, were coming out of the building to see what was going on. Cliff was busy making sure they didn't get too close. All around me, people were asking questions. No one offered any answers.

"You said it was Betty Jean," said Aunt Peg. "I wasn't sure . . ."

I nodded. "Bertie and I saw her earlier inside the grooming room. Do you know what happened?"

"No." My aunt's shoulders were slumped, her hands running up and down her arms as though she were cold. "I'm guessing she fell and hit her head on the planter. But nobody seems to have seen it happen."

I thought about that as a vehicle topped by a flashing red beacon entered the hotel lot. The light's reflection skittered eerily across the dark windows of the parked cars as the ambulance pulled around the building. "Who screamed?"

"I have no idea. I suppose it could have been Betty Jean herself, although . . ." Aunt Peg left the thought unfinished, but I could guess what she was thinking. The scream we'd heard had been long and full, not cut off abruptly as Betty Jean's would have been. "Several people reached her before me. I imagine it was one of them. Finding her like that must have been quite a shock."

"It sounded like a woman," I said.

Peg thought for a minute. "Charlotte Kay was here. You know who she is. She's in charge of the trophy committee."

She nodded toward a middle-aged woman who was standing off to one side now that the crowd had grown. Tears streamed down her pale face. She'd removed her glasses and was trying to wipe the moisture away with the back of her hand.

"And I thought I saw Rosalind . . ."

"Your psychic?"

Aunt Peg frowned. "I could have been wrong, though. We've only met once, briefly, earlier this evening when she checked in. And in the darkness . . ." She had another look around. "If it was her, she seems to be gone now."

"Step back, please. Coming through."

The crowd parted for the ambulance crew. Hastily I withdrew, pulling the two big Poodles with me. As the EMTs went to work, the crush of people closed in again. I couldn't see what was going on. I wasn't sure I wanted to.

Aunt Peg had stepped aside to confer with Cliff Spellman. After a few minutes, she returned. "There isn't anything else we can do here. Cliff will wait and talk to the police. He's called Nancy Hanlon. She's going to find Edith Jean and break the news to her."

I gulped suddenly. Edith Jean. I'd forgotten all about her. Even in the brief time I'd known the sisters, I'd seen how clearly each identified herself as half of a pair. What would Edith Jean do now?

At least for the short term, I knew that Nancy Hanlon would make sure Edith Jean got whatever she needed. Nancy was the club president. She ran a tight ship and PCA had prospered under her leadership. She delegated judiciously, took the stewardship of the Poodle breed seriously, was known to remain calm in the face of crisis and controversy. I didn't envy her her task tonight.

Aunt Peg reached over and unwound Hope's leash from around my cold fingers. "Now what?" I said.

"I guess we go back to our rooms and go to bed."

"But what about tomorrow? The dog show?"

"The show will go on as scheduled. Betty Jean will be missed, of course. I'm sure the club will plan some sort of tribute."

Was that all? It didn't seem like much, in the face of this sudden, unexpected tragedy.

"This is PCA," Aunt Peg said gently. "The national specialty. Preparations have been going on for months. People come from all over the world, they plan their vacations around the show. They look forward to it all year. Most of them have never even met Betty Jean. Right or wrong, her death won't make much of an impression on the event."

"What about Edith Jean?" I asked. "Do you think she'll go home now? Will Bubba still show in his class? What will happen to the raffle?"

"Nancy will find out the answers to your first two questions tonight. As to the raffle, it will most certainly go on. If Edith Jean chooses to leave, the club will simply make do." Peg looked at me meaningfully. "Perhaps with somebody new in charge."

I guessed I should have seen that coming.

Aunt Peg and I parted for the night. As she had said, there wasn't anything more we could do. I took my puppy upstairs and went to bed.

I awoke the next morning with a vague sense of unease, though it took me a moment to remember why. Then the events of the previous night came flooding back. I hoped Edith Jean was going to be able to cope on her own. The sisters weren't young; and from what I'd seen they relied upon one another heavily. I wondered if they had family at home, someone who could look out for E.J. now that B.J. was gone.

My thoughts were cut short by the realization that once Eve was awake she needed to go outside. Exhibitors lucky enough to have rooms that opened directly onto the exercise area, had been known to walk their Poodles in their pajamas. With a room on the other side of the building and up a floor, I didn't dare take such liberties.

I jumped in the shower, dressed quickly, and had Eve out behind the hotel in under fifteen minutes. The exercise area was mostly empty. The few people who were outside with their dogs seemed subdued.

Usually there was a lot of chatter going on; that morning, nobody seemed to have much to say. Most kept glancing over at the corner where Betty Jean had been found. After I'd left, the police had cordoned the area off. Yellow tape fluttered in the early morning breeze, warning onlookers to stay away. No one, including me, went near.

Business attended to, I cleaned up after Eve and took the puppy back to the room. I'd been looking forward to attending Mary Ludlow Scott's presentation that morning, but now it seemed that the club's interests would be better served if I drove over to the show site and opened up the raffle table. With no idea of where Edith Jean was, or what she might be doing, I decided I'd better assume I was in charge.

Eve went with me, as she had the day before. As we were cutting across the parking lot and heading into the building, Terry Denunzio hailed me. "I heard you had some excitement at the hotel last night."

"That was quick."

"Oh, honey." Terry rolled his eyes. He loves dramatic gestures, and executes them with flair. "What are you, new around here? News travels at a dog show faster than a Beagle can scarf down a table scrap. I hear the police have been questioning suspects. Now *that's* something I wouldn't mind getting in on, especially if they send around a detective who looks like Vincent D'Onofrio." Need I mention that Terry is a *Law and Order* addict?

"Suspects?" I stopped in my tracks. "Do they think Betty Jean was murdered?"

"Don't know yet, though I'm sure someone will fill us in shortly. Word is they've been talking to people who were there last night when she was found."

I supposed that meant the police would get around to me eventually. I started walking again. "Those are witnesses, Terry. Not suspects. Big difference."

"You should know, doll. How's Edith Jean holding up?"

"I don't know, I haven't seen her. I imagine she's back at the hotel, maybe making preparations to go home. That's why I'm here. I figured someone should see to the raffle table during the obedience trial."

"Good thought. You know how those obedience people are."

"No." I stopped again, turned around and looked back at him. "How are they?"

"Let's just say I wouldn't leave *my* valuables lying around unattended."

"Don't be ridiculous." I knew that Terry, like many people who showed in breed, tended to look down on the dogs that showed in obedience. I hadn't realized that his prejudice extended to their owners as well.

"Scoff if you will, but I seem to recall an incident several years ago where something went missing early in the week."

"Really? Something from the raffle? What was it?"

"Who remembers? It was hushed up rather quickly at the time. But I'm pretty sure it never turned up."

As far as I knew, all the valuable stuff had gone back to the hotel the evening before with the sisters. Surely no one would have been tempted to help themselves to Poodle dish towels or key chains in our absence. I hurried inside to find out

Since it was my call, I made the executive decision that Eve didn't have to spend the day in her crate. Instead she could lie beneath the raffle table and keep me company. My first order of duty after getting her settled was to remove the sheet and make a thorough inspection.

Unfortunately, this effort was hampered by the fact that I hadn't looked all that closely at the table the day before. With so many prizes on display, it was hard to tell if anything might be missing when I didn't have a clear idea of what should have been there in the first place. Plus, the sisters had packed some things away in boxes for the night. After pulling those items out and placing them on the table, I still had gaps to fill.

I got out the partial list I'd been carrying in my basket the day before and had a look at it. Since the point of the list, however, was to brag about the high-ticket items, noting that most were missing didn't do me much good. Those were exactly the sorts of prizes that Betty Jean and Edith Jean would have taken back to the hotel with them.

The loudspeaker came to life with a brief burst of static as the announcer welcomed the exhibitors to the annual Poodle Club of America obedience trial. Then all activity stopped for a few minutes while a club member sang the national anthem. Even the Poodles, waiting by their handlers' sides, seemed to stand at attention.

The competition began with the first class, Utility A. The majority of the people currently in the arena were down at the other end of the ring, most of them exhibitors awaiting their turn to show. With the symposium going on back at the hotel, the obedience trial hadn't drawn nearly as many spectators as agility had. If I'd had someone to mind the table, I could have taken my basket and gone prospecting for ticket sales. As it was, I couldn't do much more than watch the class and wait for someone to approach me.

In the ring, a parti-colored Toy Poodle was heeling happily at its owner's side. According to the breed standard, a Poodle had to be a solid color to be shown in conformation. Obedience, however, placed no such restrictions on its entrants. This black and white Toy, with four white feet and a black patch over one eye, was adorable.

I got so caught up in watching the little Poodle perform that it took me a minute to realize someone was making her way slowly in my direction across the wide, turf-covered expanse of the arena. I glanced over, then looked again quickly in surprise. It was Edith Jean.

Not only had she come to the show, but she was drag-ging a dolly along behind her. It bumped up and down in the grass, slowing her progress to a crawl. When she stopped to adjust her hold on the rope handle, I saw that one of her hands was swathed in what appeared to be a bright pink bandage. Quickly instructing Eve to stay, I hur-ried out to help.

"Edith Jean! What are you doing here?"

"Running the PCA raffle, just like I promised I would." She stared at me hard, as if daring me to refute that fact. "I'm afraid time got away from me this morning. You were a dear to come and open up."

Up close, I could see her eyes were rimmed in red, and her complexion was blotchy. It looked as though she'd been crying, and no wonder. Yet she'd still come to fulfill her duties. Edith Jean must have known the club would find a way to cover for her. At least I hoped she did.

"I'm so sorry." The words sounded, and felt, wholly in-adequate. I reached out my arms and gathered the small woman in a hug. "I know we'd just met, but your sister seemed like a wonderful person."

"She was." Edith Jean sniffled loudly. "Sister was every-thing to me, just as I was to her."

"Why don't you go home?" I said gently. "You don't have to be here. I can cope with the raffle. I'm sure the club will find someone to help me."

"You don't know what it's like." Edith Jean's voice quiv-ered slightly, but her shoulders were straight and strong. "Where else would I go? What else would I do? This is where I belong right now."

I wasn't sure I understood, but I certainly wasn't about to argue. "Then this is where you should be," I said.

7

I reached around her and took the rope handle. Edith Jean winced slightly as I brushed past her bandaged right hand. She held it up out of the way as we began to walk. The dolly wasn't heavy, but it was cumbersome on the grass.

"What happened?" I asked, nodding toward the bandage.

"It's nothing. Just a silly accident I had this morning in the hotel room. I was making myself a cup of coffee and I guess I wasn't paying as much attention as I should have been. I burned my hand on the hot water."

Of course she'd been distracted, I thought. The woman's sister had died less than twelve hours earlier. "Did you see a doctor?"

Edith Jean snorted. "Now where would I find a doctor around here? You young people think every little bump and scrape has to be seen by a specialist. No wonder the medical profession is such a mess. I ran it under cold water, then I bandaged it up and got on with my life."

I peered at the wrapping on her hand. If I wasn't mistaken, it consisted of a layer of gauze held in place by vet wrap, a stretchy product that Poodle people used to contain their dogs' ear hair. "Yes, but—"

"But nothing. I'm fine. End of discussion."

When we reached the table, Eve stood up and came out

to greet us. Edith Jean spared me a withering glance. "Second day on the job, and already you're making the rules?"

"Sorry. I wasn't expecting you. I didn't think anyone would even notice she was here."

Despite her objection, Edith Jean didn't seem overly concerned. She gave Eve a long, assessing look. "Very pretty. Is she one of Peg's?"

"Peg's breeding, yes. But I bred her myself." As I said the words, I realized it sounded as though I were bragging. "My first litter," I added, so she wouldn't get the wrong idea.

She reached out and scratched the puppy lightly under the chin. Any Poodle person knows better than to put their hands in a dog's long hair. Caresses, by necessity, are confined to the clipped areas. Eve responded by leaning toward her and arching her back.

"You did a nice job for a beginner. I remember when Sister and I were starting out. Years ago, that was. We would have been delighted to have something this nice right off the bat."

Abruptly Edith Jean fell silent. I wondered if she was thinking about the good times she'd shared with her sister. Good times that had suddenly come to an end the night before.

"You don't have to stay here," I said again. "I'll take care of everything until the club finds someone else to take over. Do you have family in Georgia? Wouldn't you feel better going home to them?"

"Sister was my family," E.J. said softly. "We only had each other. There was a time when things were different . . ." She paused, gazed off into the distance, then continued after a minute. "Sister and I had been looking forward to this show all year. She would be very disappointed in me if I left now. We came here to do a job, didn't we? Well by damn, I intend to see it through to the end and nobody's going to stop me."

"Of course not. Not if that's what you want."

"Thank you, dear." Edith Jean patted my hand. "I know you're only trying to help. But Sister and I thought of our Poodles and the Poodle community as our family. I'd much rather stay here and fulfill our obligations than go home and wallow in self-pity. There will be plenty of time for that when the show is over."

Her words made me feel worse than ever. According to Aunt Peg, most of the PCA members barely knew the Boone sisters. None saw them more than once or twice a year. It was sad to think that these were the people whom Edith Jean regarded as those closest to her.

The older woman marched over to the box she'd brought in on the dolly and began to unpack the raffle prizes. I hastened to lend a hand. Literally, since we only had three between us.

"You know, I'll bet there's a doctor here somewhere," I mentioned. "A couple of PCA members are doctors, aren't they? Maybe the announcer could make a request over the PA system."

"Stop worrying about me," E.J. said over her shoulder. "That's an order. Keep going on like that, and you'll drive me right around the bend. I may be old, but I'm not incapacitated."

"I never—"

Her quelling look shut me up. Instead, I simply pitched in and went to work beside her.

Business was slow for the remainder of the morning. Most people who came by, did so to offer their condolences. Edith Jean accepted everyone's good wishes with grace and the firm assertion that she had no intention of abandoning her post, even under such trying circumstances.

After a while, she got out the basket, loaded it up, and sent me and Eve on a tour of the show site. I suspected she was more interested in getting us out of her hair than she was in ticket sales. If Edith Jean wanted some time to herself, however, I was happy to oblige her.

By noon, Eve and I had sold tickets to every person in the arena who was even remotely interested in the raffle, and probably some to those who weren't. I'd missed the morning seminar, but now that Edith Jean was back on the job I was hoping to head back to the hotel for the afternoon. Aside from wanting to catch a glimpse of Aunt Peg's psychic, it was time to start grooming Eve in anticipation of her class Thursday morning.

"You go on," Edith Jean said when I broached the subject. "Of course I can handle things here. It's not as if we're even busy. Things will start perking up tomorrow when the breed show opens. Everyone will be here for that."

"What time is Bubba's class?" I asked.

The dog (or male) classes in all three Poodle varieties would be judged on Wednesday. For the first two days of the breed competition, two rings were set up in the arena and they ran simultaneously. Standard Poodles, with the biggest entry and one that usually took all day to judge, had a ring to themselves. Miniature and Toy Poodles were judged in the other ring—one variety showing in the morning and the other in the afternoon. Which size went first, alternated years.

"Minis are first this time," said Edith Jean. "Which puts Bubba in the second class after lunch. You'll be here then, right, so I can go to the ring and watch?"

"Right," I agreed.

The raffle table had an excellent location on the arena floor. In fact, if the crowds weren't heavy, we could see the ring from where we stood. But being able to casually peruse the judging from afar, and analyzing the competition in your own dog's class down to the most minute detail, were two distinctly different things.

Not only that but most dog owners went into hiding when their dogs were being shown by a professional. It's extremely important that a dog focus on his handler while he's in the ring. The handler knows how to present the dog to its best advantage; he watches the judge and positions the dog accordingly. A dog that's inattentive to its handler's cues or distracted by its owner in the audience, is unlikely to give the winning performance.

Bearing those factors in mind, Edith Jean would need to position herself in such a way that she had an unobstructed view of the class but that Bubba could neither see, hear, nor smell her. The quest to achieve such a goal often led to comical antics at ringside, with owners bobbing up and down, and into and out of sight, depending on which direction their dogs were facing. Wherever E.J. was planning to go, she certainly didn't need to be tied to the raffle table.

"Keep your fingers crossed for us," she said. "Now, after what's happened, I want Bubba to win more than ever. What a nice tribute that would be to Sister's memory."

"Yesterday you seemed to think he had a pretty good shot."

"Yes, well . . ." Her gaze slipped away. "Harry Gandolf's been lobbying pretty heavily for that dog of his, Vic. And Leo Mancini, the Toy judge, comes from the Midwest, so he and Harry are pretty tight."

Judging dogs is supposed to be a totally objective exercise. Judges should enter the ring carrying nothing but a mental image of the breed standard in their minds. More often than not, however, the dog that has generated the ringside buzz is—deservedly or not—the one that ends up at the head of the line.

E.J. was right to be wary of advance, word-of-mouth promotion. It had worked to dogs' advantage many times in the past. Now she shook her head.

"Something's up with Harry and that puppy of his," she said. "I wish I knew what it was. Sister and I don't go to many shows and Harry Gandolf's never said two words to me before in my entire life. But don't you know, there he was bright and early this morning, standing outside my hotel room and wanting to ask me if I was going to pull Bubba from the competition on account of what happened."

"That's pretty rude. What did you tell him?"

"I said, 'Son, they don't call southern women steel magnolias for nothing. My sister was looking forward to watching Bubba win PCA and if I have anything to say about it, that's exactly what our boy is going to do.' Then I just pushed right past him and left."

"He's a professional handler," I said thoughtfully. "I imagine he probably brought a whole string of Poodles to this show. I wonder why winning with that one puppy is so important to him?"

"Beats me," said Edith Jean. "All I can say is that Sister's and my lives were a whole lot calmer before Bubba started winning this spring and Harry started making threats."

I turned and stared. "Wait a minute. I thought you just said you'd never spoken to him before this morning."

"That's right. Leastways, not in person. But I sure as hell knew who he was. Just like he knew me. Roger, our handler . . ." She stopped, glanced my way. "You know Roger?"

I nodded. I knew who he was.

"Roger heard from Harry a month or so ago. Right after Bubba did all his winning on the Cherry Blossom circuit. Harry said he had a client who was interested in Bubba and was he for sale. Hell, no, Sister and I said. Bubba's the best thing that's happened to us in years. He's not for sale."

"And then?"

"Next thing Roger knew, someone had put the word out that Bubba was oversize. Now you Standard people don't have to worry about that, but with Toys it's a big deal."

I knew about that. It was important with Miniatures as well. The Poodle breed standard is exactly the same for all three varieties except in one aspect: size. Toy Poodles are those that stand ten inches or under, measured at the highest point of the shoulder. Minis are between ten and fifteen inches. Standard Poodles are those that are taller than fifteen. Any Poodle that doesn't fall within those parameters is disqualified from competition.

In theory, a Poodle that is oversize for its variety can be shown in the next larger division. But practically speaking, that simply doesn't work. Fair or not, bigger is considered to be better in the dog show ring and bigger is what wins.

For the most part, Toy Poodles that become champions usually stand within a quarter inch on either side of that ten-inch mark. Winning Minis are seldom less than fourteen and a half inches; the majority are taller. And since breeders breed for Poodles that are "right up to size," exhibitors tend to push those limits to the breaking point.

That was where the size disqualification became a factor. A judge who felt that a Poodle being shown to him didn't fall within the size parameters for its variety, could call for the wicket and take a measurement in the ring. If the judge was correct, the dog was disqualified. Three disqualifications from three different judges resulted in the Poodle being barred from competition permanently.

Many judges refused to measure at all, especially since those who were known to be sticklers for size usually drew smaller entries. Other judges preferred to eyeball the participants, making their own estimation of eligibility rather than performing an official measurement. However you looked at it, the fact that someone was spreading the rumor that Bubba was oversize couldn't help but be damaging.

"Is he over?" I asked. Anyone who had shown for any length of time had been faced with the prospect of finishing one that grew bigger than anticipated. It was luck of the draw as much as anything else that made a puppy fall just under the disqualification line rather than just over.

"No, Bubba's just in. Fortunately. He was measured twice after that," said Edith Jean. "Both judges got the wicket over him with no problem. Next thing we knew, somebody told Roger word's going around that Bubba's been dyed."

Another potentially disqualifying act. *If* it could be proven. I found myself frowning. This all sounded like a great deal of commotion to go through over the show career of one small Toy Poodle puppy.

"How did you know Harry was the one who was behind all the rumors?"

"Dog people talk," said Edith Jean. "You probably know that for yourself. First time around, we figured it was probably a disgruntled competitor. But the second time rumors started flying, Roger got mad and did some digging. Again and again, Harry Gandolf's name kept popping up. I don't mind telling you that Sister was getting pretty steamed about the whole situation. And she had a bit of a temper, that gal."

As if Edith Jean didn't.

"Just yesterday afternoon, when Harry was hanging around the show schmoozing with everybody, Sister looked at me and said, 'If that man doesn't back off and leave our puppy alone, I'm going to give him a piece of my mind.' And she was serious about it, too."

And now she was dead, I thought.

What were the chances that that was a coincidence?

8

The first person I ran into when I got back to the hotel was Aunt Peg.

I'd parked my car and taken Eve inside through the lobby, which was unexpectedly crowded. After a moment, I realized why. The morning's symposium, held in a meeting room that opened off the entryway, was just ending. Aunt Peg was standing in the doorway as people left, handing out questionnaires for feedback, accepting congratulations for a job well done, and basking in Mary Ludlow Scott's reflected glory.

I sidled over to where she stood. "I gather things went well?"

"Superb." Peg was beaming. "There were so many questions, the program ran long by an hour. Mary stayed at the podium until every single person got an answer. There's barely time now for people to grab a quick lunch before the afternoon session starts. That's why everyone's in such a rush to get out."

Maybe. Or perhaps the stampede had something to do with the fact that the expert was being followed by a charlatan. Not that I said as much, of course.

"I noticed *you* didn't think it was worth your time to attend," Aunt Peg sniffed. She hates it when her relatives fail to meet her expectations.

"I'd have been thrilled to hear Mary Scott speak. But in case you've forgotten, someone needed to go over to the show and open up the raffle table."

"Oh." Aunt Peg pondered that. I sensed that my lapse was being forgiven. "Speaking of which, do you happen to know where Edith Jean is? She hasn't checked out, but she doesn't seem to be in her room either. Everyone's been looking for her."

"I just left her back at the arena. She showed up there this morning, determined to run the raffle, just as she and Betty Jean promised they'd do."

Aunt Peg stepped back out of the flow of pedestrians. She pulled me aside with her. "You can't be serious. Surely Nancy or Cliff must have told her that they'd find someone else to take over."

"I imagine they did, but Edith Jean doesn't want anyone else doing her job. She said she and Betty Jean had been looking forward to the show all year, and there was no way she was going home before it was over. She's hoping to watch their puppy, Bubba, go Winners Dog tomorrow."

"That's the silver Toy I told you about yesterday," Peg remembered. "I judged him in Virginia in April. I'm pretty sure I put him up, too."

"Just about all the judges did. To hear the sisters tell it, he was the star of the circuit. So much so that Harry Gandolf started making trouble for them."

Aunt Peg waved merrily at several departing participants, then turned back to frown at me. "Harry Gandolf is based in Illinois. I don't recall seeing him in Virginia at all. Roger Carew was handling the puppy there."

"Harry isn't on the Boones' team, he's a competitor. Apparently he's convinced that his Toy puppy is the one that ought to go Winners Dog tomorrow. He tried to buy Bubba earlier in the spring, and when that failed, he started all sorts of rumors about the dog."

"Like what?"

"That he was oversize, that he'd been dyed. You know, disruptive stuff meant to put an end to his winning streak."

"Hmmm." Aunt Peg tapped her lip thoughtfully. "Now that you mention it, I suppose I did hear something about that. At the time I just passed it off as circuit gossip. Perhaps I should have paid more attention. It came up at the judges' dinner, the night after I'd done Poodles. I was seated next to Rollie Barnes."

Roland Barnes had started his career in Basset Hounds and bore an unfortunate resemblance to his favorite breed. He was squat in stature, dour by nature, and almost entirely lacking in finesse when it came to judging Poodles. He seldom found the best dog in his entry; and some exhibitors claimed he judged by the pound, as his winner was invariably the fattest dog in the ring.

"Rollie was doing Poodles the next day," said Peg. "He asked whether I'd had a silver Toy puppy and if so, what I'd thought of him. Well you know we're not really supposed to discuss such things but, of course, it does happen. I thought perhaps he wanted my opinion since Poodles are my breed. In the same way that I might have gone to him to ask about a Basset Hound."

"No, you wouldn't." I grinned.

After a moment, she smiled too. "You're right, I probably wouldn't have. Nevertheless, Rollie said someone had told him Roger's Toy puppy was big, that the judges weren't doing their job in letting him slip by. Since I'd already had him, he wanted to know what I thought.

"It's the nature of dog shows, I suppose. People are always talking about one another's dogs, and they're not killing them with compliments, either. I hate that aspect of the sport. Why can't the dogs simply be allowed to speak for themselves? I told Rollie I thought the puppy was lovely and well within size."

"Well within?"

"I had a point to make," Peg said innocently.

"And after you'd given Bubba your seal of approval, did he put the puppy up?"

"I have no idea. My assignment was over. I left for home first thing the next morning. Until you mentioned that Harry had been causing problems, I hadn't given the incident another thought. But while we're on the subject of the Boones, there's something else you ought to know. Cliff got an update from the police this morning."

"I heard they were questioning people. Did they talk to you?"

"Yes, last night. They came to my room after we split up. Cliff had told them I was one of the first people on the scene. And of course, I *had* touched Betty Jean. Turned her over, actually. So they wanted to know what I thought I was doing."

"As if that wasn't obvious."

"That's what I thought. I told them I was trying to see if she needed help. Just as any responsible person would have done. At the time, they weren't overly concerned. Apparently they were thinking she might have had a heart attack. But this morning I heard from Cliff that that theory's been ruled out."

I felt a chill. "What did Betty Jean die of?"

"It was the blow to the head that killed her. When she hit the planter, it fractured her skull."

"How awful. You mean she tripped in the dark and did herself in?"

"Not exactly. There was a bruise on her chest that doesn't look as though it was caused by the fall. The police told Cliff that they're looking into the possibility she might have been pushed. It seems it wasn't an accidental death after all. Betty Jean Boone was murdered."

You'd think news like that would take my appetite away, but it didn't. Not even close. Instead, I left Aunt Peg to her hostessing duties, dropped Eve off in my room, then went

off in search of Bertie. My new sister-in-law, Peg had informed me, had been sitting front row center during the
morning's program. I wondered if she'd been taking
notes. Maybe I could still gain some of Mary Scott's knowledge, even if it wasn't firsthand.

Not unexpectedly, I found Bertie standing in the buffet
line in the hotel coffee shop. These days, she was hungry
all the time. And since it was probably the first time in her
life that she wasn't keeping an eye on her figure, Bertie
was eating with gusto. I grabbed a plate and joined her.

We caught up over a hurried lunch, which mostly meant
that Bertie rhapsodized over Mary Scott's vast wealth of
knowledge, skill, and generosity while simultaneously stuff-
ing her face with pasta. "I'm going to start handling Poodles," she said. "I can't imagine why I haven't already."

"Possibly because of all the extra hours you'd have to
spend grooming?" Watching her eat was fascinating. I didn't
think I'd ever seen linguine disappear so fast.

"Like I don't do that now with some of my other breeds."
Bertie used her fork to wave away my objection. "Besides, I
can pass along the costs. I guess I've always been intimi-
dated by all that hair. And the trims that aren't like anything else I do. I figured if you weren't practically born
into the breed, you'd never be able to make a success of
it."

"I wasn't born into it," I pointed out. "I never even went
to a dog show until I was thirty."

"Yeah, but you're different."

"Thanks a lot."

"No, I mean it." She stopped and looked at me. "You
came into the dog show world with Peg. That's kind of like
having the queen bring you in and introduce you around
the palace."

"I thought Mary Ludlow Scott was the queen."

"All right, a duchess then." Bertie clung to her meta-
phor. Just on the basis of her arguing skills, I could tell she

was going to be a great mother. "You didn't have to start at the bottom, like most people do."

"I'm pretty sure I resent that," I said, thinking about it. "I had to pay my dues. It took me more than two years to finish Faith's championship. That's a long time."

Bertie was shaking her head. "It's all relative. Most people don't finish their first show dog at all. Either because they lack the handling skills, or because they're too new to the sport to be able to figure out who the good judges are. Or because some breeder saw that they were novices and sold them a puppy that wasn't show quality in the first place. Having Margaret Turnbull on your team gave you a leg up on the whole process."

Put that way, she was probably right. Breeding and showing dogs wasn't a sport for those who lack perseverance or determination. Especially Poodles.

"So now it's your turn to give something back," Bertie said.

I put down my fork and braced myself.

Really, what else could I do? Bertie was my favorite sister-in-law. Well, my only sister-in-law actually; but I was sure that if I'd had more than one, she would still have been my favorite. Whatever she wanted, I knew I'd help if I could.

"What?" I asked.

"Teach me to trim a Poodle."

"You must be joking."

"Why? You don't think I could do it?"

"*You'll* be fine. I'm the one who couldn't do it. I don't know enough."

"Sure you do. You finished Faith. And you've got points on Eve from the puppy class. So how bad can your trims be?"

"As you just so eloquently pointed out, they're not *my* trims, they're Aunt Peg's. In the beginning I was barely allowed to touch a pair of scissors to my own dogs."

"And now?" Bertie prompted.

"Now she considers me almost competent," I grumbled.

"See? You're halfway there."

"Which is why I shouldn't be dragging you down with me. You need to learn from the best."

"The best don't have time to teach me." Bertie held up a hand to stop me from interrupting. "I know, you don't either. But that's the beauty of this plan. I'm a member of the family. It's not like you can get rid of me."

Good point. "You really want to show Poodles," I said.

"I'm here, aren't I?"

"All right then. You've got a deal." I glanced at her stomach. "I hope this means you're going to name your firstborn after me."

"What if it's a boy?"

"Mel."

"Give me a break." Bertie grabbed the check and signed it to her room.

"It works for Gibson."

"Now Gibson," she said, "I'd consider."

The coffee shop was emptying fast. We got up and joined everyone else, heading back to the conference room. Oh yeah, this partnership was going to be fun.

Rosalind Romanescue's program started out with a bang.

Despite the brevity of the lunch break, Aunt Peg's meeting room was full. All the chairs were taken; more people stood in the back. As Bertie and I had found our seats, I wondered what had caused the psychic to be such a draw. I wouldn't have guessed that the inexact science of animal communicating would find such a large and enthusiastic audience at PCA.

Then Aunt Peg introduced the woman, and after a brief, polite round of applause, a question was shouted out from the side of the room. "Since you see visions and stuff like that, can you tell us what happened to Betty Jean Boone?"

Rosalind had just stepped up to the podium to begin her talk. She was a mild-looking, middle-aged woman with bright red hair that was half tamed into a French braid. She wore faded blue jeans, a denim shirt, and sturdy leather boots. Small silver earrings sparkled in the light. Her fingers, nails bare of polish, gripped the sides of the speaker's stand as she glanced over at Aunt Peg.

"I'm sorry," she said, looking suddenly flustered. "I'm afraid I don't understand."

Peg stepped over and the two women conferred for a minute. The audience waited silently.

"Gee," I leaned over and whispered to Bertie, "who knew solving mysteries could be this easy?"

"Ten to one she doesn't know the answer."

"That's a sucker bet. She didn't even know the question."

Rosalind straightened as Aunt Peg backed away. The psychic stared out over her audience. Her expression was frosty.

"The question you have just heard," she said, "illustrates a basic misconception about animal communication. I do not see visions. I do not predict the future. I cannot connect with your long-lost great-grandmother on the other side."

There were several titters from around the room. Rosalind did not look amused. Nor did Aunt Peg. Clearly she'd expected better from her seminar participants.

"What I can do . . ." Rosalind paused to let her gaze sweep over all of us, "if you have an open mind and a desire to investigate phenomena that may not have been readily apparent to you until now, is put you in touch with your animal companions in a way you haven't been able to achieve before. I can use my gift for telepathy to talk to your Poodles, and to let you talk to them through me."

The laughter had died away. Now there was only silence in the room. Rosalind may or may not have been an imposter; I was still reserving judgment on that. But she sure knew how to work an audience.

"None of you would be here today if you didn't love your dogs. As participants in your national specialty, you've reached the pinnacle of your breed. I dare say that each and every one of you has evolved a system for communicating with your Poodles. You know how to talk to them, but do you know how to listen to what they have to say?"

A hand shot up in the front row. "I'm more than willing to listen," said a Mini breeder from Florida. "I'd love to have a better feeling for what my dogs are trying to tell me. But it seems as though they understand me better than I understand them."

"That's because humans are accustomed to communicating with words," Rosalind replied. "Animals communicate with each other telepathically; they send pictures, they visualize. Every one of you has the ability to use telepathy. We're all born with it, but most of us never develop our gift."

Her voice rang out clearly across the big room. Those who'd been fidgeting in their seats now sat still—Bertie and me included.

"When I talk to an animal, I receive pictures back in turn. It comes to me like a movie playing in my head. I hear the animal's thoughts, I feel their feelings. And it becomes my job to interpret what they are telling me. This is an incredible quest, a fascinating journey. I hope that each and every one of you here today will make the effort to take it with me."

9

"Wow," Bertie breathed under her breath. "She's good. I wonder if she can talk to babies."

"I doubt it," I whispered back. "At least not babies who aren't born yet."

Rosalind gave examples of her work. She read glowing testimonials from pet owners. She explained that most often she was consulted for medical problems. "The animals tell me where they hurt. They're glad to know someone is listening to them, that someone cares about their needs. My job is to bridge the gap in understanding between humans and canines. I hope you'll agree that that's a very worthwhile undertaking."

The animal communicator spoke for another half hour. After that, Aunt Peg had arranged for people to set up individual consultation sessions. I slipped out of the conference room when those began.

It was time to start working on Eve. I still had to clip the puppy's face and tail, give her a bath, and blow her coat dry. I'd already clipped her feet earlier in the week. For a smaller show, I might have been tempted to cut a few corners or rush through some of the preparations. Not at PCA.

The national specialty was as much a breed showcase as it was a competition. Of all the exhibitors that gathered there each year, only a handful would win points. Slightly more would take home a ribbon. The rest would be content with the knowledge that they'd shown off their Poodles, and their breeding programs, at the biggest Poodle extravaganza on earth.

I wasn't holding out undue hope that Eve would win a ribbon in her enormous puppy class. But I was determined that she would look good for the knowledgeable spectators standing at ringside. For this show, Eve's grooming had to be perfect. Or at least as perfect as I could make it.

When I reached my room, the message light on my phone was blinking. I'd been hoping to hear from Sam but instead the voice mail was from a man who gave his name as Detective Mandahar. He'd been told I was one of the people present the night before when Betty Jean had died and he wished to speak with me at my earliest convenience. He was, he said, currently at the hotel and would check my room again before departing.

I wrote down the detective's name, then ran Eve downstairs for a quick visit to the exercise area. Blowing a Standard Poodle's coat dry takes several hours and I wanted the puppy to be comfortable during the long process. On the way back, I intended to stop at the front desk to ask where I might find the detective. As it turned out, however, several policemen were gathered in the corner where Betty Jean had been found the night before.

After Eve had had her run, I went over and asked for the detective. A tall black man detached himself from the group and came over. His close-cropped dark hair was graying at the temples; his eyes, slightly bloodshot, were covered by a thick pair of glasses.

I held out my hand as he approached. "I'm Melanie Travis. You left a message in my room?"

The detective nodded. He appeared to be thinking. My guess was that he'd left many such messages and was trying to remember exactly who I was. To fill the moment of silence, I added, "And this is Eve."

That made him smile. His teeth were even and very white. "Do all you people start conversations by introducing your dogs?"

"They're not just dogs," I replied. "They're Poodles."

"You're not the first person to tell me that. I gather you have a big dog show going on here this week?"

"That's right. The show itself is at the Prince George's Equestrian Center. But this is our headquarters hotel. There are Poodle exhibitors here from all over the world."

I knew I wasn't telling him anything he hadn't been told before. To his credit, the detective managed to look interested. "Do you have a few minutes to talk? This shouldn't take long."

We sat down on one of the benches that lined the walkway behind the hotel. Eve lay down at my feet. Detective Mandahar pulled out a small pad to take notes, then asked me what I'd been doing outside behind the hotel after dark the night before.

"The same thing as just about everyone else," I said. "Walking my dog before going to bed. This field back here has been designated as the exercise area for the Poodles."

"Exercise meaning that you bring the dogs out here and run them around?"

"Not exactly, though most of them do get to play a bit. This is where we bring our dogs so they can pee and poop. For obvious reasons, the club doesn't want us to making a mess all over the hotel. Everybody pitches in back here to keep the area clean."

I gestured toward the row of pooper-scoopers lined up against the building. He glanced at them briefly. "This club you're talking about, that would be . . ."

"PCA. The Poodle Club of America. They're the ones who are putting on the dog show. Some of the people here are members, others aren't. But nearly everyone staying at the hotel is involved with Poodles in one way or another."

Detective Mandahar made a note. "Is there any sort of rivalry between this club and any other Poodle clubs?"

"None at all." The question made me smile. "The other Poodle clubs are local ones. They're called affiliate clubs. Most people here belong to an affiliate club in the area where they live. And then some belong to the national club. But we're all just Poodle lovers. It's not like belonging to a rival gang or anything."

"I see."

I wasn't entirely sure that he did. His next question confirmed my suspicion.

"Are some club members more important than others?"

"Well . . . yes. We have elected officers. But everyone's vote counts equally. And holding an office is hard work. Not everyone wants to do it, or has the time to get that involved."

He consulted an earlier note. "I understand there are committees, too. And that Miss Boone was one of the committee heads?"

"Yes, she and her sister have cochaired the raffle committee for the last several years." I tried not to sound impatient. As far as I could tell, this line of questioning was getting us nowhere. And I was wasting time that could be more productively spent working on Eve.

"But it's not like someone would have killed her in order to get that position," I added. "Believe me, with a show this size, there's plenty of work to go around. Most of it is handled by volunteers."

My puppy was getting restless. I dropped my hand from my lap and scratched behind her ears. "I was told you think Betty Jean was murdered."

"Let's just say we're uncertain that she died of natural causes. So until that determination is made, we'd like to keep our avenues of investigation open."

An official sounding mouthful that told me exactly . . .
nothing. As was undoubtedly intended. Next, Detective
Mandahar walked me through the events of the previous
evening. I was willing to bet that my version sounded
pretty much like everyone else's. I'd been outside with a
dog and heard a scream. By the time I got there, Betty
Jean was already dead.

"How long have you known the deceased?" he asked at
the end.

"Since yesterday morning. My aunt, Margaret Turnbull,
volunteered me to serve on the raffle committee and I
met the sisters when I arrived at the show."

"Did anything unusual happen at the show yesterday?"

That would depend, I thought. There were those who
would say that everything that had to do with showing dogs,
especially Poodles whose trims rendered them somewhat
of an oddity in the present-day world, was highly unusual.
Not that I had any intention of debating that point.
Instead I mentioned that the Boones had been concerned
about a professional handler who'd been trying to get
their dog disqualified from competition.

Detective Mandahar looked interested, but only briefly.
"Could he have succeeded?" he asked.

"No. Because the dog wasn't guilty of the infractions
he'd been charged with."

"Then what was the problem?"

"It was one of perception. Of influence. Of wanting the
judges to think twice before using that particular dog."

"Yes, but . . . bottom line, it's still just a bunch of
Poodles running around a ring, right?"

"It's important to us," I said quietly.

"I'll keep that in mind," said the detective.

I hoped he would.

Interview finished, I bathed Eve in the bathtub in my
room.

According to the rules set forth by the club, I wasn't supposed to be doing that. But considering that the grooming room had plenty of outlets for blowing dry and not a single tub, where did they think all the wet Poodles were coming from? It wasn't as though we were going to take them outside and spray them with a hose. Besides, I'd brought my own towels from home. I figured that ought to count for something.

Bath complete, we headed back downstairs. Not surprisingly, the grooming room was crowded. With the conformation classes starting early the next morning, there was plenty of work to be done. I saw a number of familiar faces as I hopped Eve up onto the rubber-matted grooming table and laid her gently on her side.

Some exhibitors were blowing their Poodles dry, others were clipping or scissoring. A number of people were simply standing around talking. Coffee and doughnuts had been set out on a side table, a gesture greatly appreciated by those who found themselves grooming at all hours of the day and night.

Even though she was still a puppy, Eve had been shown enough to know what was expected of her. She lay quietly as I went to work. I started by drying the all-important hair on the top of her head and back of her neck. That was the hair that would give Eve's trim its luxurious outline.

At eleven months of age, Eve had an excellent coat for a puppy. Still, there wasn't a Poodle exhibitor anywhere who didn't constantly wish for more. The better the job I did with the dryer, the thicker and more impressive her coat would appear. Important as the task was, however, it was still basically mindless work. Even as I brushed and straightened, I had plenty of opportunity to look around the room.

Dale Atherton had a table set up not too far from mine. He was scissoring a white Standard Poodle who stood like a rock while he rounded the bracelets on her hind legs. Nina Gold was standing off to one side, chatting with the handler as he worked. Her designer suit and Jimmy Choo shoes looked out of place in a room where Poodle hair floated through the air and gathered in piles on the floor. Nina had yet to realize that, at PCA, what the Poodles looked like counted for a great deal more than what their owners did.

A man was standing next to Nina, his arm slung casually around her shoulders. Christian Gold, I assumed. The Mini breeder from California; the man with a bundle of money. He wasn't the fashion plate his wife was. Indeed, if he hadn't been touching Nina, I probably wouldn't have noticed him at all.

Christian was shorter than his wife. Just slightly, but enough to make the arm around her shoulders a stretch. Yet he made the effort. That said something, though I wasn't sure I knew exactly what.

As I watched, Nina laughed at something Dale said. Nina tipped her head to one side and glanced over at her husband. Christian didn't even smile.

"Excuse me, are you Melanie Travis?"

I reached for the off switch on the dryer with one hand and placed the other on Eve's neck so she wouldn't get up. "Yes—" Turning, I saw who'd asked the question. My reply died in my throat.

"I'm Harry Gandolf." The Poodle handler glanced at my hands, both of which were busy, and didn't offer his.

"I know," I said.

"You do?"

"The Boone sisters pointed you out to me."

"Ahh, well . . ." Harry smiled. The expression didn't transform his pugnacious features. Now he just looked like a happy Rottie. "I hope you don't believe everything you hear."

"That depends who I'm talking to."

"Fair enough." The smile faded. If he licked his chops, I was going to take a step back. "I'm a big fan of your aunt's."

"Really? I'll be sure and let her know."

"I wish you would. Even the best breeders don't always make good judges. Peg Turnbull's got what it takes, though."

He was right, she did. Although considering what I'd heard about Harry, I wouldn't necessarily credit him with knowing about that. Or caring.

Even with the damp towels I'd spread over the portions of Eve's coat that I wasn't currently working on, the puppy's hair was starting to curl. In the warm room, with all the other dryers blowing, her hair was air-drying too fast. Stopping to talk mid-process was not allowed. At least not with the likes of Harry Gandolf.

"Is there something I can do for you?" I asked.

"I was told you're working on the raffle committee."

"That's right. Would you like to buy some tickets?"

I'd been joking. Harry didn't look amused.

"I was hoping you might be able to tell me where I could find Edith Jean Boone. Nobody seems to know where she is."

"Why?" I asked. It wasn't any of my business, but what the heck. Her whereabouts weren't any of his.

"I wanted to pass along my condolences on her terrible loss."

Right. If that were the case, he could have done so when he'd waylaid Edith Jean that morning.

"I'm afraid I can't help you," I said.

He stared at me for a long minute. "Thanks anyway. I guess I'll go check with Roger."

As he walked away I realized that Edith Jean's handler, Roger Carew, was also in the crowded room. There was a silver Toy puppy on his grooming table. The fact that several people were standing around admiring the dog indicated that it was probably Bubba. If I hadn't been busy with Eve, I'd have been tempted to take a closer look myself.

Instead, I turned the blower back on and maneuvered myself around to the other side of Eve's table. Now I could watch the proceedings while I worked.

Roger, his attention focused on the silver puppy, didn't see Harry coming. He was scissoring Bubba's front—delicate and exacting work, especially on a dog as small as a Toy. One careless slip could totally alter the look of a trim; an accidental gouge would remove a Poodle from competition until the hair grew back. The blades of Roger's scissors flashed open and shut as he nicked off hair in incredibly tiny increments.

A couple standing by the table glanced at Harry as he approached. Roger never even looked up. With each gliding cut from the scissors, the angle of the puppy's front grew more exact, more perfect.

I saw Harry lift his hand. With sudden horror, I realized he was about to slap Roger's shoulder in greeting. That thump would travel straight down the handler's arm and into the blade of the scissors, now positioned so precisely against the puppy's hair. In mere seconds, Harry would succeed in destroying months of work.

There wasn't time to stop him. Nor to warn Roger. The room was too noisy. I was too far away . . .

Like hell, I thought. I opened my mouth and screamed.

10

Immediately the room went still. Aside from the persistent whine of the blow-dryers, everything was abruptly silent. It was that kind of scream. All eyes turned in my direction.

Including Roger's. He straightened, lifting his arm away from the puppy as he rose and looked around. Harry's hand, already mid-descent, landed harmlessly on his shoulder.

"Sorry," I said, fumbling hastily for an excuse. "I thought I saw a mouse."

"A mouse?" a woman shrieked. She danced in place, trying to lift both feet from the ground at the same time. "Where?"

I gestured vaguely toward the food table. That seemed likely enough. What I hadn't counted on was that several men would feel obliged to rush to the rescue: striding toward the table, lifting the cloth that covered it and peering underneath, then inspecting the doughnuts in the box as if looking for signs of tiny mouse tracks.

Meanwhile, out of the corner of my eye, I saw Roger try to brush Harry off. He returned the other handler's greeting curtly before turning back to Bubba. Purposely he angled himself so that his body was between Harry and the silver Toy. Roger didn't resume scissoring. Instead, after a minute, he lifted the small dog up off the table and placed him under his arm. Good move, I thought.

"I don't see anything," said one of my would-be rescuers. They all turned and looked at me again. "Where did you see it?"

"I could have been mistaken." I plastered a sheepish smile on my face. "Maybe I saw some blowing hair and got carried away."

"See?" The shrieking woman's husband patted her shoulder soothingly. "False alarm."

She didn't look convinced. In fact, she really looked as though she wished he would pick her up and carry her out of the room. I was sorry for upsetting her needlessly; but not half as sorry as I would have been if Harry had succeeded in ruining Bubba's chances at tomorrow's show.

On the other side of the room, Harry continued to try to talk to Roger. Roger continued to ignore him. Still cradling the Toy in his arms, he began to pack up his equipment. The people he'd been talking to drifted away.

And all that time, I realized belatedly, my dryer had been running with the nozzle pointing in Eve's direction. Her long hair, which needed to be straightened with a pin brush as it dried, had, while my attention was elsewhere, curled and kinked all on its own. I'd have to get out a spray bottle of water, wet that section down, and start all over.

I sighed. Then jumped. Before I could even reach for the spray bottle in my tack box, a hand was holding it out to me.

"You saw a mouse." The voice that came with the hand sounded amused. Also familiar.

Crawford Langley was Terry's boss in their working relationship, his partner in life. The two of them suited one another remarkably well. Crawford was the older, more experienced half of the pair, as distinguished in his de-

meanor as Terry was flamboyant. Crawford had been a top
Poodle handler for decades. His skills were beyond dispute, his discretion legendary, his kindness often hidden
behind a stern exterior.

"Yes," I repeated, perhaps a tad defensively. "I saw a
mouse. Is that so impossible?"

"The mouse, no. That scream, yes. You could have
given Janet Leigh a run for her money with that one." His
gray eyes considered me thoughtfully. "Though you're not
half the actress she was."

"I don't know what you mean."

"Sure you do. But I'll elaborate if you want. In the three
years I've known you, you've gotten into more trouble
than most people do in a lifetime. You've been shot at,
half strangled, knocked out, and nearly burned to a crisp.
And that only counts the stuff I know about. I'd be willing
to bet that's the first time you've let out a blood-curdling
yelp like that."

The man had a point. Which apparently was that he was
getting to know me all too well. "So?"

Crawford's tone softened. "Is everything okay?"

"Just fine, now."

"You're sure?"

Dragging his stuff behind him on a dolly, Roger was
leaving the room. Bubba's small face peered out from behind the mesh door of a wooden crate that was perched
on top.

"Positive."

"Okay." Crawford glanced in Roger's direction, then
back at me. "Just checking."

Impulsively I reached out, wound my arms around his
shoulders, and gave him a quick hug. "Thank you."

Now Crawford looked embarrassed. As soon as I released
him, he spun on his heel and walked away. "Women," I
heard him mutter under his breath.

Eve, the model of Poodle patience, was waiting for me on the table. I sprayed down her hair and went back to work.

Dinnertime had come and gone by the time Eve's coat was perfectly blown dry, her topknot and ears rebanded and wrapped, her face and tail clipped. Before heading back upstairs to our room, I took the puppy for another walk outside. After the hours she'd spent lying still on the table, I knew she'd appreciate the chance to stretch her legs.

Just like the night before, the evening had grown chilly. Accustomed to the humid warmth of the grooming room, I found myself shivering as I slipped off Eve's leash and watched her bound away.

The exercise area was mostly empty. The police were gone, although their yellow tape remained. A couple of sightseers stood at the perimeter and stared at the small grassy corner. I couldn't imagine there was anything to see.

As I waited for Eve to circle back to me, my stomach started to rumble. Loudly. It felt as though I'd eaten lunch eons ago. No doubt Eve was hungry too.

I was about to call her when one of the men standing near the corner turned around. Light from an overhead lamp fell across his face and I recognized Damien Bradley. For a man who'd supposedly been banned from the hotel, he seemed to spend a lot of time there.

I wondered whether morbid curiosity had drawn him back today. Or whether he'd come for another reason, then decided to have a look at the place where Betty Jean's body had been found. Aunt Peg was convinced that the man had a propensity for stirring up trouble, but he didn't seem to be causing any problems at the moment. In fact, he wasn't doing much of anything.

Then he noticed Eve. While I'd been watching Damien, the puppy had wandered toward the end of the field that bordered the parking lot. Immediately Damien moved to intercept her.

"Hey, sweet girl," he called out, his voice low and inviting. "What are you doing out here all by yourself?"

"Sorry," I said, stepping quickly out of the shadows. I hurried to cover the distance between us. "She's with me."

Eve, meanwhile, stopped and stood, waiting to see what we wanted her to do. Damien reached the puppy first. As a precaution, he looped his arms loosely around her neck, confining her, yet not causing any damage to the hair.

"Thanks, but she's okay." The puppy wagged her tail at my approach. "She won't run."

Professional handlers deal with all sorts of dogs: some trained, many untrained, others willful or disobedient. They take whatever their clients send them. Clearly Damien wasn't irresponsible enough to let any of *his* charges run loose. I counted that as a point in his favor.

"I didn't see you over there," he said, unwinding his arms. "And I was afraid she'd head toward the road. A black puppy on a dark night . . ."

He didn't have to spell it out. We both knew the worst that could happen.

"Thank you," I said again. There was a cotton show leash in my pocket. I slipped the lightweight collar on over Eve's head. "I should have been watching her more closely. I guess I got distracted."

"Hard not to," Damien said, glancing back at the corner. "Under the circumstances."

"Did you know Betty Jean?"

He nodded. "We were old friends. I used to handle the sisters' dogs."

I hadn't known that. "Not anymore?" Purposely I kept my tone light.

"No. Things change, don't they?" Damien didn't sound too upset by the loss. "Now they use Roger Carew. I don't think the sisters knew too many people in the dog show world. What happened was a real shame . . ."

"Yes, it was."

We had yet to introduce ourselves, but it didn't seem to matter. One of the things I'd always liked best about PCA was that everyone in attendance shared a common bond in their love of Poodles. It was easily possible to share an interesting conversation with total strangers. People did it all the time.

Damien didn't seem in any hurry to leave. I decided I wasn't either. "Are you a guest at the hotel?" I asked.

"No. I'm staying down the road. I guess I don't measure up to PCA's standard of good behavior. They requested that I go elsewhere."

At least he was honest.

"How about you?"

"I'm here. My aunt wouldn't have it any other way."

"Who's your aunt?"

"Peg Turnbull."

"Ah." Damien nodded knowingly. "One of the dragons in charge."

"I gather you don't get along too well with them."

"Let's just say I don't enjoy kowtowing to authority and leave it at that." He peered at me in the half-light. "I guess you've heard the stories."

"I'm beginning to think you might have enjoyed starring in them."

"Maybe I did, at that." Abruptly Damien's gaze shifted away from mine. His expression froze.

I looked to see what had caught his attention. Sam Driver had come out of the hotel and was walking toward us. Damien's face hardened; mine lit up. Sam was my best friend, my lover. My one-time fiancé. I'd known he was arriving this evening, I just hadn't been sure when.

Nor had I expected him to greet me with a scowl. Then, as he approached, I realized that he wasn't looking at me at all. The snarl on his face was aimed at the handler.

"Bradley," he said curtly.

"Driver," the other man replied.

So the two of them declined to be on a first name basis, that was clear enough. Nothing like a little male posturing to get things off to a good start.

Oblivious to the undercurrents humming in the air, Eve demonstrated her lack of manners by jumping up on Sam and trying to lick his face. Absently, he smoothed a hand over her cheek and down her neck. The puppy wiggled with joy. It's a sad thing when your dog gets a greeting before you do.

"Hello," I said loudly. Just in case everyone had forgotten I was there.

Sam didn't exactly answer. He did reach out and take my hand. His fingers, warm and strong, wrapped around mine and gave them a squeeze.

Damien didn't miss the possessive gesture. I assumed he wasn't meant to. "I guess I'll be going now," he said.

As the handler walked away, I tipped my face up to Sam's. "How about a kiss?"

Sam was still distracted. He stared after Damien. "What were you doing out here with *him?*"

"Talking. What did it look like?" I took a step back. So much for the kiss.

"Do you know who he is?"

"Damien Bradley. The bad boy of PCA."

"Precisely. Whatever he wanted, you shouldn't have anything to do with him."

"He didn't want anything," I said. My patience was beginning to fray. "We were just talking. Despite what I've heard, he seemed nice."

"Of course he seemed nice. That's what he does."

"Hard way to make a living."

I was kidding. Sam wasn't in a kidding mood.

"I mean it, Mel. The man is scum. You shouldn't let him flirt with you."

"What makes you think he was?"

"I know Damien. When I lived in Michigan, we used to cross paths at shows all the time. He's very good at conning gullible women."

Annoyed, I snatched my hand back. "Damien wasn't conning me. And I'm not gullible—"

"No, you're not." Sam took a step to close the distance between us. He pressed his body to mine; his voice softened as he said, "You're beautiful. And desirable. And if Damien Bradley wasn't flirting with you, he'd have to be a stupid man. Which I happen to know he isn't . . ."

Ahhh. The kiss. It was worth waiting for. It warmed my skin and curled my toes. And stole my breath away.

"You know I don't flirt with other men," I said several minutes later when I'd started to breathe again.

"That doesn't stop them from hoping you're available." Sam's hand curled around the back of my head. His fingers tangled in my hair. His thumb skimmed back and forth over my ear. "You should be wearing my ring."

At moments like that, with both our bodies humming in harmony, it was hard to remember why I wasn't.

Sam had offered me a diamond on the occasion of his second proposal. There'd been another proposal since. That time, I'd taken the ring though I hadn't put it on my finger. Sam had said he was willing to wait until I was ready. Now I had something to show him.

"I am wearing your ring," I said.

His gaze dropped to my unadorned finger, then fol-

lowed as I lifted my hand and opened the collar of my
shirt. A slender platinum chain hung around my neck.
The diamond ring dangled from it, only inches from my
heart.

Sam's sudden smile was achingly, heartbreakingly intense. I felt something inside me twist, then soften.

"Progress," he said softly. "I'll take it."

So would I, I thought. Dear God, so would I.

11

"Where's Tar?" I asked Sam as we walked back into the hotel.

Tar was Sam's Standard Poodle. Like Faith, he had originally come from Aunt Peg. The big, black Poodle had finished his championship from the puppy class and was now competing as a specials dog, meaning that he entered the Best of Variety class in the hope of defeating the other champions and going on to represent Standard Poodles in the Non-Sporting group and Best in Show.

Though he'd only been on the circuit a few months, Tar had already compiled an enviable record. He'd won half a dozen groups and his first BIS. Too young and too new to be considered one of the favorites in Friday's highly competitive Best of Variety judging, Sam was nevertheless hoping that Tar might manage to win an Award of Merit.

"Asleep in my room," said Sam. "Believe it or not, we actually got here an hour ago. After I finished unloading, I went looking for you and got sidetracked in eight different directions. I saw Peg and Bertie, and ran into at least two dozen other people I know. I've seen pictures of someone's new stud dog, helped to socialize a puppy, been asked my opinion of the new test for PRA, and offered a chance to have my dog's thoughts read. I'm still not sure what that last thing was all about."

"Welcome to PCA," I said with a grin. "The greatest show on earth."

"You can say that again. Bertie told me you left the seminar early to go give Eve a bath. You must have been working all afternoon. She looks terrific."

Like many dogs, Eve didn't like elevators. Automatically, Sam and I headed for the back stairs.

"Thanks. Have you eaten yet? I was about to go looking for some dinner. I just want to take Eve up to my room and give Davey a call . . ."

"I just saw Davey," said Sam. "He and Faith are both doing fine."

"Where did you see them?"

Reaching the landing for the second floor, I pushed the door open. Eve dashed through and ran on ahead down the hallway. Though she'd only been in residence for two days, she stopped outside the right room. Maybe she read the number on the door.

Sam fell into step beside me. "I stopped in Stamford on my way down here. I thought you might want an update."

"I'm dying for one. I spoke with Davey briefly last night. Aside from the fact that he and Faith were still alive, what I heard wasn't entirely reassuring."

"That's what I figured." Sam was grinning. "Davey told me to tell you that the s'mores were great and the firemen let him ride the truck around the neighborhood."

"Perfect," I muttered. As I lifted my card key from the lock, Eve pushed the door open with her nose and scooted past us into the room.

"Davey also said that you shouldn't bother to call tonight since he and Bob are going out to a video arcade."

"Bob doesn't have enough video games for them to play at home?" I turned in the doorway as I asked the question and found Sam standing much closer than I'd realized.

"Apparently not." He moved closer still. My back was braced against the door. His arms came up on either side of me, trapping me there. Sam lowered his head to mine. His lips hovered next to my ear. "Can we stop discussing your ex-husband now?"

I swallowed heavily. I could feel the heat and the hardness of his body. The slightest move brought friction. I heard Sam's breath catch.

One hand skimmed down over my shoulder and settled on my breast. My heart thudded beneath his palm. Sam's lips sought mine but I pulled my mouth away.

"Close the damn door," I said.

Wednesday morning the PCA National Specialty opened in earnest. Earlier in the week, things had been fairly low key. With the start of the conformation classes, the pomp and pageantry of the event increased exponentially. A full slate of activities was planned. First came the judging of the dog classes in all three varieties. At their conclusion, the Parade of Champions and Obedience Title Holders would be held, followed by the Affiliate Club Council Meeting.

The parade was a perennial favorite. Open to any Poodle that had achieved either a breed or obedience title, it was a showcase for winners from the past as well as an opportunity for breeders to give retired favorites another taste of the limelight. Each Poodle was introduced in turn and a resume of its accomplishments read. Each was then gaited around the big ring to the sound of appreciative applause.

Poodles are born performers; they love being the center of attention. Though most of these dogs now lived the pampered lives of cherished pets, that was set aside as soon as they entered the show ring. Heads and tails snapped up eagerly. They adored being back, and it showed. By the time the entire group, usually a hundred Poodles or so, did their final lap together to the accompaniment of the music from *Fame,* more than a few spectators would be sniffling happily.

The day's judging started promptly at eight A.M. The Standard and Miniature Poodle Puppy Dog classes, 6 to 9 Months of age, were up first. Entries were large, and as always the competition would be incredible. Winning a ribbon of any color was an honor; even making the cut was a thrill.

By the time Eve and I arrived at the show site at seven-thirty to check in with Edith Jean, the arena had not only been open for several hours, it was bustling with activity. As soon as we entered the building, I could feel the excitement in the air. Already most of the ringside chairs had been staked out. The catalog table was doing a brisk business.

I got Eve settled in her crate and hurried over to the raffle table. It looked as though Edith Jean had just arrived as well. She was unpacking and setting up.

"Good, you're here," she said.

My gaze swept over the table. "Is something wrong?"

Edith Jean shoved a box under the table and looked up. "Not that I'm aware of. I just wanted to make sure we got everything ready in time. It looks like today's going to be busy." Her right hand was still bandaged. Today the vet wrap was neon yellow.

"How's your hand? Does it still hurt? I'm sure I could find a doctor—"

Edith Jean stood up straight and propped both fists on her hips. "If I needed a doctor, I guess I could figure out where to get one myself, now couldn't I? Quit bugging me about it, I'm managing just fine."

That might have been an understatement. The woman was a bundle of frenetic activity. My left hand is practically useless when it comes to fine motor skills, but Edith Jean was not only coping with her handicap, she was working at top speed. Already she had the cash box open and counted, the rolls of tickets out, pens lined up neatly beside them. All that remained was to finish setting up the table.

"Here," I said, taking another box from her. "Let me do that."

"Tell the truth," E.J. confided, "I'd rather keep busy. I'm so nervous about today's judging I could just about spit."

"There's no point in being nervous now. Bubba's class won't even be held until this afternoon."

"Try telling my stomach that."

The older woman did look pretty wound up. "Do you want me to get you some coffee?" I asked. "Or maybe a nice cup of tea?"

"Sure, that's just what I need. A good jolt of caffeine."

At least she hadn't lost her sense of humor.

"I saw Harry Gandolf at the hotel yesterday afternoon. He was looking for you." Best not to mention what I'd seen him try to do, I decided. Edith Jean was doing enough worrying already. "I didn't think you wanted to see him so I didn't tell him where you were."

"I appreciate that, dear. I imagine he'll find me soon enough, though. Hard not to know where to look, now."

She was right. Word would get around soon enough that despite the tragedy that had befallen her, Edith Jean had not abandoned her post. We'd probably be swamped with well-wishers again today. With luck, we might sell raffle tickets to all of them.

"Do you mind if I ask you something I've been wondering about?"

"Shoot," said Edith Jean

"It's about Betty Jean."

She glared at me, her eyes narrowing. "You know what I wish? I wish everyone would stop walking on eggshells around me. I don't mind talking about Sister. Hell, I'd rather talk about her than pretend like she didn't exist. Why does everyone think I'm going to faint if they say her name?"

"They're trying to be sensitive," I said.

"Do I look like I *need* sensitive?"

Not particularly, I thought. Right that minute, Edith Jean looked like a feisty old southern broad who could wake up with the sun, shoot her own breakfast, skin it, fry it, and slap it on a plate. Possum, probably.

"I was just wondering what Betty Jean was doing outside the hotel the other night. Apparently she was by herself, and she didn't have a dog with her . . ."

Edith Jean nodded. "I see what you're asking. Sister and I were both outside at first. This was after we'd been in the grooming room for a couple of hours. You know how time just sort of gets away from you when you're working on a Poodle?"

Did I ever. My marathon grooming session with Eve the day before had been proof of that. "Sure," I agreed.

"That's pretty much what happened to us. Not that Bubba needs a lot of work at this point. Or that Roger would even let us touch a pair of scissors to that puppy."

I looked at the cagey expression on Edith Jean's face and ventured a guess. "You weren't grooming Bubba at all, were you? You just took the puppy down to the grooming room to show him off."

"Let's just say that Harry Gandolf isn't the only one who knows how word of mouth works."

Gamesmanship. PCA was rife with it. Though we all stayed at the same hotel, the judges were banned from mingling with the exhibitors in an attempt to prevent them from succumbing to influence. That didn't stop the exhibitors from trying to psych each other out, or gather public opinion to their side.

"Then what happened?" I asked.

"We were down there a good long while. Plenty of time

to let everyone get an eyeful. After that, we took Bubba out back behind the hotel. He'd been on the table a while and needed to pee."

Just as I'd done with Eve. In their own way, certain doggy rituals were entirely predictable.

"I was watching the puppy and you know Sister, she was always looking to make herself useful. She went and picked up a poop-scoop. After she'd picked up Bubba's mess she just kept on going, cleaning up after all the other dogs whose owners hadn't had the good sense to do it for themselves.

"Bless her heart. There she was, wandering around in the dark and scooping away like she thought she had a prayer of seeing what she was doing. 'Sister,' I said. 'Y'all come along inside now. Bubba's getting a chill.' You remember it was cold out there the other night."

Chilly, yes. Cold, no. But the sisters came from Georgia. This far north, they probably felt as though they were on the verge of the polar ice cap.

"Of course Sister didn't pay any mind to me. That was the way she was. She thought she was doing the club a favor and she figured I'd just wait until she was done. Well it's not like I was going to stand around forever. 'Fine,' I said. 'Stay out here all night. I'm going to go take Bubba inside.' And I did."

"So she wasn't with anyone when you left?"

"Oh, there were other people out there, all right. Most of them had Poodles and they were wandering around the field in the dark just like Sister was. Maybe she stopped to talk to someone after I was gone . . ." Edith Jean dropped her gaze and looked away.

I was about to ask another question, but I never got the chance. The loudspeaker came on, putting an end to our conversation. The announcer welcomed us to the show and asked us to rise for the singing of the national anthem. At the song's close, someone in the building let out a joyous whoop of anticipation. PCA was officially open for business.

In the rings, the Standard and Miniature judges stood ready to do their jobs. Ring stewards called their first classes. A dozen entries filed into the Mini ring; nearly two dozen into the Standard.

Edith Jean had already packed the raffle basket for me. Now as I stood up on my toes and tried to see over the spectators standing between us and the ring, she put it into my hands. "You're dying to watch some, aren't you?"

"Yes," I admitted guiltily. Especially with Betty Jean gone, I was supposed to be Edith Jean's right hand. But with the best Standard Poodles in the country gathered right under my nose for the next three days, how could I *not* be intensely interested in seeing them?

"Go on," she said, giving me a gentle push. "Take the raffle basket and do some mingling around the ringside. And if you happen to watch a bit of the judging while you're in the neighborhood, well, nobody ever said you had to be hard at work every single minute."

"But—"

"Go. Enjoy yourself. I'll see you in a couple of hours."

The basket felt heavier on my arm than it had the previous day. I was halfway to the ring before I glanced down and saw why. Edith Jean hadn't just filled it with the essentials I would need to sell tickets. She'd also added the thick dog show catalog that I'd stashed beneath the table with my purse. It was placed right on top for easy reference.

I turned and looked back. Edith Jean was already busy, showing off the money tree to a potential customer. Waving the catalog, I mouthed my thanks. E.J. used her bandaged hand to wave back and kept right on working.

I spent the next hour selling tickets and keeping an eye on the judging in the Standard ring at the same time. The puppy classes were of particular interest to me since that was where I would be showing Eve the next morning. I wanted to see how the judge set up his ring, find out what gaiting pattern he favored, and see if I could make a stab at discovering what he was looking for in a Poodle puppy.

Whether we had a chance of winning or not, I wanted Eve to make a good impression. One of the best ways to insure that was to be prepared. I already knew from checking the catalog that there would be thirty-six entries in Eve's class. Sorting them out correctly would be a huge task.

Being selected to judge at the national specialty is an enormous honor. It's also a lot of work. Judges have to hold their focus through class entries that are larger than the total number of Poodles they would see at a normal show. The caliber of the dogs they're deciding among is higher as well; often only the tiniest difference separates a blue ribbon from a white one. Tommy Lamb, the Standard judge, was managing his ring with flair and authority. He looked well up to the task.

Aunt Peg and Sam were seated at the corner of the Standard ring opposite where Mr. Lamb was standing. Their placement was no accident. When the judge sent his puppies straight out and back to check their movement coming and going away, they would have the same view that he did, the best in the house.

As the judge made his cut in the first class, I headed over to join them. Sam stood up as I approached. "Peg said not to save you a seat. She seemed to think you'd be working at the raffle table."

"I *am* working," I said, holding up my basket. "Can't you tell?"

Aunt Peg never even tore her gaze away from the action in the ring. "Quiet," she said.

"Why? The judge isn't saying anything."

"He might."

Hard to argue with logic like that.

"Take my chair," Sam whispered. "I'll stand behind you. Do you want me to buy some tickets while you're here?"

"That would be great." I scooted around him and sat. Sam took the basket and rummaged around for the supplies he needed.

"Who are we rooting for?" I asked Peg under my breath.

"That one." She flicked her finger discreetly in the direction of a big black puppy. "Yoko's dog. Check your catalog. He's Eve's half brother, sired by the same dog you bred Faith to."

Of course Aunt Peg had been in charge of making that decision. Just as when she planned her own litters, she'd chosen a stud dog after weighing a variety of important factors including health, genetic test results, and temperament, as well as good looks. The litter of puppies I'd gotten as a result had been everything I'd hoped they would be.

In the ring, Mr. Lamb pulled Yoko's puppy out of the line and put him in third place. He looked up and down his entry again, then sent them all around one last time.

"Good," Peg said as the judge lifted his hand and pointed, awarding the puppy the yellow ribbon. "That means you'll have a chance tomorrow."

"You mean I might win?" I asked, shocked.

"No." Peg sounded equally shocked by my presumption. "I mean you might get noticed in your class." She turned and looked at me sternly. "He'll like Eve's type. As long as you don't blow it, of course."

Of course, I thought. Wasn't that always the way?

12

"**D**o I have to buy more raffle tickets?" Aunt Peg asked.

Now that the first class was over, there was a lull in the ring while the judge marked his book, handed out the ribbons, and took a few minutes to speak into a tiny tape recorder about his placements. PCA requested that each judge write up a critique of his or her entries. Taping their impressions as they went along helped them remember what they'd been thinking at the time. With the ring momentarily empty, Peg had deigned to notice my presence.

"If you want," I replied. My aunt was one of those club members who believed in supporting her club to the fullest. And I wasn't about to turn down a sale, especially not one that gave me a good excuse to continue sitting and watching.

"Here, let me," said Sam. Though he'd finished his own transaction, he still had the basket. He lifted out the roll of tickets and began to unspool a dozen.

"You handle that like a pro."

"I should, I've had enough experience. You're not the only one who's served time on the raffle committee."

I turned in my chair and stared up at him. "You worked for the sisters, too?"

"No, this was a while ago. Ten years at least. It was before the Boones took over."

"You were on Rhonda Lowell's committee." Aunt Peg smiled at the memory. "She was a taskmaster." Her gaze shifted my way. "*She* didn't allow any sitting down on the job."

"No lunch or coffee breaks either," said Sam. "She had three assistants and by the second day, we were all dead on our feet."

"I don't think I know her," I said. The name didn't sound familiar.

"You wouldn't. She didn't last," Aunt Peg said. "Gave up showing dogs and found herself a new hobby."

"Something more challenging," said Sam. "Something faster paced."

"Lure coursing?" I guessed.

"Olympic bobsled team."

Ahhh. Suddenly, being indentured to Edith Jean's raffle table didn't sound like such a bad thing after all.

The next Standard Poodle class, Puppy Dog, 9 to 12 Months, began to file into the ring. The big group followed catalog order, handlers finding their place in line according to the numbers on their armbands.

Aunt Peg was already making notations in the margin of her catalog. While the class got organized, she spared me a quick glance. "Speaking of helping with the raffle, are you sure you shouldn't be over at the table with Edith Jean?"

"She was the one who sent me away," I said.

A woman sitting near us got up and left and Sam snagged the empty chair. "I heard about what happened to Betty Jean. I'll have to stop by and offer my condolences."

"Did you know Betty Jean?" I asked.

"No. I'm sorry to say I don't even remember what she looked like."

"You're not alone. The sisters don't appear to have known

anyone in the dog show world very well. They shipped their good puppy off to a handler this past spring and have kept tabs on his career from afar. Aside from coming to PCA each year, I get the impression that they pretty much kept to themselves. Which will make it even harder on Edith Jean when she has to go home alone."

"What about family back in Georgia?"

"Apparently there's nobody else," I said quietly. "Just the two of them and their Poodles. I wonder if Edith Jean has a job to go back to. At least that might help a little."

The puppy having its individual examination in the ring was a gangly apricot that bounced around like a jumping jack. Presumably having written off his chances, Aunt Peg spared me a bit of attention.

"Neither of the sisters worked," she said. "That's why they had so much time and energy to devote to running the raffle. That committee is one of the most labor intensive. The job starts in March when they begin soliciting donations and goes on through the end of June when they send out thank-you notes. The club offered to give the sisters a break after they'd done it a couple of times but they declined. I'm not sure how they support themselves, perhaps there's a bit of family money keeping them going. But I know they didn't have jobs."

The apricot puppy was sent around to the end of the line. According to the information I'd gleaned by watching Mr. Lamb's first class, that meant he wasn't going to make the cut.

Sam had finished filling out Aunt Peg's ticket stubs, which meant that I was fast running out of excuses for lingering. "I guess I'd better be going."

Sam stood up and handed me back my basket. Aunt Peg, concentrating once again on the action in the ring, was oblivious to my departure.

The start of the conformation classes had drawn a whole new crop of spectators. Like the others I'd spoken to earlier in the week, most were happy to support the club by purchasing raffle tickets. Twice over the next several hours I had to return to the table to empty my basket of cash and ticket stubs. Edith Jean was delighted by my progress.

"Don't forget now," she said when I checked in for the second time. "The Toy judging starts at one o'clock sharp. I'll need you to take over the table so I can go watch."

"I'll be here," I assured her. I fully intended to watch the showdown myself, even if I had to stand on the chair behind the raffle table and look over the crowds to do so.

Back at the Standard ring, the Novice class was being judged. At most shows, this class goes unentered. Here there were four in competition, one of which was handled by Damien Bradley. I checked out the Poodles, decided none was likely to figure in the day's outcome, then glanced across the ring to where Sam and Aunt Peg were sitting. They'd been joined by Rosalind Romanescue.

According to Aunt Peg, the animal communicator's seminar had turned out to be a bigger success than anyone could have anticipated. Indeed, interest in her services had been so strong that Rosalind had decided to stay on for the remainder of the show, using the extra time to schedule additional consultations. I wondered what she thought about as she watched the dogs in the ring. Was she trying to talk to the Poodles or merely enjoying the show?

The judge was handing out ribbons once again. Damien's entry took second. The popular Bred-by-Exhibitor class was next. Jostled by the moving crowds as I turned away, I bumped into someone standing behind me.

"Sorry," I said automatically. The basket was slung somewhat negligently over my arm. I reached out to steady it so its contents wouldn't spill.

"That's quite a load you're carrying," said Christian Gold. "What have you got there, muffins?"

"Raffle tickets."

Nina was standing beside her husband, her hand tucked through the crook in his elbow, her rose-tipped fingers resting lightly on his arm. "We met on Monday," she said, peering at me and offering a small smile.

Christian handed her his open catalog and reached for his wallet. "I guess we'd better have some."

"I've already sold your wife two dozen tickets," I felt obliged to mention.

He waved a hand. "Make it a dozen more."

"Do you want to hear about our prizes?"

"Let me guess. Whatever they are, I bet they've got Poodles on them."

"Pretty much, yes." I found myself smiling with him.

"That's about what I figured. Can you tell I've been here before? I'm Christian Gold, by the way."

"Melanie Travis. Pleased to meet you."

"Same here." Christian fished a pen out of the basket. I picked up another. Between us, we filled out all the stubs.

Nina, perhaps unwilling to risk her manicure, didn't offer to help. Instead, she stared past us into the Mini ring. Her face bore such a look of intense concentration that I wondered for a moment if one of the Golds' Poodles was being shown in the class. Almost immediately, I discounted the thought. If Christian had had a dog in the ring, he would never have allowed himself to be distracted by something so mundane as raffle tickets.

I took his money and handed him the rest of his stubs. "Thanks."

"Don't mention it." Christian was already turning back to the ring. "How're we doing, honey?"

"He's made the cut," said Nina.

"Damn."

Interesting reaction. "Do you have a dog in the ring?" I asked.

"No, next class," said Christian. "Ours is an Open Dog.

Our handler's in there, though. We're waiting for Dale to get done here so he can go back to the setup and work on our Mini. It looks like he's going to be held up a few more minutes."

For a professional handler, PCA was a continual juggling act. Though only two rings ran at the same time, the top handlers had entries in nearly every class. Excellent backup crews of assistants, and judges who were understanding about handlers slipping into and out of the ring as needed, were what made the system work.

"Good luck," I said.

"Thanks." Christian smiled. "We'll need it."

Nina merely nodded.

I didn't take it personally. PCA has that effect on most people, Aunt Peg included. People were secondary here; it was all about the dogs.

By the time I took one last pass around the two rings, grabbed Eve and ran her outside for a walk, then headed back to the raffle table, it was nearly one o'clock. Time for me to take over from Edith Jean. I hadn't eaten since grabbing a protein bar for breakfast, but it was looking as though lunch was going to have to wait.

To my surprise, as I approached the table, I didn't see the older woman anywhere. Several people were browsing among the items; picking them up, examining them, then carefully placing them back on the table. Edith Jean should have been answering questions and keeping an eye on things. I wondered where she'd gotten to.

The trophy table was next to ours. As I walked past, Charlotte Kay, chairman of the trophy committee, waved me over. "Edith Jean told me you'd be by any minute. She just scooted down to the ladies' room before the start of the Toy judging. I'm watching your table for her."

She glanced down, frowning slightly as she looked at

her watch. "Actually, Edith Jean left a good ten minutes ago. She should have been back by now."

"I'll go find her," I said.

Judging by the expression on Charlotte's face, we were both thinking the same thing. One Boone sister dropping dead was bad enough. Two would be two too many.

I handed Charlotte my basket for safekeeping and headed toward the far end of the large, sod covered arena. The dog show was set up on the ground floor of the building. Tiers of permanent seating rose on all sides above us. On one end, behind the grooming area, an enormous garage door led outside to the unloading zone. At the other end, wide concrete tunnels burrowed beneath the seats and led to the exits. Restrooms appeared at intervals along the tunnels; I knew from experience that the nearest ladies' room was right around the first corner.

I hadn't gone two steps inside the tunnel before I heard voices. One I recognized immediately as Edith Jean's. It took me a moment to place the second, perhaps because I wasn't expecting it: Harry Gandolf. I hesitated before rounding the corner, not wanting to intrude.

That didn't stop me from listening, though.

"Three hundred," Harry was saying. "And that's the easiest money you'll ever make. Just tell Roger to pull the puppy."

"I said no once and I'll say it again. Bubba came to PCA to have his shot and that's what he's going to do."

If Edith Jean had sounded worried or upset, I'd have barged around the corner and confronted them. Instead her tone was scornful; the older woman was more than capable of holding her own with a scoundrel like Harry Gandolf. I shrank into an alcove and pressed myself against the wall. Thanks to all that concrete, the acoustics were great.

"Five hundred," said Harry. "And that's my final offer."

"You could offer me ten times that much. The answer is still no."

"Look, I'm trying to be reasonable here. There's a lot riding on what happens today. I can't afford to lose. All you need to do is be reasonable too. After what happened, everyone will understand if you decide not to show."

"Roger won't," Edith Jean snapped. "He's down at the other end, getting Bubba ready right now."

"Roger works for you, he'll do whatever you say. Just take the money and tell him you changed your mind. Tell him you're distraught. Tell him anything you want."

"How about good luck and God bless?"

I chuckled quietly. You go, girl, I thought.

"What's the matter with you?" Harry demanded. "Don't you understand what I'm offering? Even in the backwoods of Georgia, people must know that five hundred dollars is a lot of money."

"I'll tell you what else we know, sonny. We know that sometimes it's not about the money."

"Don't be ridiculous," said Harry. "It's always about the money. You and your sister sure had me fooled. I didn't expect you to be such hard bargainers. Seven hundred."

"Keep your money, I don't want it."

"I'll bet you need it, though. With your sister dead and gone—"

"Shut up!" cried Edith Jean. "Just shut your mouth, do you hear me?"

I took that as my cue. Pushing away from the wall, I strode around the corner. Harry looked surprised to see me, but Edith Jean was the one who grew pale.

"There you are," I said, keeping my voice light. Impulsively, I reached out a hand to steady her. "We've been waiting for you back at the raffle table. Is everything all right?"

"Just fine." Her eyes darted back and forth between me and the handler. I knew she was wondering how much I'd heard; I wondered why it mattered. She wasn't the one who'd been doing something wrong.

"You go on back and take over from Charlotte," she said. "I'll be along in a minute."

"I'd rather wait." I glared at Harry for good measure.

Edith Jean patted the hand I'd placed on her arm. "There's no need for that."

"I think there is."

"Don't mind me," said Harry. "You two may have time to stand around chatting, but I have things to do."

"What a creep," I said as he walked away.

Edith Jean sighed. "You can sure say that again."

13

Edith Jean and I walked out to the raffle table together. "You're sure you're okay?" I asked.

She snorted contemptuously. "Don't you worry about me. I'm a tough old bird. Anyway, Harry Gandolf sent himself on a fool's errand, coming after me like that. It doesn't matter if he gets me all riled up, I'm not the one showing the dog. As long as Roger stays calm and gets the job done right, everything will be just fine."

"Good luck," I said. "I'll be rooting for Bubba."

Edith Jean gave me a jaunty thumbs-up and disappeared into the crowd. I went to retrieve the ticket basket from Charlotte and thank her for watching out for us.

"Don't mention it," she said. "I was happy to help out. Besides, with all these trophies on display, I'm stuck here anyway. I don't dare take a single step away." She had a point. The value of the silverware spread out on Charlotte's table, some of it decades old, dwarfed what the raffle had to offer.

"Edith Jean is on her way to the ring," I said. "Her puppy is in the next class."

Charlotte nodded. "I know both sisters were all excited about Bubba's chances. For Edith Jean's sake, it would be nice to see him pull off the win."

Something in her tone nagged at me. "But?"

She looked uncomfortable. There was a long pause before she spoke. "Bubba's a cute puppy, and he certainly had a lot of buzz going for him in the spring. But just between you and me, he's no world-beater. If he does go up—and he very well might—let's just say that sentiment will have played a part in the judge's decision."

"You really think Mr. Mancini might be influenced by Betty Jean's death?"

"Under the circumstances, it would be hard for him not to be. Look at the setup: we have two older women who've been involved in the breed for years. This is the first time they've ever had a Poodle of this caliber, and one of the sisters dies unexpectedly on the eve of the puppy's PCA debut. I'm sure the spectators will be on Bubba's side, and frankly I'd be surprised if the judge didn't give him a little extra credit too.

"I know Edith Jean thinks very highly of that puppy and why shouldn't she? We all love our own dogs. But three days ago, an objective observer probably would have told you that Bubba didn't stand a chance much beyond maybe taking his own class. Now he's one of the favorites."

I'd been curious to watch Bubba's class before; now I couldn't wait for his appearance in the ring. Walking back to the raffle table, I thought about Charlotte's assessment of the situation. Like most PCA committee heads, Charlotte's credentials were impeccable. She was both a breeder and a judge; in Poodle circles, her opinion mattered. And if she thought that Betty Jean's murder had advanced Bubba's cause, she probably knew what she was talking about.

By the time the first Toy class had ended, I'd eaten the box lunch that Edith Jean had left for me, modeled a Poodle necklace for a woman who wanted to see what it looked like on an actual neck, searched in vain for a signature on the Poodle print, and sold a respectable amount of tickets. So far, it was just another afternoon at the office. But when Bubba's class was called into the ring,

I sat up and began to pay attention. I hauled my catalog out from beneath the table and opened it up to the appropriate page.

There were seventeen puppy dogs entered in Bubba's class. The high number on Roger's armband placed the two of them near the end of the line. Judges are expected to judge at a pace of roughly twenty-five dogs an hour, and Mr. Mancini was known as someone who liked to move right along. Even so, it wouldn't be Bubba's turn to be examined for at least twenty minutes.

Thumbing ahead several pages, I found Harry's dog, Ro-Mac's The Vindicator, listed in the entries for the Open Class. Though Vic was close to the same age as Bubba, Harry had chosen to enter his puppy in a more competitive class, one that was open to Poodles of all ages. Choosing to put a puppy there was a handler's way of saying to the judge: *Look at my dog. He may still be in puppy trim, but he's ready to take on the older dogs. Don't make the mistake of thinking that he's just another youngster.*

The strategy was a sound one. More often than not, it had been known to succeed.

Reading Vic's listing in the catalog, I noticed something I hadn't realized before. Harry Gandolf wasn't just the puppy's handler, he was also its owner. I wondered if that had anything to do with why he was so determined to see his Toy Poodle go up. Being awarded the purple ribbon at PCA conferred an enormous amount of prestige upon the recipient, but there wasn't any financial gain attached to the win. I'd just heard Harry offer Edith Jean seven hundred dollars to pull her puppy from the competition. It's always about the money, he'd said, but in this case, I'd have been hard-pressed to figure out how.

Fortunately, there was a lull in the activity at the raffle table during Bubba's class. I may have been partially responsible for that since I'd spent much of the time ignoring my duties. Instead, I stood on a chair and gazed over the heads of the spectators between me and the ring. I did draw a few stares, but most were sympathetic. At PCA, nobody wants to miss out on the action when a Poodle they care about is being shown.

Generally speaking, silver Poodles are prized for their gorgeous color, but not necessarily for their showmanship. Obviously no one had told Bubba that. The little Poodle was clearly enjoying his moment in the spotlight.

Not having had my hands on Bubba, I had no idea how well built the puppy was, but he certainly knew how to play to the crowd. In the world of Poodles, black and white are the most common colors. The remaining colors—browns, blues, apricots, and silvers—find their way to the show ring much more rarely. In the entire Toy entry, Bubba was one of only a handful of silvers. In his class, he was a standout.

I'd never seen Roger Carew handle a dog before, and now I was impressed. He presented the Toy with flair and finesse. He also possessed that rare skill that the best professional handlers hone to a fine art: the ability to blend into the background, to show off a dog with such subtlety that it looks as though the dog is presenting himself.

Nobody was surprised when Bubba made the cut after his individual examination. Good as that was, however, it was only the first baby step in the long road to success that Edith Jean hoped to see her puppy travel. Mr. Mancini quickly finished going over the rest of his class, dismissed the ones he wasn't interested in, and settled down to have another good look at the eight he'd kept in the ring.

Due to his number, once again Bubba was positioned at the end of the line. Another handler might have been content to bide his time and wait to be noticed. Not Roger. The other seven exhibitors were on their knees in the grass behind their small charges, stacking them in anticipation of the judge's next pass. Roger was on his feet.

Standing slightly in front and off to the side of Bubba,

baiting the puppy with a piece of liver, he accomplished two things. One, he showed the judge that he didn't have to prop his puppy up with his hands to make it look good. And two, by angling his body away, he forced Mr. Mancini to step out of his path, walk around, and take a deliberate look at the puppy.

Mr. Mancini smiled slightly as he acquiesced. Every person in the ring, and most of those standing ringside, knew how the game was played. Besides, Bubba was doing his part as well. Standing like a statue at the end of his slender show lead, he had his head and tail bang up, his tiny feet planted solidly on the ground, and a mischievous sparkle in his eye.

He was worth a special look.

Bubba cocked his head and gazed at the judge as he approached. The Toy Poodle's expression was charming, the contrast between his silver skin and deep black eyes and nose, irresistible. His tail whipped back and forth in greeting, drawing a burst of appreciative laughter from ringside.

Leo Mancini had a lot of Poodles to judge that afternoon. He wasn't about to waste anyone's time. With a flick of his finger, he pulled Bubba out of line and sent him to the other side of the ring. Four more picks followed, until his top five choices had been arranged in the correct order. The remaining three filled in at the end.

There'd been a smattering of applause when Bubba was placed at the head of the new line. When the judge raised his hands, telling the handlers to rise to their feet and gait around the ring for the last time, the applause swelled. Spectators sitting by the Standard Poodle ring next door, looked over to see what was happening.

Still standing on my chair, and for once in my life head and shoulders above everyone in the crowd, I searched the throngs for Edith Jean. I knew she was tucked away out there somewhere. As the line began to move with Bubba dancing exuberantly in first place, I found her. The older woman was flushed with excitement. She held up one hand to cover her mouth, the other wiped a tear from her eye.

Then Mr. Mancini pointed, officially awarding the blue ribbon to the little silver Toy, and brought the house down.

After that, it was hard to settle down and go back to work. It would be at least a couple of hours before Bubba would return to the ring to compete for Winners Dog. In the interim, Mr. Mancini had five more classes to judge: 12 to 18 Months Dogs, Novice, American-Bred, Bred by Exhibitor, and of course, Open, where Harry's puppy, The Vindicator, would be in competition.

In theory, any one of those intervening classes could contribute the day's eventual winner. Everyone who'd witnessed Bubba's performance, however, knew they'd seen a dog who was going to be a contender. Now there was nothing to do but wait.

An hour later, Bertie wandered by. "This show rocks," she said. "How come you never made me come sooner?"

"You were always busy."

"You might have insisted."

"You weren't that interested in Poodles."

"There was that," Bertie admitted. She pulled out a chair and sat for a minute. "I guess it only goes to show how wrong a person can be. Maybe I'll specialize in Toys. Did you see that silver puppy? Wasn't he the cutest thing?"

"Absolutely. That was Edith Jean's puppy, Bubba. Remember, you saw him the other night in the grooming room?"

"I guess." She gave her profession a plug. "He looks different with a handler."

Sad to say, that was true of almost every show dog.

"I suppose I need to buy some raffle tickets." Bertie perused the table with the practiced eye of someone who'd been to many specialties. "Any chance I might win something that doesn't have a Poodle silk-screened, appliquéd, or embroidered on it?"

"There's a money tree," I said. "But to get that, you have to have one of the first tickets pulled. It goes pretty fast."

"How about if I know the person drawing the tickets, does that help?"

"Not much. Ask Sam. Last year he went home with Poodle pot holders."

Good sport that she is, Bertie got out her wallet anyway.

Next person to stop by was Aunt Peg. "Why aren't you stuck like Velcro to the Standard ring?" I asked.

"Mr. Lamb took a bathroom break. I thought I'd come over and congratulate Edith Jean."

"She hasn't won yet," I pointed out.

Aunt Peg looked faintly outraged. "Bubba won his class. At a show of this caliber, that is an enormous honor."

It wasn't as if I needed to be reminded of that. But Edith Jean had made it clear that she had bigger honors in her sights.

"Do you want to hear something interesting?" I asked. "Harry Gandolf offered Edith Jean a whole lot of money to pull that puppy from the competition." I related the conversation I'd overheard.

"How very odd," Peg said at the end. "Why on earth do you suppose Harry would do something like that?"

"Because he was afraid Bubba would beat his Toy dog, obviously."

"Even so. There are sixty-five Toy dogs in contention today. Any one of them might beat Harry's puppy. All it takes is one."

"Yes, but none of the others has as good a chance as Bubba does. Anyway, if you still want to find Edith Jean, try looking in the grooming area. She left me in charge here. I'm not expecting her back all afternoon."

"I started in the grooming area," said Aunt Peg. "Roger's

setup is being mobbed by well-wishers, but Edith Jean wasn't among them. Not surprising when you consider that Roger wouldn't want her there distracting the puppy when he has to go back in the ring later."

The announcer called Standard Poodle Open Dogs to the ring and Aunt Peg vanished. Several more Toy classes were judged. I left Charlotte watching the raffle table briefly and ran outside to give Eve another walk. Thank goodness my Poodle had an understanding nature.

When I returned, Winners Dog was being judged in Standards. Due to the importance of the award, the Toy ring had shut down for the duration. Every spectator in the arena was giving the Standards their full attention.

Tommy Lamb was a judge who thoroughly enjoyed the spectacle of showing. Obviously he intended to give his audience a class to remember. There were seven Standard Poodles in contention, one to represent each of the earlier classes, and he made each of them feel like a winner.

Factions quickly sprang up among the audience. Applause accompanied the Poodles' every move. And through it all, Mr. Lamb kept his own counsel, giving no hint of whom he favored until the end when he pointed, finally, at a sparkling white dog from the Bred-by-Exhibitor class.

The crowd, who'd been holding their breath, all exhaled at once. Thunderous applause followed. The owner-handler wept. Mr. Lamb gallantly offered her his handkerchief.

As they set up to take pictures, the interrupted judging in the Toy ring resumed with the Open Class. At most dog shows, Open is the strongest class. At national specialties, however, there was so much quality to go around that it tended to get spread out. Now I saw that there were fewer entries in Open than there had been in Bubba's class.

Ro-Mac's The Vindicator looked good. I thought so, and so did Leo Mancini. The black puppy was well up to the competition offered by the twelve adult Toys in his class. Vic wasn't as flashy as Bubba, but he didn't have to be. The quality was there in spades. The puppy, quite simply, shone.

The Vindicator prevailed in what looked to the ringside like an easy decision. Harry pocketed the blue ribbon. He took a minute to brush out the puppy's ears and fluff the pompon on his tail. Then he calmly took his place at the head of the Winners' line. One by one, the earlier class winners filed into the ring to join him.

Once again, all activity outside the ring came to a halt. All eyes were drawn to the competition within. The moment of truth had arrived.

14

"Mind if I join you?"

I'd been staring so hard at the ring, I hadn't even seen Sam approach. I was, of course, still standing on a chair. For the first time in my life, rather than being eight inches shorter than Sam, I was nearly a foot taller. That didn't last, however, as he was dragging over a chair of his own. When he stepped up next to me, the added height made him tower above the crowd.

"If Aunt Peg sees us, we'll probably catch hell," I mentioned. My aunt doesn't take anything lightly when it comes to decorum and her favorite dog show.

"She's already seen you." Sam was grinning. "Hard not to, the way you're sticking up over here."

He reached over and took my hand. His fingers laced through mine and held on tight. I decided to interpret that to mean that if I had to suffer the consequences of Peg's wrath, Sam would be at my side.

"Who are we rooting for?" he asked as Mr. Mancini sent the line of Toy Poodle class winners around for the first time. Sam had been watching Standards all day with Aunt Peg and was oblivious to the drama unfolding in the Toy ring.

"The silver puppy, second from the end. That's Edith Jean's Bubba. The one I told you about last night." Over dinner, I'd filled Sam in on everything that had transpired before his arrival.

"The black puppy at the head of the line is gorgeous. The one with Harry Gandolf."

I nodded, not taking my eyes from the ring. "That's Ro-Mac's The Vindicator, probably Bubba's chief competition, though I didn't get to see the rest of the classes. Harry wants desperately for his puppy to beat Bubba. Earlier I overheard him offering E.J. money to withdraw her dog from competition."

Sam didn't comment. He'd been involved in the dog show world long enough to know that just about anything was possible. He and I watched as, one by one, the Toy dogs were brought out of the line and moved again. That exercise was performed partly to refresh the judge's memory, partly to honor each one as a class winner, and partly to allow the ringside to show support for their favorites. Each of the Toys was drawing applause from the crowd, but Vic and Bubba were clearly the two favorites.

Harry's puppy, first to go, seemed to feed off the spectators' enthusiasm. The louder the response, the more he began to sparkle. Harry, too, reveled in the audience's attention. As the pair stopped in front of the judge, he pulled a furry stuffed mouse from his pocket and encouraged the little black dog to play.

"That's going to be hard to beat," Sam said as the puppy gaited to the end of the line accompanied by appreciative applause.

I had to agree, though I wasn't about to abandon hope yet. "Wait until you see Bubba. That puppy shows like a pro. If nothing else, he'll make a tight race of it."

Four dogs later, it was Bubba's turn. The crowd was waiting for him, hands poised in anticipation. The silver had barely stepped out of line before someone high up in the stands whistled loudly. The shrill sound echoed throughout the arena. A few people laughed at the over-the-top commendation.

In the ring, Roger's head snapped up. He looked around as if seeking the source of the sound. At the same time, Bubba scampered forward several steps, crossing in front of his handler's feet. Distracted, still walking, Roger didn't see him in time. One loafer-clad toe kicked the puppy squarely in the ribs.

The blow was only a glancing one; nevertheless, it lifted the tiny Poodle up off the ground and tossed him nearly a foot. The spectators gasped audibly.

Bubba landed, bounced, seemed to recover. Then he scooted in a small circle at the end of the lead and dropped his tail. A horrified silence fell over the crowd. They clung to the edges of their seats as Roger immediately dropped to his knees beside the Toy puppy.

Dog shows operate on the premise that judges compare every dog before them to a breed standard. These written standards are the bible according to which every pure-bred dog is measured. Aside from offering a physical description, the standards also attempt the difficult task of defining what the essence of each breed should be. In Poodles, a dog bred primarily to act as a companion, temperament is considered to be paramount.

Poodles are naturally happy dogs. They should be out-going and friendly, never shy or nervous. Poodles are meant to enjoy being shown, to have fun in the ring with their handlers. It's expected that one of the ways they'll demonstrate that enjoyment is by holding up their tails.

Old-timers have an expression that puts it more succinctly: "No tail, no Poodle," they say

So the fact that Bubba had gotten spooked was a big deal. If the puppy was to have any hope of winning, he needed to recover, and quickly. Roger chucked the small dog under the chin. He tickled his back. He took a small red ball out of his pocket and bounced it in front of Bubba's nose.

The puppy's ears pricked. His tail began to wag. Roger handed him the rubber ball, then snatched it back. Legs stiff, Bubba bounced up and down in place. His tail snapped up. He barked twice. The puppy wanted to play.

The crowd laughed in relief. They didn't dare applaud yet. Just in case. Roger stood up and walked the puppy over to the judge. Bubba danced at the end of the slender leash. Mr. Mancini sent him down and back. The puppy strutted his stuff.

"That was close," I said.

Sam was looking up into the stands. Tiers of mostly empty seats rose above us in all directions. Nearly all the show spectators preferred the close-up view from down on the arena floor. From even the lowest of the permanent seats, a Toy Poodle would look like little more than a moving ball of fluff.

"I wonder who whistled," Sam said.

Good question. Especially since you don't hear much stuff like that at dog shows—even big ones like PCA. Considering the outcome, I had to wonder whether the whistler had been looking to support Bubba as it had originally seemed. Or had the gesture been intended right from the start to produce an entirely different result?

In the ring, Mr. Mancini gaited his final class winner. He walked slowly up and down the line one last time. Applause swelled and dipped with his progress. The audience wasn't the least bit shy about making their preferences known; and if they could manage to sway the judge's opinion in the process, so much the better.

Leo Mancini, however, looked like a man with firm opinions of his own. He pointed toward Vic and asked to have the puppy put back on the table. As Harry swept the Toy dog up off the ground and moved to comply, the judge called for Bubba. He repeated his request. Both

Poodles were to go on the rubber-matted table simultaneously for a side by side examination.

"I wish he'd hurry up," I said. The suspense was killing me.

Sam, as usual, was more patient. "Give him time. This is the toughest decision he's had all day."

On the table in the middle of the ring, Vic stood like a rock. Bubba wasn't so happy. Poodles are seldom called upon to share a table and the silver Toy didn't like it. As he had earlier, Roger stepped back and let the puppy show himself. Then it had worked; now I wanted him to stand in close and offer Bubba more support.

After a minute, the judge returned the two Toys to the ground. Now he asked them to move together. Harry's puppy seemed to think that was a fine idea. Bubba, perhaps still flustered by what had occurred earlier, saw four human feet around him when he'd been expecting two, and balked.

It was only a momentary hesitation, and Roger covered it well. Still, I knew if I had noticed, the judge most certainly had.

Bubba trotted out and back. This time his movement was more perfunctory than electrifying. Beside him, Vic was having the time of his life. Roger looked grim, his features set with concentration. Harry was smiling; he knew which way this wind was blowing.

The two puppies stopped and stacked in front of the judge. Mr. Mancini took one last look, then sent them both back to their original positions in line. That put Vic in front, and Bubba back near the end. That didn't bode well.

The judge raised his hands and sent the line around. He let the Toys gait half the length of the ring, then lifted his arm and pointed. The coveted Winners Dog award went to Harry and The Vindicator.

Cheers erupted from around the arena. Harry pumped

a fist in the air. Even though I'd been pulling for Bubba, I had to applaud the black puppy's performance. Roger came forward from the back of the line and shook Harry's hand.

"From here, that looked like the right decision," Sam said.

I thought so too. In the end, Vic had asked for the win and Bubba hadn't. That one small difference had been enough to determine the outcome.

The Toy dog who'd been second to Vic in the Open class came back to the ring to compete for Reserve Winners. No points would accompany this award, but at the national specialty the win would be an honor nonetheless. Indicating once again how close his previous decision had been, Mr. Mancini made short work of this one. He simply motioned Bubba to the head of the line, sent the dogs around and pointed immediately.

Roger scooped up his puppy and carried him over to the marker. He looked well pleased with the result.

"I've got to go," Sam said, hopping down. "A friend of mine has two Standards in the parade. I told him I'd handle one for him."

I knew Aunt Peg had Hope entered in the Parade of Champions as well. Now that Bubba was finished showing for the day, I hoped Edith Jean would come back and relieve me so that I could watch from ringside.

"Meet me for dinner later?" asked Sam.

"Of course. I'll find Bertie and see if she wants to join us."

"And I'll ask Peg."

As Sam strode away, I saw Edith Jean approaching through the crowd. Every few feet, someone stopped her to offer congratulations. Though she accepted the good wishes graciously, I could tell she was disappointed.

"Too bad," I said when she reached the table.

Edith Jean looked surprised. "Don't you want to congratulate me like everyone else?"

"I'd be happy to, if you looked like you'd be pleased to hear it. If my puppy went Reserve Winners here, I'd be thrilled. But I know you were hoping for something more."

"What I was hoping," Edith Jean muttered, "was not to have to watch my handler give the whole shooting match away."

Oh.

Her hand went to her throat, toying absently with something there. The locket, I realized after a moment. Edith Jean was wearing her sister's locket.

I was about to comment when I saw Roger Carew hurrying toward us. He must have come straight from the ring; the silver Toy puppy was still tucked beneath his arm.

Bubba saw Edith Jean and began to whimper excitedly. His small legs paddled in the air as he wiggled in Roger's arms. The handler paused, looked around to make sure it was safe, then slipped off the puppy's show leash and lowered him to the ground. Barking happily, Bubba raced the last few feet across the turf to his owner.

At the sight of her delighted little dog, Edith Jean's expression brightened. She lifted the puppy up into her arms, murmuring endearments as his small pink tongue covered her face with kisses. The look she sent Roger over Bubba's head, however, wasn't nearly as friendly.

"I'm sorry," he said quickly. He held out the purple and white rosette and a small pewter bowl, compliments of the trophy committee.

Edith Jean didn't even glance at the loot. "You should be. You could have won that, you know. You had the better dog."

Having seen the puppies compete, I wasn't so sure of that. I'd rooted for Edith Jean because I liked her. A judge, however, had to cast such preconceived notions aside and act objectively in making the decision. In this judge's place, I might well have done the same thing he had.

"I know," Roger said to Edith Jean. "And I apologize. So many people came to see him after he won his class. Everyone wanted to have a look, and I knew you'd be pleased by all the attention he was getting. It was my fault for not remembering how young he was. I should have put him in his crate and let him rest. You have every right to be angry with me. He was just too tired to show his best for Winners and I'm the one who's to blame."

Cuddling her puppy and faced with her handler's sincere remorse, Edith Jean's ire seemed to be fading. She held Bubba to her and sighed. "Who's a good boy?" I heard her whisper. The tiny pomponned tail whipped back and forth like a metronome.

After a minute, Edith Jean looked up. "Reserve is still pretty good," she said.

"In that company, it's excellent," I agreed.

"He's got a good shot at Best Puppy," said Roger.

On Friday, after the Best of Variety class was judged in Toys, the winners of each of the four Puppy classes (two in dogs and two in bitches) would be brought back to be judged for Best Toy Puppy. That puppy would go on to compete with the Best Mini Puppy and Best Standard Puppy for Best Puppy in Show. Vic, though still a puppy himself, was ineligible for the award as he had been shown in the Open class.

"That's true," said Edith Jean. "Best Puppy in Show is pretty important. Sister probably would have gotten a kick out of that."

Looking vastly relieved, Roger took Bubba back to the grooming area to undo his tight, stylized, show ring coiffure. Edith Jean took over the running of the raffle table. I headed over to the rings to watch the parade. I knew

Aunt Peg would be busy getting Hope ready. With luck, her ringside seat would be free.

As it turned out, Peg's chair was empty. The one beside it, however, where Sam had been sitting earlier, was taken. Rosalind Romanescue was waiting for the start of the parade as well. Today she was wearing a long-sleeved T-shirt, overalls, and sneakers. A chunky turquoise necklace circled her neck. Her attire was somewhat disappointing. Where were the flowing chiffon, wild colors, and gaudy hoop earrings I wanted her to affect?

I introduced myself and sat down beside her.

"I know who you are," Rosalind said immediately. "You're the skeptic."

For a moment, I was taken aback. Maybe I shouldn't have been so quick to doubt the woman's skills. Then logic prevailed. The communicator hadn't read my mind, she'd been talking to Aunt Peg.

"Not entirely," I said. "Your presentation yesterday was very convincing. I guess I'm merely reserving judgment on a subject I know very little about."

"Fair enough. If you've got any questions, ask away."

In the ring, the Parade of Champions began with the Toy Poodles. The first entrant trotted in and was set up on the table. The dog's resume was read by the announcer.

I glanced at the Poodle, then back at Rosalind. "How did you find out you had this . . . gift?"

"You mean did it come to me all at once like Dr. Dolittle?" Rosalind smiled and shook her head. "Not at all. Ever since I was a little girl, I've known that I was tuned in to the animals around me in a way that most people were not. Don't get me wrong, however. I firmly believe that everyone is born with the gift of communication. It's just that most people never use it. Eventually, they forget how. Like any skill, this one improves the more you practice it."

"That Poodle there." I gestured toward the ring. The

second Toy, an apricot, was taking its turn. "Could you tell me what it's thinking?"

"For certain, no. Usually, I set up my sessions to take place at a time when things are calm and the animal is quiet. The evening hours work well. I want the dogs to be able to concentrate on me, just as I am concentrating on them." She gazed into the ring, staring at the little apricot intently. "All I'm getting now is a vibe that goes something like this: happy, happy, happy!"

You didn't have to be a psychic to see that. The Toy Poodle had his tail so high in the air, it was curved up over his back. He was prancing with delight at his owner's side.

"Not very convincing, hmm?" Rosalind didn't sound surprised.

"Not really. What about people? Can you read their thoughts, too?"

"I wouldn't say that I read dogs' thoughts," Rosalind said carefully. "It's more that they send me pictures and impressions and I interpret them. Animals are very open to this sort of communication. They 'talk' to one another telepathically all the time.

"Humans, on the other hand, are very resistant to the idea. People value their privacy. Most keep secrets of some sort or another. Nearly all would consider an exercise of that sort an intrusion. It's definitely not something I would try to do."

As she'd been speaking, Rosalind's tone had changed. Her voice had hardened. I was facing the ring, but I glanced at her out of the corner of my eye. "Could you though, if you wanted to?"

"Excuse me," said Rosalind. "I see someone I need to talk to."

An interesting lady, I thought as she walked away. I wondered what her secrets were.

15

As the Toy entries finished and the Minis began, I pulled out my cell phone and gave Davey a call.

Unlike most people, I don't usually carry a phone with me. Generally, when I'm out of touch, I like being that way. But being separated from my son for the first time was reason enough to not only have the phone in my purse, but also to actually keep it turned on.

Of course, nearly three days had passed and Davey hadn't called me once. I was having trouble deciding whether that was a good thing or not.

"Hey!" Davey said, when he picked up the phone. "Who's this?"

"It's your mother. In Maryland. Who were you expecting?"

"Nobody," Davey said quickly. *Too* quickly.

I filed that away to worry about later. "How are things going?"

"Great. Dad and I are having an awesome time. We went to the beach today. Tomorrow he said we could go to Playland."

Ah, the joys of part-time parenting. There was probably no point in asking if he was eating well unless I wanted to hear about a diet of cotton candy and Creamsicles. "How's Faith doing?"

"Well . . ."

The word dragged on entirely too long for comfort. I had the vet's phone number on speed dial if he needed it. "Yes?" I prompted.

"She likes it here," said Davey. "But I think she misses you."

My shoulders relaxed. Horrible mother that I am, I was comforted by the thought that at least *one* of them did. "Are you letting her sleep on your bed at night?"

"Of course." He sounded insulted by the question. "She's been doing that practically since she was born."

"And she's eating okay?"

"Fine. I just think she'd rather be with you than with me."

"Tell her I'll be home on Saturday, okay? Tell her I miss her too."

"I will." Davey didn't see anything odd about my request. Clearly I was raising him right.

We talked for another few minutes, and I spoke with Bob briefly. He didn't volunteer any information about the fire engine episode and I didn't ask. He said they were sending out for pizza for dinner. That sounded safe enough to me. I told him Eve and I would be back over the weekend and hung up.

The Miniature Poodles in the parade soon gave way to Standards. Sam did a creditable job of showing off his friend's dog. When their turn came, Aunt Peg and Hope looked as though they were having a better time than they had in the agility ring. At the end, when all one hundred champions crowded back into the ring for their final lap together, the audience stood and cheered.

I stopped by the raffle table after that, finding that Edith Jean had already packed things up for the night. Over in the grooming area, I ran into Bertie as I was releasing Eve from her crate. Sam and Peg had already invited her to dinner, she said. We were meeting in the hotel restaurant in an hour. It was nice that *someone* thought to clue me in on the plan.

An hour gave me plenty of time to drive back to the hotel and give my Poodle a long, luxurious run in the exercise area before going to meet everyone. Spending a week on the road was hard on a puppy, especially one who was accustomed to living in a home, not a kennel. Faith might be missing my company, but I knew she was better off at home with Davey than she would have been with us.

Back in our room, I mixed Eve's dinner in her big, stainless-steel bowl and took a quick shower while she ate it. I still had a few minutes before heading downstairs to the restaurant when a knock came at the door. Immediately Eve jumped off the bed and ran to see who it was. She sniffed at the crack beneath the door and her tail began to wag. I took that as a good sign.

Sam was standing in the hallway. Obviously he'd gotten delayed at the show longer than I had. He looked hot, and rumpled, and somewhat harried. I had cold beer in my refrigerator. I wondered if that was what he'd come for.

Then he wrapped his arms around me and pulled me close. His mouth came down and covered mine. The stubble on his jaw rasped along my cheek. His fingers tangled in my hair. For a full minute, the world seemed to spin in circles around us.

"Ahhh," said Sam when he finally pulled away. "Much better."

I tilted my head and gazed up at him. "And here I thought you'd come for the beer."

"What beer?"

"I have Coors in the mini fridge with Eve's food."

"You didn't mention *that*." Sam strode past me and helped himself. He popped the top off the bottle and took a long cold swallow. "Ready to go down to dinner?"

I was. Sam carried the beer with him, drinking it as we wound through the hallways. Thankfully he finished it just before we reached the restaurant. Aunt Peg would not have been amused.

She and Bertie had already gotten a table. They were perusing their menus when we joined them.

"Thank goodness you're here," Aunt Peg said. "Maybe you can talk some sense into her."

Bertie rolled her eyes. I suspected she was beginning to realize that being a member of the Travis/Trumbull family was not always the easiest game in town. Sam grinned and pulled out my chair for me. He'd seen the worst my relatives had to offer and still kept coming back. Go figure.

"Now what?" I asked.

"She thinks she's having an ice cream sundae for dinner."

"Suddenly *she* thinks she's in charge of my life," Bertie retorted.

"I think the whole thing's none of my business," said Sam. He buried his face behind his menu.

"An ice cream sundae sounds good," I said. "I'm on vacation, after all. Maybe I'll have one too."

"Steak," Sam muttered. He might have been speaking to himself. "Thick and rare. Maybe a baked potato on the side."

"You can't eat ice cream for dinner," Aunt Peg said pointedly. "Not in your condition."

"If I had wanted to listen to the food police"—Bertie's tone was equally sharp—"I'd have brought Frank with me."

Sam's menu was vibrating. I suspected he might have been laughing.

"I have an idea. Let's talk about something else. Betty Jean Boone, for instance." I looked around the table. "Amazing isn't it, that there's been a murder in our midst, and nobody even talks about it? The show just goes on as if nothing happened."

Aunt Peg looked at me reprovingly. "Now, Melanie. It is PCA after all."

Most people reserve that hallowed tone for referring to the Vatican.

"Besides," said Bertie, "the police are handling things. Aren't they?"

"I suppose. I spoke with Detective Mandahar yesterday."

"I met him Monday night," said Peg. "I understand from Cliff that they're still nosing around and conducting interviews. I don't know what they've turned up, however. Nobody seems inclined to keep the board informed."

A grievous oversight on the part of the local police, I thought. But hardly surprising when you stopped to consider that they might still be exploring the possibility of interclub warfare.

The waitress came and took our orders. Aunt Peg sighed loudly, but didn't interfere when Bertie and I both ordered ice cream. At least Bertie went for the banana split. The only fruit I asked for was extra cherries.

"That was too bad today for Edith Jean," Bertie said when the waitress had gone. "I was hoping Bubba would win."

"Edith Jean was very disappointed," I said. "Roger came over afterward and apologized. He said the loss was all his fault."

"That's a hard call to make," said Peg. "But his handling in the winners ring certainly didn't help matters any."

"He fell over his own dog," Bertie snorted. She was an accomplished professional handler herself. She could afford to throw stones. "No wonder Edith Jean was upset. That's a beginner's mistake."

"He was looking for the biggest win of his life," said Sam. "Maybe he was nervous."

"Or maybe someone distracted him on purpose," I said. "Harry'd already tried several times to remove Bubba from the competition. Maybe he sent someone up into the stands to take one last shot at keeping the puppy from winning."

"If so, it worked," said Peg. "Not that Harry's puppy wasn't a good one. I imagine there's every possibility that Vic would have won anyway. But after that initial mishap, Bubba never really recovered. He didn't show nearly as well in the winners ring as he had earlier in his own class."

"Roger told Edith Jean that the puppy was tired. He said he'd let too many people come and look at him after he won the puppy class."

"He did," Aunt Peg agreed. "There was a crowd around that table all afternoon. I don't know why Roger didn't put a stop to it."

"Because this is PCA," said Sam. "And the things you might think to do at a regular show go right out the window when you suddenly find yourself the center of attention here. It's a heady feeling. Not that Roger made the right decision, but I can see how he might have succumbed to the temptation to bask for a little while."

"Nevertheless," Bertie interjected, "Harry Gandolf kept his eye on the ball, and he's the one who got what he wanted. I went by his setup earlier today when I was in the grooming area. Did you know he brought a string of thirteen Poodles to PCA? You'd think that would give him plenty of chances to do well. I wonder why he was so determined to win with that particular puppy."

Before the rest of us could offer opinions, the waitress appeared with our food. I'd chosen a butterscotch sundae with butter pecan ice cream. It tasted wonderful. I decided I ought to have ice cream for dinner more often.

My bowl was half empty when I paused with a spoonful of whipped cream on the way to my mouth. "I saw something odd this afternoon."

"What's that?" asked Peg. Oddities are her specialty. She was eating very proper pork chops, but I'd have been willing to bet she wasn't enjoying her dinner half as much as I was.

"Did you ever happen to notice that one of the Boone sisters wore a locket around her neck?"

"Now that you mention it, yes." Aunt Peg frowned briefly. "Though I could never remember which one it was. She had a habit of playing with it which caused some comment once among the committee members. It probably seems unkind now."

"What does?" asked Bertie.

"I'm afraid we began to speculate about whose picture might be inside. None of us, as you might imagine, knew enough about their personal lives to hazard an informed guess. Someone thought that perhaps, being a southerner, Sister was keeping a picture of Elvis near and dear to her heart. In the end, consensus among the group was that the locket probably contained a photo of their favorite Poodle."

Sam was laughing again. Maybe that was why he kept coming back. Never a dull moment around here.

"So?" he asked me. "Who is inside?"

"I have no idea. That wasn't what I was wondering about. Earlier I could have sworn that Betty Jean was the sister who wore the locket. Today I saw it on Edith Jean."

"Maybe they both had lockets," said Bertie. Her banana split had vanished. The bowl it had come in couldn't have been any cleaner if she'd licked it. "They seemed to do everything else alike."

"Or maybe you got it backwards," said Peg. "Maybe Edith Jean was the one who's had it all along."

"Since we're speaking of the Boone family," said Sam, "and the police investigation, does anybody know who stood to profit from Betty Jean's death? Who's going to inherit?"

"I would think everything would simply go to the surviving sister," said Aunt Peg.

"There's no other family back in Georgia," I said. "That's why Edith Jean wasn't anxious to go home after her sister died."

"So if no one back there had anything to gain from Betty Jean's death," Bertie mused, "then the murderer must have been someone who had something to gain here."

"Harry Gandolf," I said quickly.

"Not necessarily," Aunt Peg came right back. "Harry may have expected that Edith Jean would pull Bubba from the competition after her sister died. In fact, we probably all did. But when she didn't, things could have gone the other way with the sympathy vote working to her advantage."

"Harry wouldn't have known that ahead of time though."

"I agree that he doesn't seem like a particularly pleasant man," said Bertie. "But that's a long way from being capable of committing murder."

"If not Harry, then who?" I asked.

"The way Betty Jean was killed seems to indicate that the act wasn't premeditated," Sam said thoughtfully. "Whoever it was, simply saw their chance and took it."

"I'll tell you who comes to my mind," Aunt Peg said. "Damien Bradley."

"He always comes to your mind," I retorted. "While you're at it, are you sure you wouldn't like to try to blame him for global warming and deficit spending?"

"Melanie's feeling a little touchy where Damien Bradley is concerned," said Sam. "They were having a cozy chat when I arrived the other night. I gather he charmed her socks off."

Aunt Peg's brow rose. "Not literally, I hope."

"Trust me." I snorted. "There was nothing cozy going on. Our chat took place in full view of the entire back of the hotel. I have to admit, however, that I didn't find him to be the demon that everyone makes him out to be."

"He must have wanted something from you," said Peg. "That's what brings out Damien's charming side."

"Same thing I said," Sam agreed.

The two of them were united in their obstinacy. I glanced at Bertie, who shrugged. She didn't know Damien Bradley any better than I did.

"He told me he used to handle the sisters' Poodles for them," I mentioned.

"There you go, then," said Peg.

"There you go, what?"

"He makes a perfect chief suspect. Who better than a shady character with a past connection to the dead woman?"

Who better, indeed.

"What about Rosalind Romanescue?" I asked.

Aunt Peg's head whipped around. "What *about* Rosalind?"

"Don't tell me you don't think she's a little strange."

"Not at all. She's merely different. It wouldn't hurt you to try and keep an open mind."

"And an open wallet," I said. "Do you know she's charging seventy-five dollars apiece for those private consultations she's been doing? Your bringing her here to do the seminar has given her the implied backing of the Poodle Club of America. She's taking in money hand over fist."

Aunt Peg's shoulders stiffened. "She is not."

"Ask her yourself. A number of her customers have stopped by the raffle table. Everybody's talking about her."

"Are they satisfied customers?" Bertie asked curiously.

"For the most part, I think so. But who's to say whether or not the information she's giving out is right or wrong, since no one else claims to be able to read dogs' minds?"

"I can see I'll have to have a little chat with Rosalind," Aunt Peg muttered. "I certainly didn't bring her here with the intention of letting her manipulate our exhibitors for profit."

"I know she was a last-minute substitution," I said. "How did you manage to find her so quickly?"

Peg looked thoughtful. "Crawford was the one who told me about her. I'm afraid I was so grateful for any suggestion that I didn't ask as many questions as I otherwise might have. I simply called Rosalind, found out she was available, and asked her to come right down. Which of course, she did. At the time, I thought that was terribly obliging of her."

"Did you pay her for her program and her expenses?" asked Sam.

"Of course. And then she seemed so interested in the Poodles and the show that the club offered to pick up her hotel room if she wanted to stay on until the end of the specialty. No wonder she was anxious to remain."

With regret, I finished the last of my sundae and put down my spoon. I wondered if I dared to order dessert. "Crawford Langley doesn't seem like the type of person to have much use for the services of an animal communicator."

"He doesn't, does he," Aunt Peg mused. "I'm beginning to think that perhaps I should have looked into things a little more closely than I did."

"We need to get back to our original question," said Bertie. Three pairs of eyes turned her way. "Harry wanted to win at all costs, Damien is apparently not a nice man. Rosalind believes in free enterprise. But what does any of that have to do with Betty Jean's death?"

"We don't know," I said. "That's the fun part."

"Fun?" Sam sent me a look. I wondered if he was remembering the last mystery I'd gotten myself tangled up in. That adventure had gotten me shot.

"Don't worry. I'm just a bystander this time around." Absently my fingers went to my throat. They rubbed back and forth over the ring that hung there, warming it between them like a talisman. "I'm just here to sell raffle tickets, show my puppy, and mind my own business."

"Sure," Bertie muttered under her breath. "If you believe that, I've got some swampland, a bridge, and a one hundred percent can't-miss, Best in Show prospect I'd like to sell you."

16

Thursday morning, six A.M.

Most normal people were asleep at that hour. I was blow-drying a Standard Poodle puppy's legs. The rules of normalcy tend not to apply when you're showing a Poodle at PCA.

Not only that, but I wasn't the only person in the hotel grooming room. Indeed, when Eve and I arrived—fresh from a morning run in the field, where dew-tipped grass provided the necessity for another session with the blow-dryer—someone had already started the coffeemaker and poured the first cup. Some professional handler's long-suffering assistant, no doubt. Perhaps someone who'd been up all night grooming. I exchanged bleary-eyed nods with the others in the room and went to work.

Maybe it was the two cups of coffee I tossed down while I straightened and dried Eve's coat. Maybe I had a case of preshow nerves. But for whatever reason, I felt jittery and tense. Hot and cold at the same time. The puppy, who'd been groomed a hundred times before and usually lay still as a stone, squirmed on the table beneath my hands.

Whatever was in the air, she felt it too.

The tension didn't go away when we reached the show site just before seven. If anything, it intensified. The grooming area at the arena was already full, a hive of frenetic activity. Dryers hummed, scissors flashed: Poodles were unwrapped, banded, shaped.

Both the Mini and Standard rings would open in little more than an hour. Thursday, the day the bitches were judged, traditionally drew the largest entries of the specialty. Nearly four hundred Poodles would be judged over the course of the next twelve hours. The stakes, already high on Wednesday, ratcheted up another notch.

I set up my portable grooming table next to the two crates Sam and I had left in the building: Eve's, which had been in place since Monday, and Tar's, added Wednesday morning. Quarters were tight, with everyone jockeying for a little extra space. Mostly I was hemmed in by people I didn't know, or whose faces were familiar only from the Poodle magazines I subscribed to. Dale Atherton's setup was in the next aisle.

Eve's class, Puppy Bitches 9 to 12 Months, was second on the schedule. I knew that Sam and Aunt Peg would arrive in time for the start of judging at eight. Hopefully one of them would come and help me with scissoring and hair spray. In the meantime, I needed to get Eve thoroughly brushed out, unwrap her ears, and put in the tightly banded topknot that she would wear in the show ring.

Quickly I went to work. As I unpacked supplies from my tack box and lined them up on the table, Eve stood on the rubber-matted top and peered around the arena curiously. Finally she was beginning to relax. I wished I could say the same for myself. When I asked her to lie down so I could begin brushing, she complied happily.

"If it isn't the lady from the other night."

I looked up and found Damien Bradley standing in the aisle. He was holding a steaming cup of coffee and looking very relaxed. Either the handler had excellent assistants, or he didn't have any morning classes.

"Melanie," I said, remembering that I hadn't introduced myself the last time we'd met.

"Yes." He gazed at me speculatively. "I know."

Something about the way he said the words made my spine stiffen. Like maybe he'd been checking up on me. I wondered what had piqued his interest: our brief meeting, my association with Aunt Peg, or the fact that Sam had chased him away. Or there was always the possibility that—due to Sam's and Aunt Peg's repeated warnings—I was simply imagining things.

"Showing this morning?" Damien asked. As conversational gambits went, it wasn't terribly smooth. We both knew the answer was obvious.

"Puppy 9 to 12," I said and went back to my brushing.

"I won't take much of your time, then. I only wanted to say that I didn't realize when we met the other night that you were a friend of Betty Jean's. I'm sorry. I should have offered my condolences."

"That's quite all right. She seemed like a very nice lady, but I didn't know her well."

"I understand you're helping the sisters with the raffle. That's a big undertaking. The three of you must have been working together all spring."

"Actually, no." My hand stilled. I wondered what he was getting at. "The sisters did most of the work. My aunt only got me involved a couple of weeks ago. I met Edith Jean and Betty Jean when I arrived on Monday."

"I see." Damien almost smirked. All at once he was looking very pleased about something, though I had no idea what that might be.

Then he noticed my interest and shuttered his expression. "What happened to Betty Jean was a terrible, terrible tragedy," he said piously. "I'm afraid poor Edith Jean may be lost without her sister's guidance. I'll be sure to offer my assistance."

"She seems to be handling things well so far. In fact, she's dealing remarkably well."

"I'm sure that's what she wants you think. I'm sure that's

what she wants everyone to think. But now that Edith Jean is on her own, she'll need someone to look out for her . . ."

As he was speaking, Damien had placed his hand on my shoulder. I supposed the gesture was meant to indicate the sincerity of his feelings. Instead, it had the opposite effect. When his thumb began to move, stroking back and forth, I pulled away sharply.

As I did so, Dale Atherton leaned across the low wall of stacked crates that separated my aisle from his and tapped the handler on the arm. He gestured toward the other end of the room. "Hey, Damien, isn't that one of your assistants waving at you?"

Damien turned to look. "Where?"

"Right there. See?" Dale slid me a wink as his hand pushed Damien around. "You'd better go check it out."

"Yeah, I guess I will."

"Don't mind him," Dale said affably as Damien walked away. "He's an idiot."

Then he went back to work. Time was passing, so I did the same.

The first notice I had of Sam's arrival was when Eve lifted her head off the grooming table and woofed softly. Moments later, Tar came trotting down the aisle. His long ear hair was wrapped in bright blue plastic, his enormous topknot loosely contained in bands of the same color. Two long, thick pony tails drooped off either side of his head. Tar wasn't showing until the next day; for now, he was still in his civvies.

The two Poodles touched noses in greeting. Sam and I did the human equivalent.

"Thank God the troops have begun to arrive," I said as Sam tucked Tar into his big wooden crate. "I was beginning to think I was going to have to get this puppy ready all by myself."

"Are you kidding?" Sam chuckled. "At PCA? Peg would have a fit if she didn't get to do the finishing touches.

She's gone to the ring to check out the first puppy class. I'm supposed to make sure you've got everything under control and that your topknot's in tight enough. She'll be along in a minute."

Now that the responsibility for making Eve look perfect had been lifted from my shoulders, I told myself I could begin to relax. It didn't help much.

Predictably my aunt took the scissors out of my hands the moment she appeared. She glanced at the line I'd been working on, tsked under her breath and said, "Go make yourself useful, dear. Check in with the ring steward and pick up your armband."

That was a job for unskilled labor. A five-year-old with good manners could manage it. On the other hand, with Eve's show time drawing nearer, anything that kept me moving around and thinking of other things was preferable to simply standing still and worrying.

Sam opted to come with me. In case I got lost? I wondered. Or in case I passed a door to the outside and decided to bolt through it, escaping before anyone noticed I was gone? I'd been a spectator at PCA many times, but this was my debut in the ring. It wasn't an experience for the faint of heart.

As we passed by the Mini ring, Sam paused for a look. That variety had a smaller entry and their second puppy class was already in.

Dale was showing a brown puppy. The line had been sent around for the first time; now the judge was beginning his examination of those near the front. The puppies and handlers at the end were standing at leisure to await their turn. Dale leaned outside the ring and said something to one of the spectators.

Christian Gold, I realized, as we came up next to them. Nina was on his other side.

"One of yours?" Sam asked, glancing down at the brown puppy. Christian nodded. Nina smiled. "Good luck."

"Thanks," Christian replied. "We don't have much of a shot in this class, might make the cut if we're lucky. We're saving our big guns for later in the day."

"Open Bitch," said Nina. "GoldenDune Dorian. Watch for her."

"We will," Sam promised.

"Dorrie's a little young for this competition," said Christian, "but we think she's going to be something special."

"If I can wean her away from her owner long enough to make that happen," Dale said, glancing at his client's wife. "Nina's turned her into a bit of a pet."

"So she's a little spoiled." Nina looked down. Her eyelashes fluttered. "You're good with spoiled. I'm sure you'll manage, just like you always do."

We'd lost Christian's attention; he'd gone back to watching the Minis in the ring. When the line moved up, he poked Dale and pointed, sending him on his way. The handler moved up into place. Sam and I headed on to the Standard ring.

"Dale better watch his step," he said under his breath.

"Why?"

"Did you see the way he looked at Nina?"

"No." I paused and glanced back. The handler was kneeling beside his puppy, flicking a long comb through its rounded tail. "I wasn't really paying attention. How did he look at her?"

Sam leaned down, pressing his lips close to my ear. "The same way I look at you. Like he was picturing her naked in his bed."

Oh.

Well that got my mind off the dog show. The heat that pooled in the pit of my stomach drove the butterflies straight away. My soft gasp was lost in the noise of the crowd around us. And Sam, damn him, just kept walking.

By the time I caught up he'd reached the Standard ring

and picked up my armband. I ran two rubber bands up my arm, and snapped the cardboard number into place.

"Feel ready yet?" Sam asked.

"Not exactly."

"Don't worry. Eve will do fine."

"She's not the one I'm worried about," I said.

Back at the setup, Aunt Peg had worked wonders. My puppy looked like a potential star. Too bad her handler was feeling like the rank amateur she was.

Aunt Peg consulted her catalog. "There are thirty-six puppies in your class," she said, just in case I needed an update on how many people were going to be trying to beat us. "Don't let Eve get lost in the crowd."

While I filled my pockets with bait, a squeaky toy, and a greyhound comb, Sam read over her shoulder. "You start out fifth in line, so pay attention right from the beginning. Don't relax until after Mr. Lamb's gone over her. I'll meet you after that with a bowl of ice water."

The water was for Eve, needless to say. A class of thirty-six would take more than a hour to judge. That's a long time for adult dogs to spend in the ring, much less puppies. All would get tired and thirsty. Once Eve had been seen for the first time, we'd have a long wait until we were needed again. Many handlers simply sat down in the grass with their puppies lying beside them. Eve and I would probably follow suit.

The first call for my class came over the loudspeaker. A few minutes later, the announcer gave the placements for the younger puppies. Aunt Peg cupped Eve's muzzle in her fingers and helped her jump gently down to the ground. The puppy shook out her coat. Thanks to Peg's masterful scissoring, the trim fell right back into place when she was done.

Sam balled up the slender show lead and pressed it into my hand. "It's only a dog show," he said.

"No, it's not." I licked my suddenly dry lips. "It's PCA."

"Hold that thought," Peg said gaily, "and you'll do just fine."

Either that or collapse where I stood.

Somehow Eve and I managed to get ourselves up to the gate. I imagine Sam and Aunt Peg had something to do with that, though I don't exactly remember. Briefly I showed my armband to the steward before being hustled into the ring by the next handler standing behind me. Mr. Lamb was already going down the line, checking off the numbers against the list in his judge's book.

I moved Eve into place and set her up so that she was standing square on all four feet. Her front legs were dropped straight beneath her shoulders; her hind legs extended slightly to show off their angulation. This part was old hat for Eve. At eleven months of age, she'd already been to a dozen shows and done well enough to accumulate seven points.

She dipped her head toward the inside of the ring, her dark eyes seeking out the judge. Once stacked, I knew she'd hold her pose. Mr. Lamb had moved past us, still working on his book. We'd have at least a minute or two before the actual judging began. I took some time to scan the line myself.

I knew about a third of the exhibitors; another third looked familiar. The rest were probably owner-handlers like myself who'd traveled to PCA from other parts of the country. That impression was confirmed by the number of frozen smiles I saw plastered onto pale faces. I wasn't the only one who was nervous.

Then Eve tilted her head back and gazed up at me. Her tail, tipped by an outrageously big black pompon began to wag back and forth. *This is fun,* she seemed to be saying.

There's nothing more infectious than a Poodle puppy in a good mood. All at once the knots that had tangled in my stomach began to loosen. PCA might be the Holy Grail of dog shows, but what happened in that ring in the next few minutes wasn't going to change the world. And win or lose, at the end of the week, I still got to take home the puppy that I loved best.

Mr. Lamb was finally making his first judging pass down the line. He paused opposite us. Eve gave him the come-hither look she'd perfected in the whelping box. He smiled slightly before moving on.

We'd passed step one; we'd gotten ourselves noticed. I reached down and slipped Eve a piece of bait. She scarfed the dried liver down and looked for more. I showed her my empty hand. She shoved her nose into it, then jumped back playfully as Mr. Lamb asked the first half of the class to take their puppies around the big ring. Perfect timing.

"Let's show him what we've got," I said to Eve. The puppy's ears pricked.

We were ready to rock and roll.

17

Eighteen big Poodle puppies, eighteen handlers, all trotting in unison around a ring large enough to give everyone room to move out. It could have been chaos. Amazingly, it worked pretty well.

Over time, I'd perfected the savvy exhibitor's skill of keeping one eye on the judge and the other on where I was going. It seemed to me that Mr. Lamb's gaze lingered, ever so briefly, on Eve as we gaited past. So far, so good.

As we awaited our turn to be examined, I pulled out my comb and ran it through Eve's long silky ears. The added grooming didn't do much for her appearance. It did, however, give me something useful to do with my hands.

When the puppy ahead of us began its individual pattern, I brought Eve forward out of line and stacked her again. One of my hands rested lightly under her chin, supporting her head; the other held her tail. When Mr. Lamb spun around to see who was next, we were ready for him.

After all the hours of worry and preparation that had gone into getting us to that point, our turn seemed to pass in a blur. I know I didn't fall down or otherwise embarrass myself. And I know Eve showed well because Aunt Peg clapped for us at the end. My aunt doesn't offer praise lightly. Related or not, she wouldn't have applauded unless our performance warranted her approval.

As promised, Sam met us afterward with a bowl of water for Eve and some encouraging words for me. Then he melted back into the crowd of spectators. I took Eve off to one side and tried to get her to relax. All around us, other exhibitors were doing the same thing. Some chatted in small groups; others were watching the competition. Poodle puppies variously stood next to their handlers or lay down in the grass; sitting wasn't allowed as it would pull apart the carefully sprayed neck hair.

Twenty minutes later a burst of enthusiastic applause accompanied one entry back to the end of the line. I looked up to see who'd merited such approbation and saw Roger Carew heading our way. His puppy was an elegant cream with flowing movement and a beautiful face. Judging by the audience's reaction, she'd be one of the ones to beat in the class.

"Pretty puppy," I said as Roger found an open spot near me and settled in to wait.

"Thanks." He glanced over. "You, too."

"Congratulations on yesterday."

"Yesterday?" The handler moved closer. Our puppies touched noses, checking each other out. Roger and I both kept a cautious eye on the situation. One unexpected leap, even offered playfully, could pull down a topknot.

"Bubba's Reserve," I said.

His mouth flattened into a thin line. "Thanks. But under the circumstances, it didn't feel like much of a win."

"I think Edith Jean was pleased."

"I hope so."

He looked past me for a moment, gazing up into the stands. I wondered if he was looking for potential whistlers.

Roger's puppy lay down carefully on the turf; Eve opted to do the same. With the two of them settled, neither Roger nor I would be going anywhere for at least a few minutes. I decided to ask some questions to pass the time.

"I saw you in the grooming room at the hotel with the sisters on Monday night," I said. "Did you go outside with them afterward?"

Roger glanced back in my direction. He still looked distracted. "You mean when Betty Jean was killed?"

I nodded.

"Originally, yes. I had Bubba with me and I thought he might want to stretch his legs. The sisters were bickering about something." A tight smile played over his lips. "As usual."

"Cleaning up the field, I think."

"Could be. I do know that one or the other of them was complaining about the cold. Anyway, we got separated in the dark. Bubba took off in one direction. The sisters headed in the other. I probably wasn't outside for more than ten minutes, tops. Then I picked Bubba up and headed back to my room. I didn't see the sisters to say good night, but I figured it didn't matter since I'd be seeing them first thing in the morning anyway."

He paused, then blew out a breath. "Of course, it did matter. But I had no way of knowing that at the time."

"You had Bubba with you," I said, repeating what he'd just told me.

"That's right. I took him upstairs and put him to bed."

"Edith Jean said that she had Bubba. She said that was why she went inside and left Betty Jean out in the field by herself."

Roger shook his head. "She must have been confused. Bubba's been living with me since early March. I brought the puppy here ready to show. I wasn't about to jeopardize his chances by letting those two spend the night babying him. The sisters understood that. They agreed the puppy should stay with me."

As would most owners. I didn't dispute the logic of his decision, only the fact that his story didn't jibe with what Edith Jean had told me. On the other hand, she had had plenty on her mind over the last several days. She could hardly be blamed for forgetting one small sequence of events on a night that she would surely be anxious to forget.

While we'd been talking, Mr. Lamb had worked his way steadily through the rest of the large class. Around us, exhibitors were beginning to stand up, brush the grass off their clothes, and smooth their puppies' hair back into place. It was time to go back to work.

Comparing armbands, we re-sorted ourselves back into numerical order. I headed toward the front of the line where I'd started out. Roger aimed for the middle. Eve trotted dutifully beside me. Much as she loved to show, I could tell she was tiring. The long, unaccustomed, mid-judging break had taken its toll. The puppy had lost her edge; now it would be up to me to see if I could bring it back.

For the second time, the entire class stood nose to tail in a long line that took up two sides of the ring. Mr. Lamb started at the front. Walking at a measured pace, he passed the puppies, one by one. A flick of his finger indicated who had made the cut. Those lucky exhibitors left the old line and formed a new one.

The first puppy was called; the next three passed by. By the time Mr. Lamb reached Eve, I'd been holding my breath for so long that my chest hurt. When his hand beckoned us forward, I nearly stumbled in my haste to comply. Then it took me a moment to figure out where to go.

Thankfully, thinking wasn't required on my part. All I had to do was follow the first puppy's lead. I hurried Eve out to the middle of the ring and set her up again.

In all, ten puppies made the first cut, including Roger's cream bitch. The remaining twenty-six were excused. Once they'd filed out, Mr. Lamb got down to the business of choosing his ribbon winners. The spectators pressed closer, marking their catalogs and choosing their favorites.

Ten puppies, four ribbons; it didn't take a genius to see that my odds weren't very good. But now that we were up and moving again, Eve was beginning to revive. We weren't going to concede without a fight.

We moved again, one by one. The ringside applause meter rose and fell with each entry, a telling bit of feedback as to how we were faring. When our turn came, Eve gave it her best shot. She gaited away from the judge straight and true, then headed back with head and tail high. No matter how things turned out, I knew I'd be proud of the effort she'd made.

Mr. Lamb took his time. He stared for a long, final minute at the entries, assuring the spectators that the gravity of his decision befit the size and caliber of the class. Then he picked out his top six. Roger's puppy was pulled second. To my utter delight, Eve was beckoned out sixth. She wouldn't win a ribbon, but she'd made the final cut. As we gaited around one last time, it was easy to believe that the resounding applause was for us.

I left the ring with a goofy grin on my face, and a tired but happy puppy at my side. Several bystanders offered congratulations. We hadn't won anything, but we'd been in consideration. In such exalted company, it was more than enough.

Aunt Peg was beaming when she came to find us. "Well done!" she said. "I'd hoped you would make the first cut. Getting pulled at the end was definitely a nice bonus."

Nice, indeed. I'd be reliving the high of this moment for weeks.

By noon, I was back at work at the raffle table. In the interim, I'd taken down Eve's show ring hairdo, rewrapped and rebanded her topknot and ears, and given her a long walk outside. When I slipped her into her crate an hour later, the puppy looked relieved at the prospect of finally getting some downtime.

I wouldn't have minded having some myself. Since Edith Jean had been in charge of the raffle all morning while I'd been busy with Eve, however, I knew she'd be ready to take a break. As I headed toward the table, I saw Edith Jean approaching from the other direction. She was carrying a large cardboard box. It balanced awkwardly between her two hands, one of which was still wrapped in gauze. I hurried over to help.

"Here, let me get that." The box was heavier than I'd expected. I hefted it over to the table and set it down on a chair. "What's in here anyway?"

"Another prize for the raffle. Something that should have been here weeks ago, but wasn't."

"I didn't realize you took donations this late in the game."

"It's not like I have a choice, is it? Some people always procrastinate until the last minute. In this case, the donor said she didn't dare send the item through the mail. Hence the eleventh hour delivery. Since it's all to benefit the club, it's not like I can turn things away."

"Sure you can." I opened the box and peered inside. If I wasn't mistaken, I was looking at a pair of Poodle andirons. Presumably they were meant to hold wood in a kennel fireplace. An interesting concept, if somewhat farfetched.

Edith Jean was rubbing her bandaged hand absently. "Does it hurt?" I asked.

"No, the darn thing itches. Probably means it's healing. Another day or two and the bandage will come right off." Edith Jean tucked her hand behind her back as if she was sorry I'd even noticed. "You did a nice job in there with your puppy. She's very cute."

"Thanks. Eve's a real doll. She's always fun to show. How were things here? Did you sell lots of tickets?"

"Not as many as we will this afternoon when you get out there and work the crowd."

She reached beneath the table for the basket. We'd left most of the supplies packed inside it the night before. All I needed to add was some cash for making change. I leaned down to help her with it and as I bent over, Sam's ring, hanging on its chain around my neck, slipped out from beneath my shirt.

Edith Jean caught the diamond between her fingers and peered at it. "That's an awfully nice ring to keep hidden away."

"I know."

"An engagement ring?"

"Yes."

Her gaze dropped to my hand. "Most women like to show those off."

"In my case, it's a little complicated."

Edith Jean straightened and let out a raspy laugh. "It's always complicated, honey, and that's the truth. Maybe you're too young to know that yet, but you'll find out in time."

Her hand lifted. Fingers that had touched my ring moments before now went to the locket around her neck. I hoped she wasn't thinking about Elvis.

"A couple days ago I could have sworn that Betty Jean was the one wearing that locket," I said. "Now you have it on. Was I confused about that? Or do you each have one?"

Something came and went quickly in Edith Jean's expression. "You're right," she said. "There was only one locket, and it belonged to Sister. She kept it with her all the time. Never took it off, even when she went to bed at night. The locket meant something special to her. Now it means something special to me. I'm going to wear it every day in her memory."

Since she hadn't volunteered the information, I supposed I didn't dare ask whose picture was inside. Aunt

Peg's curiosity would have to go unsatisfied a little while longer.

"Since we're talking about Sister . . ." Edith Jean paused, gazing at me speculatively. "I was wondering if you might help me out with something."

"Of course. Whatever you need."

"The police are going to release her to me. I guess everyone's thinking I should take her home to Georgia, but that's not what I want to do. It's not what Sister would have wanted either. I'm looking to have her cremated."

"That sounds like a fine idea." I wondered where I fit into the plan. "Are you going to hold a memorial service when you get home?"

Edith Jean shook her head. "I've thought about it and I'd like to do one right here. At PCA, on Friday afternoon. I'm thinking we might could take Sister's ashes and scatter them over the Poodle ring right before Best in Show. Doesn't that sound like just the very thing?"

18

Oh, it was just the thing, all right. Just the sort of thing to give Aunt Peg and the other board members apoplexy. I could see that reaction coming from a mile away.

"Umm . . ." I said, stalling for time. "Isn't that when they usually hold the drawing for the raffle?"

"Precisely. That's what makes it so perfect, Sister and I having been in charge of the committee and all. It'll be like a double whammy service. The spectators will get two for the price of one."

A double whammy service, I thought weakly. Just what the club was looking for to lend dignity to its proceedings. I didn't know whether to laugh or run for cover. Both probably would have been in order.

Feeling cowardly, I opted for trying to pass the buck. "Have you spoken to anyone else about the idea? Nancy Hanlon, maybe, or Cliff Spellman?"

"I mentioned it to Cliff. He didn't say yes or no, just told me I needed to talk to Nancy. I haven't had a chance to pin her down yet, but I will. And of course, I'll probably have to run it past the show chairman, too. It's not like I haven't been a card-carrying member of this club for years. I know how things are done."

Oh no, she didn't, I thought. If Edith Jean had even the slightest inkling of how PCA worked, she would never have proposed such a thing. Aunt Peg would probably have a fit at the very suggestion, and hers might be one of the milder reactions.

"You know there's a good chance they'll turn you down," I said gently.

"I imagine they might try." Edith Jean's spine stiffened defiantly. "That doesn't mean they'll succeed. I was thinking about mounting a grassroots campaign. You could help me pass the word along. Like maybe this afternoon when you're out selling tickets, you could talk about the idea, and drum up some support. It will be that much harder for the board to say no if everyone else is already in favor."

That was an "if" the size of Texas, wasn't it?

"That's all you want me to do?" So help me, my knees were almost weak with relief. "Just let people know about your idea?"

Edith Jean stopped and thought. "Now that you mention it, maybe we ought to get a petition going too. People like to be asked to sign things. It makes them feel important. What do you think?"

I thought that I hadn't mentioned anything of the sort. Not only that, but finding people at PCA who were willing to put their names on *that* particular piece of paper might be about as easy as teaching a Pekingese to point. "A petition might be premature. After all, you haven't even spoken to Nancy yet."

Edith Jean didn't look deterred. "We can't afford to wait too long to get the ball rolling. After all, we've only got a day and a half to pull the whole shebang together."

I knew the woman was grieving. I knew that everyone handled grief in his or her own way. But so help me, I had to speak up. "You know, it might help your cause if when you talk to the board, you try not to refer to the memorial service as a shebang . . . or a double whammy."

Edith Jean regarded me calmly. She crossed her arms

over her chest. "I'm a good ole southern gal, sweet pea. Down in Georgia, we know how to speak our minds. We call things like we see them."

We did that in the north, too. And right about now I was ready to call this whole idea a catastrophe.

Edith Jean was silent for a moment before speaking again. I was afraid that maybe I'd hurt her feelings, but it turned out that she only wanted to change the subject. "I don't mind telling you, your police up here don't seem worth squat."

They weren't my police, I wasn't even from Maryland. On the other hand, my home was even farther north of the Mason-Dixon Line, which was probably worse in Edith Jean's mind. "They still don't have any idea who killed Betty Jean?"

"Not a one, far as I can tell. Mostly they just seem to be running themselves around in circles. I guess they've got more important things to do than worry about the death of one poor old lady from somewhere else."

"I'm sure they're trying their best." I hadn't a clue if that was true or not. After my initial interview with the detective, my involvement with the police had been limited to periodic updates from Aunt Peg. "I could try to talk to someone if you like."

"No, don't do that," Edith Jean said quickly. "I don't want to trouble anyone on my account. Besides, what's done is done. There's not much point in looking back. I'm just going to carry on the best I know how."

Carrying on was beginning to sound like a good idea to me, too. I picked up the basket and headed out. Miniatures had finished for the day in ring one. Toys were about to start. In the Standard Poodle ring, the Novice Bitch class was ending. It would be followed by a lunch break.

Day by day, raffle tickets were becoming harder and harder to sell. For one thing, due to our diligent efforts, most exhibitors and spectators had already had an opportunity to purchase them. For another, everyone had now had several days to browse the concession stands in the hallway outside the upper tier of seats. Spare cash, hoarded all year to bring to the specialty show, was going fast.

I sold some tickets in the grooming area, and a few more to the dealers manning the concessions. Then I headed out the upper doors to the parking lot where the professional handlers had parked their big rigs. Many had opted not to unload inside and were prepping dogs beside their motor homes.

As I'd hoped, I found Terry and Crawford at home. Crawford was using the lunch break in the Standard ring to grab a bite to eat. He was seated in a director's chair in the shade; jacket off, tie loosened, munching on a tuna fish sandwich. Terry, who'd set up a boom box and tuned it to a local rap channel, was standing at a grooming table nearby, working on a Toy Poodle.

Terry flashed me a big smile; Crawford was more reserved. "Checking out here for mice?" he asked. One silver brow lifted archly.

"Mice?" Terry squeaked. He took a hasty look around. "I should hope not."

"Melanie thought she saw one the other night at the hotel." His eyes never leaving me, Crawford stood up, reached over and turned off the radio. The sudden silence came as a relief. "Or maybe she was mistaken."

"Actually it wasn't a mouse." I plopped the raffle basket down on an empty grooming table and helped myself to a seat. "What I saw was a rat."

"Ahhh." Terry nodded knowingly. "Plenty of those around."

"Harry Gandolf," I said.

Crawford considered that. "Harry made you scream?"

"You screamed?" Terry turned to stare. "I would like to have heard that."

"I can demonstrate."

"No need," said Crawford. "Once was plenty. What did Harry do?"

"Roger Carew was scissoring his puppy, Bubba, and Harry was about to knock into him. He'd been trying all week to get that puppy out of his way. Roger didn't see Harry coming. It was the only way I could think to warn him in time."

"It must have worked," said Terry. "Bubba looked fine yesterday. Until Roger tripped over him, that is. So Harry ended up getting what he needed anyway."

"Needed?" My ears perked. "You mean wanted, don't you?"

"Kind of both the same in this case. Last month, Harry made a deal to sell Vic to a breeder in Japan for mucho yen. The Japanese breeder had been burned before, however. He'd bought dogs from overseas that turned out not to be the quality he'd been promised.

"Apparently Harry'd done some bragging about Vic. He told the Japanese breeder that he was good enough to win at PCA. 'Fine,' said the breeder. 'Prove it. I'll pay you after the puppy wins.' So you might say that Harry was feeling the heat. No Winners, no sale."

I nodded slowly. "That explains why he offered Edith Jean money not to show Bubba."

"What he offered her was probably only a fraction of what he expected to get for Vic," said Terry. "Toy Poodles are a hot commodity in Japan, and with the strength of the yen against the dollar, there's plenty of shopping going on. The same breeder had approached us earlier in the year; that's how we knew he ended up with Harry. And the money he had to spend—"

Crawford cleared his throat loudly. He leveled his assistant a look.

"Thousands," Terry whispered out of the side of his mouth. "Enough to make even someone like me think twice."

"We didn't have what he was looking for," said Crawford. "Period."

"Too bad," I said. "And a lucky break for Harry."

"As long as he could make it happen," said Terry.

Indeed.

I turned and looked at Crawford. "Aunt Peg told me you were the one who recommended Rosalind Roman-escue to her for the seminar."

"Yeah. So?"

"So I was surprised by that. I can't imagine you talking to an animal psychic."

The older man's mocking look was back. "Why is that?"

"Well . . . because I've always thought of you as being more practical than that. I can't imagine you're the kind of person who'd be taken in by sleight of hand and hocus pocus."

"Is that what you think Rosalind does, magic tricks?"

"Quite possibly."

"You might consider letting her do a reading for you. There's a good chance you'd change your mind."

I looked at him in surprise. "Has she done one for you?"

"Several, actually. Though as it happens, we'd never met before this week. Rosalind usually does her communicating over the phone. That way she can get in touch with clients all over the country."

I tried, without success, to picture how that might work. "Like you hold the receiver up to the dog's ear?"

"No." Terry giggled. He was no help.

"She communicates with the animals telepathically," said Crawford. "The phone is so she can talk to the humans. You pick a time and call her. She taps into your dog's thoughts and you talk to him through her."

"And you've actually done this?"

"I just said that, didn't I? Pay attention, Melanie, and try not to look so shocked."

"Yes, sir."

That earned me a glare. Crawford doesn't do sarcasm.

"The first time was on a circuit over the winter. One of the dogs I'd brought with me to show was behaving very oddly. Up until then, he'd been the easiest Standard Poodle in the world. Suddenly he wasn't eating, he wouldn't walk on a leash. He didn't even want to come out of his crate. And if you reached in to get him, he'd snap and pull away. You can see why I was worried."

I certainly could. Fortunately, that was *most* un-Poodle-like behavior. "Did you have a vet look at him?"

"Not right away. After all, we were hundreds of miles from home. Besides, the dog wasn't running a temperature, and he didn't have any obvious symptoms. We couldn't figure out what was the matter.

"Roger and I got to talking about him one day. By then, I'd stopped showing him. I couldn't even slip the leash over his head without a fight. Roger said he had these clients, a pair of dotty sisters from the south, who'd had some luck consulting a psychic. By that time, I was desperate enough to try anything. He got the number for me and I gave Rosalind a call."

"And?" I asked.

"The dog had an infected tooth, one of the molars way in the back. The root was about to abscess. From the front everything looked fine, but the poor guy was really in pain. No wonder he didn't want us touching anything in the area."

"Wait a minute," I said. "I know Poodles are smart, but are you saying that a dog *told* you his tooth was going to abscess?"

"Not in those exact words," said Crawford. "He let Rosalind know that his head hurt. And he let her know where. We added some deductive reasoning and a visit to a canine dentist. But her assessment of the situation was what got us started in the right direction."

Hmm, I thought.

"Tell her about Stretch," said Terry.

"Who's Stretch?" I asked.

"Another client's dog that Rosalind talked to."

"You tell her." Crawford settled back in his chair. "I'm eating."

Besides, there were few things Terry enjoyed more than a good story.

"Okay, so we were showing this Standard named Stretch. A nice boy, easily finishable, though he came by his name honestly." Terry held up his hands, wide apart, indicating a more than optimal length of back.

"Let's move it along, shall we?" Crawford was a firm believer in the dog show credo that you never advertise your dog's faults.

"Good old Stretch was just about finished. He only needed his last major when we hit a month where there weren't going to be any good judges for him. Rather than have him sit around the kennel all that time, we sent him home for a break."

"That was brave of you," I said. Most Poodle handlers won't trust their clients with dogs that are in show coats.

"No, it was all right. We knew Natalie could do hair. A couple of weeks went by and we entered Stretch in some shows. But when Natalie sent him back, he was all mopey and depressed."

That wasn't entirely unusual. For some dogs, depending on their home situation, it was very difficult to make the transition between owner and handler.

"So Crawford called Natalie and asked how Stretch had been when he was home. You know, did anything unusual happen since we'd seen him last? Natalie said everything was fine. The only thing that was different was that she'd whelped a litter of puppies while Stretch was there. As it happened, they were his puppies, though she couldn't imagine how he would know that. For some reason he was fascinated by the litter and was always trying to get into the puppy room to see them."

"And hearing that made you call Rosalind?"

"Not right away," said Crawford. He'd finished his sandwich and was sipping a glass of sweet tea. "At first we figured he just needed a couple of days to adjust to being back in the kennel. Besides, this was a dog who loved to show. We had him entered that weekend, and we thought that would perk him up."

"It didn't," I guessed.

"Right," said Terry. "He showed like a bum. There was no way he was going to get a major with that kind of performance. So Crawford talked to Natalie about it and Natalie called Rosalind. Natalie was thinking maybe Stretch missed his puppies and wanted to go home and see them."

"I thought you said he didn't realize they were his puppies."

"We were just throwing out ideas," Crawford grumbled. "Work with us here, okay?"

I sat back and shut up.

"It turned out," Terry said, "that Stretch didn't miss the puppies. Instead he was jealous of them. He had an idea that while he was away, the puppies were going to grow up and take his place in the house. He was afraid that Natalie was going to stop caring about him."

"Poor guy." Even a nonbeliever like me couldn't help rooting for a happy ending.

"Exactly. So Natalie tells Rosalind to send the message back to Stretch that she loved him and missed him. She couldn't wait for him to come home. All he had to do was go that weekend and show his heart out. If he won, she'd come and pick him up right away."

Terry was grinning. I figured I knew what was coming. "He got his major, didn't he?"

"First day." Crawford nodded. "And he was asking for it,

too. Maybe I'd been a little skeptical before, but not after that. I'm not sure how she does what she does, but Rosalind made a convert out of me."

At this rate, I thought, she'd be making one out of me, too. Maybe I should think of scheduling a session. Not with Eve; the puppy and I were getting along famously. But maybe I could have Rosalind contact Faith back home in Connecticut. The Poodle would probably be happy to pass along all the juicy tidbits that Davey was carefully editing out of our telephone conversations.

The Standard Poodle as spy. The idea had potential.

I thought back to something Crawford had said earlier. He'd told Aunt Peg about Rosalind. Roger Carew had told him. And Roger had gotten the word from . . .

"Those dotty southerners," I said. "Were they by any chance—?"

"The Boone sisters," said Crawford, confirming my hunch. "Betty Jean and Edith Jean. They knew all about Rosalind. They'd used her services themselves."

Why was I not surprised?

19

Considering all the information I'd milked them for, I figured it would be greedy on my part to try and sell Crawford and Terry raffle tickets too. I left them to their work and lugged my basket back inside the arena. The lunch break had just ended in the Standard ring. The Bred by Exhibitor Bitch class was about to begin.

Looking out across the ring, I saw Aunt Peg at the other end, settling into her corner seat. The chair next to hers was empty, and I made a beeline for it.

As I sank down beside her, Peg looked askance in my direction. "There is a limit," she said, "to how many raffle tickets I can buy. Please tell me I'm not single-handedly supporting the entire endeavor."

"I'm not here to sell you anything." I shoved the basket back, out of sight, beneath my chair. "I'm here to watch. Bred-by Bitch, are you kidding? It's the best class in the whole show."

Few of the spectators would have disagreed with me, and certainly not Aunt Peg. At regular all-breed dog shows, Bred-by has largely become just another class, an additional stepping stone on the way to those all-important points. But at specialty shows like PCA, which are always judged by Poodle experts, the Bred-by Exhibitor class is a showcase for the best the country's Poodle breeders have to offer.

Aunt Peg already had her catalog open and turned to the right page. As I glanced over to check the page number, I saw that her margins were filled with scribbled notes. The information she gathered by watching at PCA would impact breeding decisions she made throughout the year.

Quarters were close at ringside. All conversations were held sotto voce. As Mr. Lamb finishing checking in his entries, Peg said quietly, "I've just come from having lunch with Nancy Hanlon. The poor woman was almost distraught. You'll never guess what's happened now."

"Edith Jean." I almost smiled, then caught myself in time. "Right?"

"You've heard about the proposed memorial service?"

"And the ash scattering."

Aunt Peg rolled her eyes. The gesture was more eloquent than a comment would have been.

"Edith Jean is afraid her request will be turned down—"

"Oh, she'll be turned down all right. There's little doubt of that."

"She wanted me to circulate a petition while I was selling tickets. She's hoping to drum up some popular support."

"Tell me you didn't!" Aunt Peg looked ready to snatch the raffle basket and paw through it, if necessary, to root out the offending paper.

"No, I convinced her to wait and talk to Nancy and the board first."

"I'm on the board," Aunt Peg said firmly. "And I can tell you right now, we're not going to approve anything of that nature. Not that we're not sympathetic mind you, but PCA is hardly a suitable instrument for someone's expression of grief. It's a dog show, for Pete's sake. It's supposed to be about the Poodles."

So presumably if a famous and well-regarded Poodle

had died Monday night, holding a memorial service would have been okay?

Aunt Peg wouldn't have appreciated the question. I went on to other matters. "I found out why Harry Gandolf was so determined to go Winners Dog in Toys."

My aunt never took her eyes off the action in the ring. She did, however, incline her head in my direction to indicate that she was listening.

"He'd made a deal to sell that puppy to Japan, provided it won. A very lucrative deal apparently."

"Rather a risky move on his part, wouldn't you think? Tying the sale to a win here?"

"I gather the Japanese buyer had been burned before. Harry didn't have any choice in the matter."

"Even so, there are an astounding number of variables that have to combine just right on the day to produce a win of that magnitude."

The Standard Poodles bitches were gaiting around the ring for the first time. A flashy black bitch, handled by Dale Atherton, caught my eye. I hadn't realized he was a breeder as well as a handler, but he had to be to qualify for entry in this class. He and his Poodle made a stunning pair.

"I'm sure Harry realized that," I said. "In fact, he spent the first two days he was here attempting to cut down on those variables by identifying his chief opposition and trying to remove the dog from competition."

"Trying to do so?" Peg's brow lifted. "Or succeeding at it?"

"Well, he did win," I said, wondering what she was getting at. "But as you mentioned, there were other, perhaps unexpected, variables that came into play. The fact that Bubba was tired from spending much of the afternoon basking in everyone's admiration. That whistle during the Winners class that distracted Roger—"

Aunt Peg shot me a telling look before glancing down

to scribble something in her catalog. Being nosy, I looked over and deciphered her script. Beside the name of the Poodle currently being examined in the ring, she'd written *flat feet*.

"I know what you're thinking," I said. "You think Harry engineered that distraction. The whistle came from high in the stands. Nobody would have been sitting up there to watch, it's too far away. Harry must have had a hand in it. But he was down on the floor at the time, and there's no way I can see of figuring out who helped him—"

"Melanie," Aunt Peg interrupted my rambling. Her tone was stern. "It doesn't matter who whistled."

"What do you mean?"

"You're asking the wrong question."

It wouldn't be the first time. "What's the right question?"

"Who whistled isn't important. What matters is, why did Roger look?"

"What?" The concept was so simple that for a moment it left me baffled.

"Why did Roger look?" Peg repeated. The judge was now examining a skittish brown bitch. My aunt noted the word *brown* in her margin as if that single word conveyed a wealth of meaning. Then, for the first time since the class began, she turned her attention to me.

"So someone made a noise, so what? It happens. Roger's a professional. Presumably he knows how to handle distractions. Upon reflection, that's what struck me as odd about the whole incident. Not that someone whistled at the puppy, but that Roger allowed it to affect his performance. Now, you may be right, perhaps Harry did set something up. Maybe he thought a loud noise like that would upset Bubba, though I can't think why it would necessarily. Or maybe Harry had nothing to do with it and he simply got lucky."

That was an awful lot of maybes. And having observed Harry Gandolf in action over the last few days, I'd come to the conclusion that he was the kind of person who preferred to make his own luck. Still, Aunt Peg had a point. One that bore thinking about.

When I didn't answer right away, Peg went back to watching the class. Dale was moving his black bitch. She sighed softly and wrote the word *lovely* beside its name.

"You want to be in there with them, don't you?" I asked.

"Of course I do," Peg said sharply. "This is the first time in years I haven't shown at PCA. Having the luxury to watch is all well and good, but it's not enough. I feel incomplete just sitting here, as though I'm only doing half what I'm supposed to do."

It wasn't that Aunt Peg didn't have anything to show. When I'd bred Faith, she'd chosen a puppy from the litter to keep for herself, a male sibling of Eve's whom she and Davey had named Zeke. Aunt Peg had started showing him in the spring when I'd brought Eve out. The puppy dog was big and handsome; already he had both his majors and needed only a few singles to finish.

PCA would have been the perfect place to show Zeke off, except for one small glitch. The Standard Poodle judge, Tommy Lamb, and Aunt Peg were old friends. Decades earlier when Peg and her husband, Max, had started out in Poodles, Tommy had served as one of their first mentors. Over the years, the relationship had developed into a strong and abiding friendship.

Under the circumstances, showing to Tommy would have been a lose/lose proposition. If Aunt Peg did well, she risked the chance of people crying favoritism. If she did poorly, Tommy would be left in the unenviable position of needing to explain why he hadn't liked a dog whose bloodlines he'd once had a hand in creating.

Either way, Aunt Peg was better off on the sidelines.

That didn't make the unaccustomed inactivity any easier for her to take, however.

"You'll miss next year, too," I said in an effort to make her feel better.

Aunt Peg thought for a moment, then smiled. The expression blossomed over her face like a flower opening to the sun. "No, I won't. Next year, I won't miss a thing. I'll have the best seat in the house."

The selection process for the following year's judges had been completed not long after Aunt Peg had received her judge's license. In a stunning tribute to the lifetime of hard work she'd devoted to the Poodle breed, Peg had been chosen on the first ballot. The following year, she would hold the position that Tommy Lamb held now. Aunt Peg would be judging Standard Poodles at PCA.

"Why do you think I'm watching so closely?" she asked. "I don't want to miss a move Tommy makes. I'll be lucky to do half the job he does."

I'd seen Aunt Peg judge. She would do a superb job; and luck wouldn't have anything to do with it. "One more thing," I said.

"Have you ever noticed that with you it's always 'one more thing'?"

"I must take after you," I said dryly.

For once, Aunt Peg didn't have a retort handy. I pressed my advantage. "Rosalind Romanescue."

"Now what?" Exasperation sharpened her tone. She frowned at a blue bitch in the ring who was backing off from the judge. *No tail,* she scribbled and left it at that.

"I talked to Crawford about her. He's a believer. Not only that, but he has the stories to back it up."

"I told you she was the real thing."

"No," I felt obliged to point out. "You told me she was all you could get on short notice."

"I found her talk delightful. I'm thinking of having her communicate with my bunch."

I was well acquainted with the six rambunctious Standard Poodles that ran Aunt Peg's house. Trying to hold a coherent conversation with that group would require an air traffic controller, not an animal communicator.

"Crawford got her name from Roger Carew," I said. "Roger got it from the Boone sisters."

"Really?" The last bitch in the class was being examined. Aunt Peg tore her gaze away. "Rosalind knew Betty Jean? I guess that explains her reaction."

"When?"

"At the seminar, remember? Right off the bat someone called out a question about what had happened the night before. When she didn't answer, I pulled her aside and explained about Betty Jean. For a moment, I thought she wouldn't be able to continue. Then she pulled herself back together and went on as if nothing had happened."

"You didn't think that was odd?"

"Why should I have? At the time, I had no idea she was acquainted with the Boones. If I had, I probably would have handled things differently. Maybe taken a small recess to allow Rosalind to regain her composure."

"Except that she apparently didn't need one. As you said, after a moment's hesitation she simply carried on as if nothing were wrong."

Aunt Peg and I both pondered that as Tommy made his cut. To nobody's surprise, Dale's bitch was pulled out on top. The audience agreed with the selection. Applause followed the black Poodle to the head of the new line.

"Maybe she and Betty Jean were merely acquaintances—" Aunt Peg began.

"Maybe she already knew Betty Jean was dead," I said at the same time.

We both stopped speaking and looked at one another.

"You might go ask," Aunt Peg proposed.

As if this murder was my problem. As if I hadn't already told Sam that this time I was nothing more than an interested bystander. As if we both didn't know that given my past proclivities, it was somehow inevitable I would do exactly that.

"Right," I said.

20

Dale Atherton won the Bred-by class to the tune of enthusiastic applause from ringside. His black bitch would be one of the favorites in the Winners ring later that afternoon. As the judge handed out the ribbons and took a minute to record his impressions of the class, I pulled out my basket. It was time to try and sell some more tickets.

I had to admit that by day four, the routine was getting old. In the beginning, it had been sort of fun—better, anyway, than the myriad other jobs Aunt Peg might have found for me. Now, however, I was growing tired of hitting people up for money, even if the proceeds did go to a good cause.

That probably explained why my tally for the next hour's work consisted of two small sales and an equal number of lost pens. On the plus side, I was able to make change for a spectator who'd lost a bet and direct a harried mother to the restrooms. I also kept an eye out for Rosalind. Unfortunately, the communicator was nowhere in sight.

As the Standard Open Bitch class was called into the ring, I went and got Eve. A half hour run around the outside of the building cleared both our heads.

The puppy was still tired from the morning's excitement. At least that was what I tried to tell myself when she didn't protest as I returned her, yet again, to her crate. Instead Eve simply walked inside, turned a small circle, and lay down. Her easy compliance made me feel guiltier than an argument would have. It was sad to think that she was coming to accept as normal the restrictions that being at the show placed on her behavior.

As I was bidding Eve good-bye and promising I'd be back soon, I heard a familiar voice coming from the neighboring setup. Dale Atherton was there, keeping a watchful eye on his bitch as they awaited their next turn in the ring. Bertie had stopped by and the two of them were chatting. I threaded my way through the columns of stacked crates that separated the aisles and went to join them.

"Thanks for saving me earlier," I said to Dale.

"Saving you?" Bertie asked. She looked lovely, as always.

Dale, no slouch in that department himself, was also charmingly modest. "It was nothing."

"Damien Bradley," I said for Bertie's sake.

"I thought you said he seemed like a nice man."

"That was yesterday. Now I've changed my mind."

Dale smiled. "That happens around Damien."

"Your bitch looked beautiful in her class," I said. "Good luck later."

"Thanks, we'll need it. The competition is pretty steep this year, especially in Standards."

"How many did you bring with you?" asked Bertie.

"Unfortunately, Olivia's my one and only. Usually I'd have a bigger string, but this year I picked up a new client who's kept me pretty busy with his Minis. I had to cut down on the number of outside Poodles I was taking."

"Christian and Nina Gold," I said.

Dale nodded. "GoldenDune is a big operation. I've had as many as ten to fifteen Poodles of theirs at a time. Of course I don't take that many to all the shows. Christian was insistent about PCA, however. He wanted his Minis to make a statement here, with entries in as many classes as possible.

"Especially with the two rings running simultaneously, that didn't leave many openings for anyone else. Livvy's different, though. I bred her myself. I figured I could make the entry and if the timing worked, I'd go ahead and show her. If not, I'd just pull her. Try explaining that to a client who expects to see their Poodle in the ring."

Bertie nodded sympathetically. She'd been there.

"Not that I'm complaining. Christian and Nina have been great to work with." Olivia, lying on her grooming table, reached out and nudged his hand with her nose. Dale rubbed the Poodle's muzzle fondly before continuing. "Just being affiliated with an operation of the size and scope of GoldenDune has been good for me. A year ago, not that many people knew who I was. Now I guess I'm moving up in the world."

Dale paused, looking somewhat flustered. On him, the look was adorable. "I'm babbling, aren't I? I do that when I get nervous. I didn't think Livvy would win the Bred-by class. Oh, I knew she'd look good, but I didn't think she'd win. And now that she has, I can't help but think that Tommy must have really liked her. Maybe we have a shot at Winners."

"I'd be surprised if you didn't," said Bertie. She wasn't a Poodle expert but like many accomplished dog fanciers, she had an eye for a good one.

"That's precisely the problem. I went in the ring thinking we were just here to have some fun. Then suddenly my no-pressure afternoon went to high pressure, just like that." Dale stopped speaking and looked at the two of us. "All right, you're still letting me babble on. Enough about me. One of you talk for a while. Change the subject."

"How about Monday night?" I asked. "We could talk about that."

"Monday night?" He looked puzzled.

"When Betty Jean Boone was killed?" Bertie guessed.

I nodded. "Dale was there. At least, right afterward, anyway."

The handler thought back. "I'm happy to talk about it, though I don't have much to say. I thought I heard someone scream and I opened my door to see what was going on."

"You got to Betty Jean before I did," I said. "And I was already outside. You must have been standing right next to your door."

"I was." Dale lifted a hand and rubbed his jaw, much the same as he'd stroked the Poodle a minute before. "A friend had been with me in my room. We'd just said good-bye—at least that's what it felt like to me—when I heard the scream. Of course, I wanted to make sure she was all right."

She? Bertie and I exchanged a quick glance. Remembering Dale's disheveled appearance when he'd come to the door, I supposed it wasn't surprising that he'd been entertaining a woman.

"Your friend might have seen something," I said thoughtfully. "Has she spoken with the police? I'm sure they'd be interested in hearing from her."

Dale was already shaking his head. He looked as though he regretted saying as much as he had. "Trust me, that's not about to happen. I heard from the police too because I was outside just as you were. But the woman in question is a very private person. She told me she didn't want to get involved and I respected her wishes."

"But—"

"Besides," Dale overrode my objection, "I'm sure she didn't have any information for the police or she'd have said something. When I came out of my room, she was already gone. The incident must have happened after she passed by."

Firm as Dale's conviction sounded, I wasn't convinced that he was doing the right thing. Maybe I'd mention something to Detective Mandahar if I saw him again.

"I guess I'd better be getting back to the raffle table," I said.

Bertie watched as I hefted the basket up and slipped it over my arm. "How's business?"

"Slow to nonexistent. I've pretty much worn out my welcome. People see me coming and run the other way."

"As if that's anything new," Bertie said with a grin. "Want me to try taking a spin around the arena with that thing?"

About to leave, I stopped abruptly. The idea had definite appeal. "It's probably against the rules."

"What rules?"

"I don't know. There must be some rule that covers it. There are rules about everything else. You aren't even a member of the club."

"Are you?"

"No," I admitted. "But I got conscripted."

"And I volunteered. So what?" Bertie took the basket off my arm and checked out its contents. "This looks pretty much self-explanatory. Okay, Dale, you're up first. How many tickets do you want?"

"Who said I wanted any?"

Bertie batted her long dark eyelashes. "Who said I was giving you a choice?"

You've got to admire a woman with moxie. As I walked away, Dale was already reaching for his wallet. Somehow I suspected *slow* wasn't a word in Bertie's vocabulary.

Since Bertie was busy doing my job for me, I decided to wander around for a while and simply enjoy the show. What a novel concept. Between working on the raffle, taking care of Eve, and then prepping and showing the puppy, I'd hardly gotten to take a deep breath much less watch more than a small sample of the competition. Many Poodle exhibitors planned their yearly vacation around the specialty show. I wondered if all of them went home as tired at the end of the week as I seemed destined to be.

Judging in the Toy ring had already finished for the afternoon. In Standards, Tommy Lamb was about to place his Open Bitch class. I saw an open spot near the gate, wriggled through the crowd, and found myself standing by the rail just as he pointed toward the striking black bitch at the head of the line. Cheers erupted around me. I hadn't been there long enough to see whether or not I liked the winner, but I joined in anyway. Any win at PCA was worth celebrating.

The bitches who'd made the final cut but hadn't received ribbons filed out. I moved over slightly to give them room to get by. With the Winners class up next, I wasn't about to cede my ringside position.

Harry Gandolf came through the gate. He handed off his Standard bitch to a waiting assistant, then paused and looked around.

I knew he'd be interested in watching what came next. Impulsively I scooted over, bumping the couple on my other side who sighed and gave way. "Hey," I said. "There's room here. Come stand by me."

Harry might have been surprised by the invitation, but he knew better than to question his good fortune. Already an announcement had been made over the loudspeaker; the earlier class winners were entering the ring. People stood seven or eight deep at ringside and those in the back were pressing forward, hoping to get a better view. Excitement and anticipation hummed in the air.

"Melanie, right?" Harry's shoulder dug into mine as we were jostled rudely from behind. He lifted his hand and cradled my elbow to steady me. "Sorry about that."

"No problem." Another shove like that and I was going

to find myself in the ring with the class winners. "Yes, I'm Melanie. We met briefly the other night."

After four intense days with all of us packed together at the show site, the arena had become like the mother ship. Everyone had begun to feel as though they knew everyone else. Even though I'd never given Harry my name, it didn't surprise me that he knew who I was.

"Congratulations on yesterday," I said. "Your puppy deserved the win."

He cast me a quick glance. Trying to determine, I decided, whether or not I was being sincere. "Thanks," he said after a moment. "I thought so."

"I hear he'll go to Japan now."

"I guess news gets around at PCA."

"Gossip, too."

In the ring, the seven class winners had been sent on their first go-round. Thunderous applause drowned out Harry's reply. I took a minute to enjoy the spectacle: seven glorious Standard Poodle bitches, all at the peak of bloom and condition, flying in unison around the big ring. It was truly a sight to behold.

"I'm sorry," I said, when the line had finished making its circuit. "I didn't hear what you said."

"That's not gossip. It's the real deal. Vic leaves next week, as soon as the new owner's check clears the bank."

"Under the circumstances, I guess it's lucky for you that he won."

Harry didn't look pleased. His heavy features settled into a frown. "You want me to rebut that, right? Well I'm not going to. I'm guessing you probably heard part of my conversation with Edith Jean. Hell, maybe you heard all of it. I had a lot riding on that win, I'm not ashamed to admit it. So I tried to stack the odds in my favor. There's nothing wrong with that. When you've been showing dogs as long as I have, you'll know one thing."

"What's that?"

"It's a game. That's all it is, just a big effing game. And the people who win in the end are the people who know how to play."

Having judged all these Poodles earlier in the day, Mr. Lamb was making short work of his decision. I kept one eye on his progress in the ring, the other on Harry. "Are you trying to tell me that the Boone sisters didn't?"

"I'm not trying to tell you anything," said Harry. "I'm trying to watch Winners Bitch."

Fair enough.

Mr. Lamb continued his judging. Due to circumstances beyond our control, Harry and I continued to stand pressed up hard against one another. Maybe that was why he felt compelled to keep talking.

"Since you brought it up, I'll tell you something else," he said presently. "Those two old birds weren't anywhere near as savvy as they thought they were. This is the big time, and I gave Edith Jean her shot at it. She should have taken the money and run."

"Funny you should think so."

"Why's that?"

"Well, because you won anyway. You didn't have to pay Edith Jean and Vic still beat Bubba. So you came out ahead."

"Yeah, well . . ." He stopped and scowled at my logic. "That's a nice thought, but at the end of the day, it ain't going to cut it. Here's the word from Harry and it's the God's honest truth. Everybody's got their hand out, and everybody pays. One way or another, everybody pays somebody in the end."

21

Tommy Lamb made his Winners Bitch award into a duel between Dale's Bred-by bitch and the Open class winner, much as the Toy judge had done between Vic and Bubba. The format encouraged the audience to choose up sides and join in the festivities, and we responded with predictable enthusiasm.

Poodles as performance art; for lovers of the breed, it didn't get much better than this.

In the end, the top award went to the Open Bitch, and Dale had to be content with the striped rosette for Reserve. He didn't look disappointed by the outcome. His face was wreathed in smiles as he accepted the lesser prize.

Just for the heck of it, I kept my gaze trained on the handler as he walked over to the marker. I wondered if there was a particular lady in the crowd with whom he'd make eye contact. But although more than a few of the women had their eyes on Dale, I didn't see him single anyone out for a special glance. He accepted congratulations from all sides and exited the ring a minute later.

As the pictures were being taken, the crowd melted away. One minute Harry was standing beside me, the next he was gone. I couldn't say that I'd miss his company.

Once photos were finished, the Veteran's Sweepstakes would follow. Veterans were older dogs, and in Poodles, any dog or bitch over the age of seven qualified. In addition, all the entrants had to be A.K.C. champions. These Poodles were truly the elder statesmen of the breed; many had been the top winners of their time.

One of the things that made the sweepstakes special in the eyes of exhibitors was that this was the only breed sanctioned competition where Poodles could be shown in any trim their owners felt would present them to advantage. Not being restricted to the Continental and English Saddle clips that were required in the breed classes, most Poodles were exhibited in the comfortable and popular kennel trim. Their hair was short and sporty; the dogs looked elegant, their owners looked happy. Someday, when Faith was old enough to qualify, I planned to show her in the sweepstakes myself.

As the first class of Toy veterans was called into the ring, spectators began to return to ringside. I dropped back from my noisy position near the gate, took out my phone and called my ex-husband's house. As I'd expected, Davey picked up. My son loved to talk on the phone.

"Hi, sport," I said.

"Hey," Davey replied. At least this time he recognized my voice. "How's the dog show?"

"Great. Eve made the cut in her class. How's home? Did you go to Playland?"

"It was awesome," Davey reported. "Dad and I went on the roller coaster six times."

"That sounds awesome all right." Thank God I hadn't been there. Roller coasters make my stomach turn over. "Did you remember to wear sun block?"

For some reason, the question made him giggle. "Davey?"

"Yeah, I put some on."

Reading between the lines, I hazarded a guess. "What about your Dad?"

"He said lotions are for sissies. Real men get tan."

That was my ex, just the sort of role model every mother

wants for her only child. I sighed. Playland was right near Rye beach. There was very little shade. "How red is he?"

"Like a pizza without the cheese. He says it doesn't hurt though."

He would say that, I thought. Since real men don't feel pain.

"Maybe you can convince him to put some aloe on it."

"Maybe Frank can," said Davey. "He's coming tonight for dinner. Not Bertie though. She's away on a trip."

"She's down here with me."

"Cool." Davey adored his new aunt. "Let me talk to her."

"Sorry, I meant she was here at the show, not here beside me. She's off selling raffle tickets."

"Aunt Peg said that was going to be your job." His tone was slightly accusatory.

"It is my job. Bertie's helping me."

"Are you going to buy me a ticket?"

"Two, if you want. How's Faith doing?"

Davey went on to give me a detailed report of how the Poodle was spending her time. When that was done he called Faith over, lifted up the flap of her ear, and held the receiver to the opening in the hope that she would understand that he was talking to me. I don't think it worked, though Davey said Faith's tail did begin to wag. Mostly I attributed that to the fact that the phone was probably tickling her. Where was Rosalind when we needed her?

By the time I got off the phone, the Minis were in the sweeps ring. Things were moving right along. I'd expected to run into Bertie sooner or later. Since I hadn't, I realized I probably ought to let Edith Jean know what had become of her raffle basket.

When I got to the table, the older woman was packing up. "Good, you're back," she said. "Your basket showed up about ten minutes ago with a very nice young lady and a mountain of cash."

I pulled out a box and began to help. "That was my sister-in-law, Bertie. She offered to help out. I hope you don't mind."

"Mind? Are you kidding? She must have some sales technique. If we put that gal on the payroll, we could double our profits."

That made me feel appreciated. "I don't think Bertie's looking for a job."

"Too bad," Edith Jean mused. "You must have lucked out, getting her for a sister-in-law. Sister and I had one of those once. Ours was a real bitch. We didn't mind one bit losing touch with her after Earl died."

"Earl?" I looked up. I hadn't heard that name before. Then again, everyone at PCA freely admitted that they knew next to nothing about the sisters' lives, except for the one week a year that was spent at the show. "Was he your husband?"

"Goodness, what a thought"—Edith Jean began to laugh, then suddenly caught herself—"what a thoughtful man he was, that's what I meant to say. Of course Earl was my husband, who else would he have been?"

Good question. I was almost sorry I hadn't asked it myself. "Were you married long?"

"Just three short years. I was already in my thirties when we met. You've got to understand that southern girls, especially out in the rural areas, they marry young. By the time Earl came along, I'd pretty much given up on finding myself a man. Then just like that, there he was. Earl was older, and very dashing. I fell head over heels."

That explained the locket, I thought. "You must have been very happy."

"We were." Edith Jean nodded. "Leastways for a little while. Earl had himself a bit of money stashed away. He said he'd always wanted to get back to the land, saw himself as a gentleman farmer or some such thing. That was fine with Sister and me. We had our Poodles and we had ourselves a fair piece of acreage. Earl moved in, bought himself a tractor, and went to work planting crops."

She smiled at the memory. "Good old Earl never did manage to grow much of anything edible but Sister and I didn't care. Plenty of food to be had in the supermarket. 'Course, as it turned out, he wasn't too handy with the tractor either. One day he managed to flip the damn thing over on himself. Sister and I were away at a dog show. Nobody found him until it was too late."

"I'm so sorry," I said.

"Thank you, dear." Edith Jean reached out and patted my arm as though I was the one in need of comforting. "It was all over and done with a long time ago. Sister and I went on, that's what people do, isn't it? We never went to many dog shows after that though. It just wasn't fun like it had been before."

I swallowed heavily as the irony of what she'd said hit home. One death had kept the sisters away from the dog show scene for decades. Recently they'd ventured back, only to be met with death again.

"By the way," said Edith Jean, changing the subject. "I forgot to mention a man came around here earlier looking for you. Tall guy, real good-looking . . ."

I grinned. "That's Sam."

"Said he'd barely seen you all day. Looked anxious to rectify that, if you know what I mean. If I was you and had that waiting for me, I wouldn't be hanging around here."

"Maybe I like hanging around with you," I said.

"Bull crap." Edith Jean's hands grasped my shoulders, turned me around, pointed me away. "You've put in enough work. Go find your man and have yourself some fun."

Actually, I wasn't sure I'd put in much work at all. On the other hand, who was I to argue with an order like that?

"Yes, ma'am," I said.

*　*　*

I found Sam over by the ring. He was watching the first of the Standard Poodle classes with Christian Gold. The two of them stood, heads tipped together, conferring in whispered tones about the entry in the ring. Sam straightened and smiled when he saw me.

"I've been looking for you," he said.

"So Edith Jean told me. What's up?" I'd intended to join them, but Sam took my hand and pulled me away.

"Come on." He headed for the exit at the far end of the arena floor where wide, empty tunnels snaked out beneath the stands.

His strides were long and fast. I had to hurry to keep up. "Where are we going?"

"Away," he muttered.

I thought perhaps I'd misheard him. "Away from what?"

"Everything."

That side of the building was deserted. Everyone who remained at the show site at the end of the long day had stayed to watch the veterans. Reaching the end of the arena, we stepped off the sod and onto a concrete walkway, away from the brightly lit show rings and into the shadowy tunnel.

Fingers laced firmly through mine, Sam dragged me around the first corner and into a small alcove. Then he stopped abruptly, his body turning and angling into mine. My back arched up against the wall; my shoulder blades braced against the cold unyielding barrier.

"God I've missed you," he said.

The air escaped from my lungs in a rush. "You saw me this morning."

"You were working then." Sam leaned closer. His breath mingled with mine. I inhaled sharply.

"Last night—"

"You were working then too." That was the nature of PCA, and we both knew it. "You had to get Eve ready."

"Tonight—"

"I'll be working on Tar." His lips nibbled around the edges of my mouth. "Hell of a vacation. Do you realize this is the first time since we've known each other that we've gone away alone together?"

"Mmmm." Usually we'd been accompanied by our seven-year-old chaperone. Sam's tongue was touching mine. I couldn't quite speak. Thought was fleeing too.

"I thought we'd have more time to ourselves. Instead, all I ever seem to do is see you on the other side of the arena. We've got to do something about that."

His long legs splayed, positioning mine between them. His fingers were still threaded through mine. Our hands were pressed together, palm to palm. When he braced his hands on the wall on either side of me, I was totally surrounded by him. My breathing quickened. I could feel my heart beginning to pound. My breasts rose and fell with each shuddering, indrawn breath.

Sam smiled silkily. "Now we're getting somewhere."

The kiss was everything I'd been waiting for, and more. Enough to make me forget for a moment where we were. Maybe even enough to make me not care.

Sam's hands released mine. His fingertips skimmed over my cheek, holding and caressing at the same time. I wrapped my arms around his body, then slid them lower. Grasping the back of his shirt, I tugged until the hem slid free. Then I slipped my hands underneath. Warm skin against warm skin.

He trembled slightly, groaning deep within his throat. The tremor acted like wildfire to the pinpricks of sensation that were already sliding along my nerve endings. I eased back slightly. Sam's eyes had darkened, his expression was intent as he gazed down upon me.

"We'll never make it back to the hotel," I said.

He buried his face in the hollow of my throat. I felt the warmth of his chuckle against my ear. "Sweetheart," he said, "we're not going to make it out of this alcove."

My pulse began to throb. My stomach muscles curled. Somewhere, far away, I heard the muted sound of ringside applause. Enough to remind me that we weren't alone.

"But—" I began.

Sam hushed the objection with another kiss. It seemed to last forever. Aunt Peg would kill us if she knew, I thought dimly. Then thought evaporated, taking sanity with it, and I forgot all about why I'd been arguing.

22

Friday morning, I was up at dawn again.

What can I say? It was PCA, and it only happened once a year. On this, the last day of the specialty show, the Best of Variety classes would be judged in Toys, Miniatures, and Standards. More than one hundred and fifty Poodle champions would compete for the honor of representing their varieties in the Best in Show ring.

In addition, a number of other prizes would be awarded, each one tremendously meaningful on this national stage: Best Brood Bitch, Best Stud Dog, Best Brace, Best Puppy in Show, and Best Bred-by Exhibitor. It was a full day's slate of judging, the culmination of everything the earlier classes had been working toward. The festivities concluded Friday night with the PCA Banquet, which would be held at the hotel.

By Saturday morning, the show was over for another year. Everyone would pack up and head home. Sam, Aunt Peg, and I would return to Connecticut. Edith Jean would go back to Georgia. And if the police hadn't figured out who'd killed Betty Jean by the time we left, I doubted they ever would.

Would you like to hear me say again that this was *not* my problem?

Even so, I couldn't help but feel for Edith Jean, who'd

kept her emotions to herself and soldiered on relentlessly with her duties. If Betty Jean's murder was none of my business, then whose was it? Were all of us—the entire Poodle community whom Edith Jean felt to be members of her extended family—going to simply disperse the next day and go on with our lives as if nothing had happened? I found that to be a dismal and sobering thought.

Even though it was early, once again the arena was buzzing with activity. The task of making so many Poodle champions look absolutely exquisite was no small endeavor. I put Eve into her crate, leaving her with the heartfelt promise that this was the last day she'd have to spend confined. The puppy merely sighed with acceptance.

Though the grooming area was full at that hour, the rest of the building was mostly empty. Judging hadn't started yet. The two big rings that had served the show all week had been opened up and joined together to form one enormous ring, which currently sat idle. Row upon row of chairs waited for the spectators to arrive.

From where I stood on the edge of the sod, I could see clear across the entire lower level of the facility. Charlotte Kay was at the trophy table. Her silver cups and bowls were already on display, a glorious array of prizes for the competition to come. Edith Jean was just arriving at the raffle table. In a few minutes, I'd go and join her. In the meantime, there was something else I wanted to check on.

As I'd brought Eve into the building, I'd caught a glimpse of Rosalind Romanescue and Christian Gold slipping out a mostly unused side door that led to one of the parking lots. I'd never managed to connect with Rosalind the day before. If I hadn't still been looking for her, I probably wouldn't even have noticed them.

Once I did, however, I realized there was something furtive, almost sneaky, about the way they'd hurried out of the arena together; something that made me wonder what they were up to. Wrapping my sweater around my shoulders, I pushed open the door and went after them.

At a glance, the exhibitors' parking lot was filled with cars and entirely deserted. No wonder, when all the action was going on inside the building. As I scanned the rows of parked vehicles, I wondered whether Christian and Rosalind had gotten into a car and driven away. Or perhaps walked through the lot and continued to the motor homes that were parked beyond. With nearly ten minutes head start on me, they could be almost anywhere.

And then I got lucky. As I stood looking out over the lot and debating what to do next, I heard the murmur of muted voices. Following the sound led me to a black Mercedes-Benz SUV parked one row over. Its tailgate was sitting open; Christian was inside the car.

Rosalind was perched on the edge of the tailgate, legs stretched out in front of her, hands folded demurely in her lap. Though she was staring in my direction, she didn't seem to see me. Her eyes gazed past me as if I wasn't even there.

As I drew near I realized that the two of them weren't alone. A black Miniature Poodle in full show coat was standing in the cargo area between them. There was a peculiar stillness about all three of them, as if their attention was so fully engaged by what they were doing that nothing else mattered.

All at once I felt like an intruder, though I couldn't, in that first moment, imagine what I was intruding on. Christian was the one who noticed me first. He looked out through the car window and scowled. His expression made it clear he was hoping I wouldn't interrupt them.

Then abruptly Rosalind's gaze focused and came to rest on me. Unlike Christian, she smiled. "Are you looking for me?"

Of course I had been, though I had no idea how she'd have known that. I nodded.

Rosalind ducked her head down inside the SUV. "We're done here," I heard her say.

"No, we're not." Christian's voice, loud and strident, carried easily.

"I told you, what you're asking is impossible."

"And I told you it isn't."

Rosalind shrugged at that, as if Christian's opinion was of little consequence. She stood up, linked her arm through mine, and began to walk away.

"Come back here!" Christian yelled after us. His hand flew to the door handle. He scrambled from the SUV.

"Odious man," Rosalind muttered. "You don't suppose he'll come after us, do you?"

I hazarded a glance back. "He hasn't yet. Though he is glaring daggers in your direction."

"Let him. Idiot."

We'd passed into the next row of parked cars and almost reached the building before Rosalind began to relax. "What was that all about?" I asked as we went inside.

She didn't answer right away. Though it was warm inside the arena, she crossed her arms tightly over her chest. Her hands rubbed up and down her upper arms. I was about to offer her my sweater when she finally spoke. "Christian Gold wants to win Best of Variety in Miniatures."

"Imagine that." It wasn't an uncommon goal. Forty other exhibitors entered that day were all hoping to do the same thing.

"He contacted me last night and asked if I could communicate with his specials bitch," said Rosalind. "He wanted me to tell her how important this show was, to make her understand that she had to win. I tried to tell him that's not the way animal communication works. The Poodles and I talk to each other in images, not words. Also, the concept of an important competition is pretty much lost on a dog."

"What did he say to that?"

"He seemed okay with my response. He said he could see why I had reservations about the idea, but he'd appreciate it if I tried anyway. Since I thought we understood each other, I agreed. I told him we needed someplace quiet to work, a place where there wouldn't be a lot of distractions. Christian suggested that we go outside.

"When we got there, I realized he'd wanted to go somewhere where nobody would see what we were doing. As if he were embarrassed to be seen with me. Fool," Rosalind growled under her breath. "His Poodle is a delight. He doesn't deserve such a nice dog."

"The session didn't go well, I take it?"

"The session didn't *go* at all. Rita, the Mini bitch, didn't want to talk about PCA. She wasn't even slightly interested in what happened in the dog show ring. Not that I can blame her."

Her eyes narrowed. "I can't force these things to happen, you know. All I can do is listen and interpret what the animals have to say. Rita told me she'd had a litter of puppies before and she'd like to have another."

I grinned. The Mini bitch wasn't exactly on topic. "What did Christian say to that?"

"He told me to just get on with it. As if Rita was some sort of wind-up toy and I was pushing the wrong buttons. So I tried again. With pretty much the same result. Rita's not the most focused show dog, apparently. When I tried to tell him that, Christian began to get ugly. He told me to tell Rita that if she didn't win today, he'd never let her have puppies again. That she wouldn't have earned the privilege of reproducing. How vile is that? He actually seemed to think I could pass the message along as if I was some sort of FedEx courier."

Rosalind's cheeks grew pink with indignation. "As if I would, even if I could! I've handled some strange requests in my time, but I've never heard anything like that. What kind of monster is that man anyway? I could tell that Rita

was getting agitated. She could feel my distress. I was trying to calm both of us down when you arrived."

"How did you know I was looking for you?" I asked.

"I didn't. But I saw you and thought maybe you'd give
me a way to escape. I needed an excuse and I was hoping
you'd play along."

So much for psychic undertones.

"I owe you one," said Rosalind.

"Perfect," I said. "I'd like to collect."

If Rosalind was taken aback by the speed with which I'd
accepted her offer, she recovered quickly. "Do you want
me to do a session with one of your Poodles? I have to tell
you I'm a little drained right now, but we could certainly
do something later."

"Thanks, but I have something else in mind." While
we'd been talking, I'd steered her up the steps to a food
concession on the upper level. "Do you have time to sit
down with me over a cup of coffee and answer a few questions?"

"What kind of questions?" Rosalind asked warily. Her
experience with Christian had put her on guard.

"Easy ones, I hope. I'm just trying to clarify a few
things."

Rosalind agreed, and we both ordered coffee. I added a
bagel with cream cheese to my request. A few minutes
later, we carried our food out to the tiered seating. Up in
the stands, it was strangely quiet; rows of empty seats
spread in all directions around us.

Down on the arena floor, the Toy judge and stewards
were preparing to open the ring. The grooming area was a
hive of frenetic activity. Spectators were streaming in the
doors and finding their seats. I sipped at my steaming coffee and pondered how to begin.

"You're not waiting for me to read your mind, are you?"
Rosalind asked after a bit.

I looked up, sputtered, then saw she was smiling.

"Sorry." Rosalind sounded entirely unrepentant. "Psychic humor. Which is odd when you stop to consider that, no matter what people believe, I'm not actually a psychic."

"You're telepathic," I said. As if I was finally beginning to get it.

"I prefer to think we're all telepathic. Some of us know how to use our gifts and others don't. Is that what you brought me up here to discuss?"

"No. I wanted to talk about Betty Jean Boone."

Rosalind looked interested in my choice of subject. "What about her?"

"I found out recently that you knew the Boone sisters before you came to PCA."

"That's right. I did several sessions for them in the spring."

"In Georgia?"

"Heavens, no. I live in New Jersey. We conducted the sessions over the phone."

"So then you'd never actually met them?"

"Not in person. It works that way with many of my clients. People contact me from all over the country. It's not at all unusual for me to do business with people I've never met."

"Even though you form a close bond with their animals?" I asked.

"It's not so much that *I* form a bond," Rosalind clarified, "as that I help my clients explore their own relationship with their pets. Dogs don't tell me things because they want *me* to know. They give me information to pass them along to their owners. I'm really more of a conduit than a participant in the discussion."

The more I understood about what Rosalind did, the more fascinated I became. I wondered how much ribbing I'd have to endure from Aunt Peg if I scheduled a session for Eve. That was for later, however. Now, I needed to steer the conversation back to the topic I'd wanted to discuss.

"My aunt wanted you to know she was sorry you had to hear the news of Betty Jean's death so bluntly. If she'd had any idea that you knew the Boones, she would never have allowed that to happen. I know the whole thing came as a shock to you."

Rosalind shook her head. "I wasn't so much shocked as I was surprised. I already knew what had happened. What I didn't expect was that someone would make a joking reference to a rather gruesome death as if it was some sort of parlor game. That was the part that startled me."

She stared intently down onto the arena floor. The Toy Poodle specials were filing into the ring. From where we sat, they looked tiny. I could tell the handlers apart, but the Poodles themselves were an indistinguishable blur. I waited, curbing my impatience, until Rosalind was ready to continue.

"I arrived at the hotel early Monday evening," she said finally. "After your aunt called me, I got in my car and drove right down. This dog show sounded like a wonderful opportunity for me. I wanted to make sure I got here in plenty of time.

"After I'd settled into my room, I went out and got some dinner. Upon my return, I walked around the back of the hotel. I'd seen earlier that that was where the dogs were allowed to play and run free. It was dark, but there were lights on. All sorts of Poodles were racing around in that big field, people wandering here and there and talking to one another."

I nodded, remembering the scene. Aunt Peg and I had probably been two of the people Rosalind had seen.

"The fresh air cleared my head beautifully and I was on my way back inside when I heard what sounded like someone running, or at least in a big hurry. Up until that point, I hadn't been paying much attention to my surroundings, but of course I looked up then. That was when I saw a body lying in the shadows. I'm afraid I let out a rather deafening shriek."

One mystery solved, I thought. "That was you?"

Rosalind nodded sheepishly. "I'm afraid so. Sad to say, I'm not good in emergency situations. There's too much turmoil, entirely too many emotions. Thankfully, other people immediately saw what had happened and began to rally around. My presence quickly became superfluous and I left. Later when I went down to the bar to get a brandy to settle my nerves, I heard someone say that the woman I'd seen outside was Betty Jean Boone."

"Did you ever talk to the police about what you saw?" I asked.

Rosalind seemed surprised by the question. "No, why would I? I didn't know anything that would help them in their investigation. I hadn't seen anything more than a dozen other people also saw. I heard later that the detectives were questioning people, but nobody ever contacted me."

Because nobody'd realized she'd been there, I thought. "You didn't see the person you'd heard running?"

"Of course not. If I had, I'd have certainly reported that. But by the time I looked up, the person was gone. All I saw was a woman's body crumpled on the ground."

"Have you spoken with Edith Jean since?"

"I saw her the next morning. Although now that you mention it, it was a rather strange encounter."

"In what way?"

"As I said, we'd never met before. And obviously we weren't meeting under the best of circumstances. Still, I felt as though I ought to introduce myself and offer whatever solace I could. But when I told Edith Jean who I was, she went positively pale. I've never had anyone respond to me in quite that way before. At the time, all I could think was that grief affects everyone differently. Perhaps Edith Jean felt my approaching her like that was an intrusion."

Rosalind's use of that particular phrase reminded me of something she'd said the last time we'd spoken. "Maybe she was afraid you could read her thoughts."

Rosalind looked horrified. "Even if I could do something like that, I wouldn't dream of it. What a nasty, vile idea. Edith Jean Boone has nothing to fear from me."

Yet that hadn't stopped her from being afraid. I wondered why.

23

Rosalind went off to watch the show and I headed down to the raffle table. By the time I got there, Edith Jean had everything set up. The prizes looked inviting; the money box was open. A spool of tickets stood ready to serve any eager customers that happened by. Despite Edith Jean's preparations, however, the area was deserted. With Best of Variety in the ring, no spectator wanted to miss a minute of the judging.

"Good morning," Edith Jean sang out cheerfully as I drew near. Her fingers flicked an imaginary speck of dust from the top of the money tree. "Isn't this an excellent day?"

"So far, so good," I said. With everything that had transpired during the week, it was hard to see what Edith Jean had to sing about. "How's the raffle going?"

"Fine and dandy. We're in the homestretch now. Just one more day of minding the store, and we're done. The drawing's all set for this afternoon. It'll take place in the ring after the Standards finish and before Best in Show. You'll be here to help out, right?"

"Right." That would be my last official duty as a member of the raffle committee. I snuck another glance at Edith Jean. She still looked way too cheerful. Something was up; I wondered what. "What exactly does helping out involve?"

"Oh, it's easy. I know you've seen how it works in the past. The tickets are put in a big barrel, and then drawn out one by one. The first person whose number is called gets first choice of the items on the table. The second ticket gets second choice, and so on and so on until all the prizes are distributed."

I looked around the crowded table. Even if people chose relatively quickly, the process was going to take a while.

"Forty-two," Edith Jean said in answer to my unspoken question. "That's how many prizes there are. And therefore, how many tickets you'll have to draw from the barrel."

"Me?"

"Who better? I can't do it. I have to stay by the table, checking the stubs and overseeing the selection process. Managing the drawing is a two-man operation. That's the way Sister and I always divided the work in the past."

Since she'd put it that way, it would probably be churlish of me to mention that I'd rather stand at the table and take ticket stubs than be the one performing out in the middle of the vast show ring.

"So I just have to draw the numbers?" I repeated for good measure.

"That's all there is to it. Danny, the announcer, will accompany you out there with a microphone. You hand each ticket over to him and he'll read off the number. That will start the stampede in my direction."

Stampede would be a mild description for what would come next. I'd seen that in the past, too. "As soon as I'm finished drawing tickets, I'll come straight back here and help."

Edith Jean mumbled something. Her words were too low for me to catch.

"Pardon me?"

"Not exactly," she said. "When you're done, Danny's going to pull out a sheet of paper and read a little something I wrote."

"I don't understand . . ." I started to say. Then all at once, I understood all too well. Dread welled in the pit of my stomach.

I knew the board had turned down the request for a memorial service. Nancy Hanlon had been given the job of delivering the unwelcome news. This, then, was to be Edith Jean's response.

She reached beneath the table and pulled out a bright red fanny pack. Dog handlers wear them in the ring all the time. Strapped around the waist, they make a handy pouch for bait.

"While he's reading," said Edith Jean, "you're going to open this up and scatter the ashes."

"No." Involuntarily, my hands came up in front of my body as if forming a shield between me and impending disaster. For good measure I took a step back. "No, I'm not."

Edith Jean didn't look the slightest bit impressed by my objections. "Of course you are, dear." She draped the pack's strap over my upraised hand. The bundle was surprisingly heavy. "You'll simply wear this into the ring. No one will even notice it's there. Then, when the climactic moment arrives, you'll just whip it off, unzip it, and let fly."

The scenario was too horrible to even contemplate. In all the fantasies I'd ever harbored concerning the Best in Show ring at PCA—and I had to admit, there'd been a few—there had never been any whipping, unzipping, or letting fly. And you can trust me on that.

"Edith Jean, I can't do that."

I'd thought Aunt Peg would kill me if she ever found out about my last transgression. At least that one had taken place in private. This one would be tantamount to treason. My death would be part and parcel of a public hu-miliation. And the PCA board would probably applaud my demise.

You think I was overreacting? Think again. This was PCA, the pinnacle of Poodledom. The specialty known for its dignity and decorum.

Edith Jean wasn't just asking the impossible. Worse, she was asking for the absurd.

"You have to," she said in a small voice. "If you don't help me, who will?"

I thought fast. There had to be someone . . . anyone . . . whose name I could invoke. Briefly, Terry came to mind. He'd enjoy the theatrical aspect of this little performance. His image was quickly followed by another, however: Crawford chasing me around the arena wielding a big pair of sharp scissors.

"I'd do it myself if I weren't an invalid." Edith Jean sounded pitiful now. She held up her right hand, still swathed in gauze and vet wrap.

Invalid my foot. The older woman had had her hand wrapped all week. It hadn't hampered her actions at all. She'd counted change and hefted big boxes with equal aplomb. Nor had it prevented her from doing anything else she'd wanted to do. If that hand still hurt, I certainly hadn't been able to tell.

"Let me think about it," I said.

Immediately Edith Jean smiled. "You're such a sweet girl."

No, I wasn't. I was a liar and a hypocrite. What I'd really be thinking about was a way to put a stop to this impend-ing debacle. Or at the very least, my participation in it.

"How did you get Danny to agree?" I wanted to know.

"Agree to what?" Miss Innocent asked. As if we hadn't just been talking about hijacking the dog show to serve her nefarious purposes.

"You know—to read your statement."

"That part was easy. Have you ever known a young man who couldn't use a little extra cash?"

"You offered to *pay him*?"

"Not at first. But eventually we were able to strike a deal. We agreed that no matter what number you drew from the barrel first, he would simply palm it and then read out a number that matched one of the stubs from his own tickets. That would give him first choice of the raffle prizes. I'd pretend to check with him, then set aside the money tree."

"You can't do that!"

"Oh, but I can," Edith Jean said brightly. "I'm in charge of the raffle. And what I say, goes."

"But that's fraud, or theft, or impersonating a ticket-taker . . . or something."

"Yes, well, desperate times call for desperate measures."

"Edith Jean, listen to me." I dumped the fanny pack on the table and crossed my arms over my chest. If I left them loose, I was half afraid I might resort to shaking her. "These aren't desperate times. And you don't have to do this. You can have a memorial service for Betty Jean when you get home."

"No, that won't work. I want everything over and done with before I leave Maryland in the morning. I want to say good-bye to Betty Jean here. When I go home, there'll only be Edith Jean. Just me, I mean. That's the only way."

Maybe she was losing her mind, I thought. Alternatively, maybe I was losing mine. I did know one thing, however. I had to find Aunt Peg—and fast. A problem of this magnitude—especially one that concerned her beloved dog show—was beyond my capabilities.

"I have to go," I said. "I'll be back in a bit, is that okay?"

Edith Jean looked in the direction of the ring. From our spot on the sidelines, we were just about able to see the tops of the handlers' heads. Vic, the Winners Dog, was still in contention. Standing second to last in the long,

long, line he wouldn't be called upon to perform for at least another hour. Even then, I doubted Edith Jean would much care how he did.

After the Toy BOV judging concluded, Bubba would return to the ring. As a Puppy class winner, he was eligible to compete for Best Toy Puppy. I knew she would want to see that, but I was sure I'd be back in plenty of time.

"You go on," she said. "There isn't much happening here anyway. I'll manage just fine."

"Thanks." I grabbed my catalog and hurried away before she could change her mind.

Even though Standards wouldn't be judged until afternoon, I'd hoped Aunt Peg might already have her corner seats staked out. No such luck. A pair of Toy breeders from Florida were sitting in the spots Peg and Sam had occupied for most of the week. They were staring into the ring with such rabid intensity that they were oblivious to my scrutiny. And my frustrated sigh.

I knew Aunt Peg was at the show site somewhere, but in a building that size, it didn't narrow things down much. Maybe a jog through the grooming area would turn something up.

"Hey," said Bertie, appearing out of the crowd. "Where are you off to in such a hurry?"

"I'm looking for Peg. Have you seen her?"

"We had breakfast together at the hotel. Her idea. For some reason, that woman feels obliged to keep pumping food into me. I ditched her as soon after that as I could." Bertie looked over, realized she was talking about one of my nearest and dearest relatives, and flushed guiltily. "Sorry."

"Don't mention it. Sometimes I feel exactly the same way. Now, however, I have to find her. Edith Jean Boone is planning an insurrection for this afternoon. Somebody has to stop her."

"Not the memorial service again? I thought the board put the kibosh on that."

"They did. Or at least they think they did. The problem is, Edith Jean isn't paying any attention."

"That should be interesting." Bertie sounded annoyingly happy about this turn of events. "I ought to come to this show every year. Are all PCAs this much fun?"

"You're perverse, you know that?"

"Of course. It's one of the things your brother likes best about me."

He would, I thought.

"If I see her," said Bertie, "I'll tell her you're looking for her."

"Thanks." We headed off in opposite directions. When I reached the edge of the grooming area, I stopped and looked around, eyes skimming quickly over the tightly packed aisles.

By now, after five solid days together, everyone at the dog show was beginning to look at least vaguely familiar. From a multitude of diverse backgrounds we'd all come together, united by a single purpose. Several people glanced up as I gazed around. Each one smiled before going back to work.

That was the beauty of PCA. Who needs goodwill ambassadors when you can have Poodles?

Standing at the head of the wide center aisle, I stepped aside to let a wide-eyed family wander past. Tourists, probably at their first dog show. Both parents stared at the spectacle in wonder. Their elementary school–age children looked similarly awestruck. They probably had a pet Poodle at home. To them, these Poodles were Fifi or Pierre with a better haircut. Today's tourists were tomorrow's exhibitors. Judging by their expressions, this family would go home with visions of sugarplums dancing in their heads.

Turning back to my quest, I bumped into a handler who'd come up beside me. "You looking for me?" asked Damien Bradley.

"No. Why would I be looking for you?"

"That's what I'm wondering."

"Well, don't," I said. "I'm not."

"Yeah, right. I'm sure you think you're pretty clever. I've heard all about you." He brushed past me and started to walk away.

I spun around and followed. "What have you heard?"

Damien stopped so abruptly that I barreled right into him. Smooth move on my part. Damien seemed to think so, too. He snorted under his breath.

"You're the lady who solves mysteries. The one who figures things out."

"Sometimes," I said. "Not always."

"Want some advice?" Damien leaned in close, making sure his words were for me alone. "Stay away from Edith Jean Boone. That old broad's nuttier than a Snickers bar."

Tell me something I don't know, I thought.

24

I finally found Aunt Peg upstairs on the concourse level, chatting with the publisher of the breed's premier magazine, *Poodle Variety*. Rather than ruin both their days, I grabbed Aunt Peg's arm and dragged her out to the tiered seating where we'd be able to talk privately.

"That was rather rude of you," she sniffed. "I suppose there's something absolutely vital you have to discuss with me right this second."

"Yes."

Aunt Peg looked startled. "I was joking," she said.

"I'm not."

She sighed and sat down. "This *is* PCA, you know. Would it be too much to ask that for once you might attend a dog show and simply enjoy yourself?"

Since I was still standing, I used the extra height to good advantage and glared down at her. "Who was the one who got me mixed up with the Boone sisters in the first place?"

"That would be me," Aunt Peg admitted.

"And who brought Rosalind Romanescue down here to fill in at the last minute, unaware of her connection to a woman who would shortly turn up dead?"

"Me again, I suppose."

"Who asked me to find out why Roger Carew looked up during the Winners class at an unidentified whistler?"

"Have you?" Aunt Peg brightened.

"Actually . . . no. But that's not the point."

"I hope you don't mind my asking, dear. What *is* the point?"

I sank down into a seat beside her. Now that I finally had Aunt Peg's undivided attention, it was hard to know where to begin. Then I realized that as I'd hesitated, she'd opened up her catalog. Now she was looking past me, squinting down at the faraway action in the Toy ring. It figured.

"The point is that PCA is in big trouble."

That got her attention fast, as it was meant to.

"Trouble? What kind of trouble?"

"The Edith Jean Boone kind. She's planning on having her sister's ashes scattered in the ring this afternoon right before Best in Show."

"Oh, that." Peg looked relieved. She snuck a glance back at the judging. "Don't worry, Nancy had a little chat with her about that. Edith Jean understands how inappropriate it would be."

"No, she doesn't. What she understands is that the board turned down her request. But that doesn't mean she has any intention of listening to you."

"What choice does she have? It's not as if she can simply commandeer the facilities."

"She won't have to," I pointed out. "The ring was already allocated to her when the show committee decided to hold the drawing for the raffle there."

"I see." Rather suddenly Aunt Peg did. "Should I ask what part you intend to play in this drama?"

"I'm in charge of drawing the tickets from the barrel. Edith Jean is also hoping that when the fateful moment arrives, I'll scatter the ashes for her."

"She doesn't think anyone will notice when you lug an urn into the ring with you?"

"Fanny pack," I said.

"Pardon me?"

I tried not to smile. "She put the ashes in a fanny pack."

"You can't be serious."

"I wish I wasn't."

Abruptly Aunt Peg stood. "I can see I'm going to have to round up Nancy and Cliff and the rest of the board, and see what can be done about this."

"You'd better hurry," I said. "And by the way, one more thing. Rosalind was the screamer."

Peg looked briefly baffled. "I thought you were looking for a whistler."

"Not then, earlier. When Betty Jean was murdered. Remember the scream we heard? That was Rosalind."

"And why didn't we know this before now?"

"Because Rosalind didn't hang around to see what happened next. She saw the body, screamed, and then went inside the hotel."

"How very odd."

"Odder still, Christian Gold seemed to think he could use her telepathic ability to threaten his Specials bitch into winning the Variety today."

"That would be a first," Aunt Peg said, considering. "At least I hope it would. Although if Christian was trying to influence the outcome by sending telepathic messages, you'd think he'd have been better off sending them to the judge."

Good point.

Aunt Peg started to walk away, then stopped. "Sam did find you yesterday afternoon, didn't he? He seemed rather desperate to know where you were."

"Umm . . . yes." My voice squeaked.

"He didn't tell me what he wanted . . ." Her eyes searched my face. I probably looked guilty as hell. "Is everything all right?"

"Just fine."

"Because if it's not—"

"It's fine, Aunt Peg."

She didn't look convinced. "Whatever it was, try not to hold it against him. He was probably just nervous about today's competition with Tar."

Now I was blushing. Heat flooded my cheeks. Thankfully, Aunt Peg had started to walk away again. She didn't seem to notice.

"I'm sure that was it," I said, following her out of the stands. "Believe me, I won't hold it against him at all."

Aunt Peg and I parted when we reached the lower level. I went racing back to the raffle table. Best of Variety had just been decided in Toys. Best of Winners had gone to the Winners Bitch, so Vic had to be content with what he'd already won on Wednesday. I doubted Harry was displeased; he'd gotten what he needed to make his sale.

"You're just in time," said Edith Jean. "Bubba's about to go back in for Best Toy Puppy. I thought I might have to shut the table down for the duration. See ya!"

Off she went to see Bubba compete. Once again, I climbed up on a chair to watch. The silver Toy was fully rested and raring to go. He showed with every bit as much enthusiasm as he had in his first class and easily defeated his two opponents. That meant that he would compete again at the end of the day for Best Puppy in Show. Presumably this time Roger would know enough to tuck him away in a crate until he was needed in the ring again.

Edith Jean must have had the same thought, and she

wasn't taking any chances. She reappeared at the table, only to send me away. "I need you to deliver a message."

"Sure." Immediately I regretted my impetuous reply. I hoped she wasn't sending me to deliver any ultimatums to the board. "To whom?"

"Roger. Obviously *I* can't go talk to him now. Bubba would get all excited and Roger would never be able to get his focus back. I want you to go over to the grooming area and make sure he doesn't do anything stupid."

"Like let half the people in the building pat your puppy?"

"Exactly." She waggled a finger under my nose. "Bubba is to rest and conserve his energy, do you hear me? You tell him the orders came from me."

"Will do," I said. It beat minding the raffle table any day.

The only problem was, when I reached the grooming area, Roger and Bubba were nowhere in sight. Miniature Poodles, up next in the ring, were out in full force on dozens of grooming tables. I saw Dale Atherton applying finishing touches to Rita's trim while Christian looked on critically. Nina stood nearby, reapplying her lipstick and checking out her reflection in a small gold compact. I saw Mary Ludlow Scott conferring with Cliff Spellman and Aunt Peg. Judiciously, I gave the group wide berth. I saw Crawford waiting to be called to the ring and looking cool and calm in an ice blue jacket and matching tie.

Terry, holding the Mini dog about to be shown, smiled and waved. "You look like a woman on a mission."

"I'm looking for Roger Carew. I thought he'd be back here with Bubba."

"Didn't he just win Best Toy Puppy?"

I nodded.

"Pictures," said Terry. "He's probably still up at the ring, waiting his turn."

I should have thought of that, and probably would have if I'd ever had occasion to have a picture of my own taken at PCA. You can go ahead and file that thought under the "when pigs fly" category. I took Terry's advice, spun around, and headed back the other way.

If anything, the crush at ringside was greater than it had been in the grooming area. Though the action was temporarily on hold as the Toys finished up and the Minis prepared to enter, none of the lucky spectators who'd already staked out good seats wanted to relinquish them. As droves of additional fanciers arrived to watch the new variety, people simply packed in tighter and tighter.

I fought my way to the front near the gate. Out in the middle of the ring, the Toy Best of Variety winner was posed with his handler in front of a beautiful floral arrangement. Mr. Mancini was holding the dog's purple and gold rosette and gazing down at him approvingly. Lined up on either side of them were various club notables holding prizes and challenge trophies. The tiny Toy was all but dwarfed by his attendants.

The Toy bitch who'd won Best of Opposite Sex was waiting in the wings. She'd be photographed next, followed by the Best of Winners. Standing over to one side, Roger Carew was holding Bubba in his arms, hands carefully positioned so as not to muss the beautifully coiffed hair. He was talking to another handler who was also waiting for a picture. That man had his back to me but as I slipped into the ring to join them I realized it was Harry Gandolf.

"I told you there was nothing to worry about," I heard him say to Roger. "Everybody ended up with a piece of the pie, including you. So it all worked out for the best."

Roger started to reply. Then he saw me approaching and swallowed what he'd been about to say. Apprehension flickered in his eyes. The hasty smile he mustered looked more than a little forced.

"Let me guess," he said. "You have a message for me from Edith Jean."

"How did you know?"

"You're the third person to arrive bearing the same instructions."

Ah, well. Edith Jean could be quite thorough when she put her mind to it.

"Then I'll just offer congratulations," I said. "To both of you."

"Thanks." Harry began to edge away. "See you around," he said.

Roger barely nodded in acknowledgment. From where we stood I could see that the BOS bitch was being photographed. It wouldn't be Harry's turn for another few minutes.

"Was it something I said?" I asked.

"No, that's just Harry. He's not a big talker."

Maybe. Except that Harry and Roger had been chatting quite amicably until I'd arrived. I'd even go so far as to say that they'd looked rather chummy. There was nothing unusual about that, of course. Professional handlers spend much of their lives on the road, and most of their time in close proximity to one another. Even the fiercest competitors inside the ring were often friends under other circumstances.

But what made me think twice was the fleeting look of concern on Roger's face as I'd approached. He'd been wondering how much I'd overheard and that made me wonder too. *Everybody pays somebody in the end,* Harry had told me earlier. Now I put that thought together with Aunt Peg's question. *Who whistled isn't important,* she'd said. *What matters is, why did Roger look?*

All at once, I was afraid I knew the answer.

"Harry offered Edith Jean seven hundred dollars to pull Bubba from the competition," I said softly. "I hope you held out for at least as much."

Roger had been staring fixedly at the photographer's setup. Now his head swiveled back around. "I don't have any idea what you're talking about."

Like hell.

"Harry needed Vic to go Winners Dog to insure the dog's sale to Japan," I said. "There was a lot of money riding on that win, and he was willing to pay Edith Jean to make sure that Bubba didn't beat Vic. She turned him down. I think he came to you next, and you accepted his offer."

"What a ridiculous idea. Bubba was Reserve Winners and best Toy Puppy. At a show of this caliber, I'd hardly call that losing."

"I agree. But Harry didn't care how much you won, as long as Vic ended up with the purple ribbon. I think when Harry approached you, you saw a way to make everybody happy, including yourself. Considering how devastated Edith Jean would be if she ever found out, I just hope your piece of the pie was big enough to make it worth your while."

"That's nothing but conjecture on your part." Roger's tone was low and menacing. "You can't prove any of it."

"I don't have to," I said. "The judging's over. Nothing can be changed now. But you'd better hope that Harry wasn't so desperate for the win that he'd have been willing to stoop to murder. Because that might make you an accessory."

"I had nothing to do with that," Roger snapped. "I don't know anything about what happened to Betty Jean."

"You don't have to convince me," I said. "Tell it to the police. They're the ones who'll be interested to hear about what you've been up to."

I felt the heat of his glare burning into my back all the

way out of the ring. I passed by Harry, who must have been watching the exchange. He looked incensed as well. I gave him a glance and kept right on walking.

It was a relief to pass through the gate and lose myself in the crowd.

25

I was debating what to tell Edith Jean when I got waylaid by Bertie.

"I need to talk to you," she said, falling into step beside me.

"Can it wait?"

"Not for long."

Across the way, the Miniature Best of Variety class was being called into the ring. Forty-four Miniature Poodles in assorted colors, all groomed to perfection, paraded out into the arena. Spectators found seats and settled in for the duration. Catalogs opened, pages flipped. A heady sense of anticipation filled the air.

I changed course, angling away from the ring and heading toward the less crowded area in the shadow of the stands. Bertie followed.

"What?" I said when we'd found a quiet place to talk.

"I know who Dale Atherton was with Monday night."

"Who?"

Even though there was no one near us, her voice dropped to a whisper. "Nina Gold."

"No!"

"Yes!" Bertie replied, just as emphatically.

"Are you sure? Dale would have to be crazy to take a risk like that. The wife of his best client—"

"The very fancy, younger wife," Bertie interjected.

"Even so, remember what Dale told us? Getting Christian Gold as a client is what catapulted him into the big time. Most of the Poodles he shows now are from GoldenDune."

"Hey." Bertie held up her hands. "I'm not defending the guy, or his intelligence. I'm just telling you what I saw."

Even as I stood there arguing, I remembered that Sam had made a similar comment. "Which was what, exactly?"

"I went to Dale's setup a few minutes ago to wish him luck with his Mini. Christian and Nina were there, doing the same thing. Except that Christian was giving Dale a pep talk which, reading between the lines, sounded pretty much like win or else."

That sounded like what I knew of Christian, especially after the episode I'd witnessed that morning. Unlike Edith Jean who lived with her Poodles and treated them as pets, Christian must have kept his Minis in a kennel. If Rita had been at all attached to him, he couldn't have been able to visit with his handler just before the Poodle went in the ring. That knowledge did nothing to elevate him in my opinion.

"How did Dale respond to that?" I asked.

"Pretty much as you'd expect." Bertie was a handler herself. She was also a pragmatist. "Yes sir, no sir. Whatever you say, sir."

"And Nina?"

"She wasn't saying much, but her eyes never left Dale. She wasn't even subtle about it. If Christian hadn't worked himself up into such a lather about the show, I imagine he'd have noticed himself."

"Okay, but that's hardly enough—"

"Don't worry," said Bertie. "There's more. So I was watching all this from the fringes and after a few minutes, I began to think that maybe I should step in and try to rescue the poor guy. I mean, it's not like Dale doesn't have enough pressure on him already. I figured he could probably use a few minutes of peace to compose himself and his dog before he was due in the ring. But as soon as I stepped forward, Nina reached out and grabbed my arm. She practically yanked me away."

"You're kidding." This was better than a soap opera. "Then what happened?"

"She was hissing at me under her breath." Bertie grinned. She has an appreciation for high drama herself. "She said she'd seen me hanging around. That she didn't want me there and I should get lost."

Nina wasn't the first woman insecure enough to be threatened by Bertie's outrageous good looks. She probably wouldn't be the last either, despite the wide gold wedding band that Bertie now wore. Of course, Nina wore a wedding ring herself, which may have explained why she didn't take Bertie's commitment to her marriage as seriously as she might have.

I considered what Bertie had said. "Still, it's not as though Nina said something totally damning like keep away from him, he's mine."

"Believe me, she didn't have to. The subtext of what she was telling me was perfectly clear. That's why Dale wouldn't tell us who he was with on Monday night, not because he was concerned about protecting the woman's privacy but because he was worried about saving his own butt."

Applause from the Mini ring kept me from replying for a minute. After it died down, I said, "That explains why Dale came flying out of his room so fast. He heard a woman scream and thought it might be Nina." Then that reminded me of something else. "Speaking of which, Rosalind Romanescue was outside behind the hotel on Monday night too." I related the conversation I'd had with the animal communicator. "I wonder if she saw Nina out there."

"If she had, wouldn't she have told you?"

"Not necessarily. Rosalind probably doesn't know what

Nina looks like. However, if we were able to point her out in the crowd of spectators . . ."

"Let's go for it," said Bertie. My sentiments exactly.

It took us a while to find Rosalind. By the time we did, the Miniature BOV judging was almost over. I'd been keeping tabs on the ring as we searched. Christian's Mini, Rita, had made the final cut; but if I was reading the judge's body language correctly, she wasn't going to win the top prize. Instead, the judge seemed to have narrowed his selection down to two heavily coated males whose handlers were battling one another for supremacy as if the fate of the western world hung in the balance.

"There!" Bertie pointed suddenly into the stands. I looked up and saw Rosalind sitting by herself in a corner seat. Up high, removed from the action on the ground floor level, I supposed she could see well enough for someone who didn't know the dogs and had no stake in the outcome.

Bertie and I raced to the tunnels, and from there up the stairs. Considering our abrupt and somewhat breathless arrival, Rosalind didn't seem particularly surprised to see us. Maybe she knew we were coming?

"Hi," I said. Bertie and I grabbed seats on either side. "Do you mind if I ask you one more question?"

"Would it stop you if I did?"

"Probably not," I admitted, ignoring Bertie's knowing smirk. "Monday night when you were out behind the hotel, you said you saw a number of people."

"That's right."

"If I pointed out a particular woman, do you think you would remember whether she was there or not?"

"I might," said Rosalind. "Then again, I might not. As I told you before, I wasn't paying that much attention to the people. Mostly I was watching the Poodles."

If my hunch was correct, Nina Gold hadn't had a Poodle with her. Still, it was worth a try. I gestured down into the crowds below where Christian and Nina had a pair of ringside seats. The two of them were fairly easy to pick out.

"The woman I want you to see is Christian Gold's wife. She's sitting right next to him."

Rosalind sat up and gazed where I'd indicated. "Spike heels," she said.

"Pardon me?"

"Spike heels, that was how I thought of her. Of course I had no idea who she was, but everyone else in the field was wearing sneakers or flats. She had on a pair of three inch heels. I don't usually notice people's shoes but she looked ridiculously overdressed. Who could help but notice that? You say she's Christian's wife?"

"That's right," said Bertie.

Rosalind had herself another look. "Good. He deserves a silly wife."

"You didn't happen to see what she was doing, did you?"

"No. I only know that when I'd just arrived she was hurrying along the walkway. I remember she had her head down, as if she didn't want to talk to anyone. She went right past me and kept going. That was when I veered off to circle the field. I didn't see her again after that."

So Dale had been right. His lady friend had left a few minutes earlier, before Betty Jean had been killed.

"Thanks," I said. "That's all I wanted to know."

Bertie and I stood up and went back downstairs. "She was there," Bertie said. "The fact that Rosalind didn't see her with Betty Jean doesn't mean she didn't do it."

"There were at least a dozen people out there. Plus probably more I didn't see."

"Yes, but not all of them had as much to lose as Nina and Dale did if their affair ever became known. If someone saw Nina coming out of Dale's room, I can see how she might have taken steps to keep that person quiet."

"But . . . murder?"

"If that's what it took," Bertie replied.

With Minis wrapping up in the ring, I knew Sam would be in the grooming area finishing Tar's preparations. The Standard Poodle had done a creditable amount of winning since Sam had started showing him as a Special early in the year. Already he'd amassed nearly a dozen Non-Sporting group wins, as well as his first Best in Show. With a record like that, he would walk into the ring a contender.

Had Tar been my Poodle, I'd have been too nervous to even breathe, much less scissor. Not Sam. He had the situation under control. Dog and handler were both ready, awaiting only the announcer's call to bring them to ringside. Both looked, quite predictably, gorgeous.

"Good luck," I said. Squeezing in beside the grooming table, I stood up on my toes and gave Sam a kiss.

"Thanks." He smiled in my direction, but I could tell his thoughts were elsewhere. In his position, I'd have been preoccupied too.

"Anything I can do to help?"

"Not right now, but if you could bring Tar some water later, in the ring, I'd appreciate it."

"No problem."

Sam was holding his catalog. It was open to the Standard Poodle Best of Variety listings. More than seventy dogs and bitches were entered, each one a champion, and all with owners and handlers who hoped that their Poodle would figure in the outcome of the day's judging. It had to be a daunting thought.

I glanced at Sam's armband. His number would place him squarely in the middle of the pack. "Don't get lost in there," I said, repeating Aunt Peg's words of wisdom to me.

"Don't worry," Sam said firmly. "We won't."

The announcer asked for the Standard Poodles. Tar stood up on his table. Sam hopped him carefully down to the ground. The Poodle shook out his coat. Sam used his comb to flick the hair back into place.

It was a familiar ritual; one I'd seen and performed myself hundreds of times. But today was different. It wasn't just another dog show. This was PCA, and everything mattered.

I grabbed Tar's water bowl and followed Sam to ringside. At an all-breed dog show, getting a fully coiffed Standard Poodle from table to ring unjostled often requires a handler to use the blocking skills of a linebacker. Not at PCA. Here, all the handlers shared the same concerns and the same objective. Of necessity, they were respectful of each other's dogs and space. Despite the huge crush of big Poodles moving simultaneously toward the ring, there was no crowding or pushing.

I watched Sam check Tar in with the ring steward at the gate. Then I raced over to the raffle table to check in with Edith Jean. In the same way that I'd freed her to watch Bubba, I was hoping she wouldn't mind if I watched the Standard judging. I was also still debating how much I should tell her about the conversation I'd had with Roger.

On the one hand, what had happened was already over and done. Edith Jean was pleased with Bubba's results so far, plus the Toy puppy still had a shot at Best Puppy in Show later that afternoon. Telling her that her handler had accepted a bribe wouldn't change anything and it might cast a pall over the pleasure she'd taken in the puppy's accomplishments.

On the other hand, Roger was Edith Jean's handler. That was an ongoing relationship, one whose duration might span years. If she couldn't trust Roger to look out for her best interests, that was something she needed to know.

By the time I'd battled my way through the crowds, I'd

come to the conclusion that I had to tell Edith Jean what I knew. It wasn't going to be easy; nor was it a conversation I was looking forward to having. So when it turned out that Edith Jean was no more anxious to listen than I was to talk, I didn't exactly insist.

Seeing me coming, she stepped out from behind the raffle table. "What are you doing here?"

"I work here," I quipped. The joke fell flat.

"Not this afternoon you don't." She looked past me, scanning the throng as though looking for someone. "I figured you'd be watching Standards."

"I'd like to, but there's something I need to tell you."

"Do we have to do it now?"

Edith Jean was all fluttery hands and fidgety movement. If I'd had to guess, I'd have said she looked nervous. But about what? I wondered if one of the board members had stopped by to talk to her about the memorial service. Or maybe I was reading her wrong. Maybe she was mad at me for turning her in.

"We can talk later if you'd rather—"

"Good." Edith Jean dragged her gaze back to me briefly. "Don't worry about the memorial for Betty Jean. It turned out things weren't going to work the way I wanted so I've made other plans."

"I'm happy to hear that—"

"Look." Edith Jean flapped a hand toward the ring as the spectators behind me began to clap. "The judging's about to begin. You're going to miss the first go-round. Isn't that Sam in there? You really ought to go and watch. He's going to think you're not interested if you don't."

Sam would understand. Luckily for me, he always did. But that didn't stop me from wanting to see. I ran around the back of the table, grabbed a chair, and hopped up to stand on the seat. Yet again. Hopefully Aunt Peg would be too busy watching to notice.

I set Tar's bowl down on the table and flipped open my

catalog. Due to the huge number of entries, Mr. Lamb had sent his bitch Specials out of the ring so he'd have more room to concentrate on his dogs. As I watched, he raised his hands and set the long line in motion.

I sighed with appreciation. The sight of that many Standard Poodles, all exquisitely groomed and presented, was absolutely breathtaking. Best of all, Tar looked wonderful. Even from my peculiar vantage point, he was a standout: tall and masculine, and every bit as black as his namesake. Muscles rippled across his hindquarter as he trotted around the ring with proper reach and drive, a beautiful example of a Standard Poodle in motion.

"See?" Edith Jean said when the dogs had finished their circuit of the ring and I'd hopped back down. "You shouldn't be here. Go away."

She didn't have to tell me again. Not when the offer was that tempting. "I'll check back later," I promised.

"You do that." She shooed me in the direction of the ring.

I found Aunt Peg in her usual seat. She'd piled her sweater, purse, and a shopping bag filled with new grooming supplies on the chair beside it to save it for me.

"You won't believe what I found out," I said as I rearranged the stuff on the grass at our feet and sat down.

"At this point, I'm inclined to believe almost anything." Aunt Peg's eyes remained trained on the ring. "But whatever it is, save it for later. I'm watching." A hallowed experience, her tone implied. One to be savored without interruption. "You've already missed the first go-round. Tar looked very good."

"I saw it," I said. "I was over by the raffle table."

The quick glance she sent my way revealed what Peg thought of that little peccadillo. "I trust you can manage to sit still long enough to watch his individual examination?"

One could only hope, I thought.

I entertained myself until Tar's turn came by looking at the dogs in the ring, then comparing them to the notes Aunt Peg made in the margins of her catalog. Nothing, not even the tiniest detail, escaped her notice. The majority of the Poodles before us were black. Aunt Peg could not only tell them apart at a glance, she could also enumerate their faults and good points. It was a rare skill, one honed by decades of careful, watchful experience.

Finally Tar reached the head of the line. Tommy Lamb approached him slowly, his eyes alight with appreciation. Sam waited until the judge had cradled the dog's muzzle in his hands, then stepped back, allowing the leash to hang loosely, letting Tar show himself. Not every dog could handle the responsibility; Tar managed it beautifully.

The gaiting pattern was a simple one. Down to the end of the ring and back, so the judge could see the Poodle's movement coming and going. Then all the way around the perimeter of the big ring and back into line. Taking his time, Sam walked Tar around in front of the judge. He checked the dog's collar, balled the skinny show leash in his hand. Then he chucked the Poodle under the chin and off they went.

For a moment, there was only silence as Tar began to move. Then someone began to clap. Others joined in until the sound swelled and built to a crescendo around us. Tar knew the applause was for him. His stride lengthened, his gait became more animated. When Tommy Lamb finished his examination and sent the Standard Poodle to the front of the ring, indicating that he'd made the cut, the spectators roared their approval.

As soon as the pair reached their assigned spot, I closed my catalog and stood up. It was time to bring Tar a drink of water. I glanced down, then around. I'd been carrying the Poodle's stainless-steel bowl earlier. Now I didn't see it anywhere. Annoyed, I realized I must have left it behind at the raffle table.

"Be right back," I said to Peg. Still engrossed by the action in the ring, she didn't even acknowledge my departure.

It wasn't until I'd pushed my way through the crowd standing behind us that I could even see the committee tables around the perimeter of the arena. When I finally broke free, I looked in that direction, then frowned. The bowl was sitting on the edge of the table, just where I'd left it. Edith Jean, however, was nowhere in sight.

While I'd been busy watching the show, she had disappeared.

26

She'd probably just run to the restroom, I decided as I strode toward the table. Still, it was unlike her to leave the raffle prizes unsupervised. The last time she'd stepped away, she'd asked Charlotte Kay to keep an eye on things. And the last time she'd gone missing for more than a few minutes, Edith Jean had been in trouble.

I believe in gut reactions. When a sense of foreboding made my skin start to prickle, I knew I needed to listen. Belatedly, I realized I probably should have been listening better earlier. *And* asking more questions. Why had Edith Jean seemed so tense the last time I'd seen her? And why had she been so anxious to get rid of me? What sort of plans was she making now?

I snatched up Tur's water bowl and zigzagged through the ever increasing crowd to the trophy table. Charlotte was holding up an enormous silver challenge bowl that would be presented to the Standard BOV winner later in the day. She was reading the engraved names of past recipients to an interested spectator.

Since the trophy had been in competition for several decades, I knew that was going to take a while. It was rude of me to interrupt, but I broke in anyway. "Excuse me, Charlotte?"

"Yes?" She lowered the big bowl and gazed at me over the rim.

"I'm looking for Edith Jean. Do you happen to know where she is?"

"She said she had to leave for a short while. I told her since you weren't available, I'd keep an eye on the table."

"I *was* available," I said. "I was right there. She sent me away to watch the judging."

"I don't know anything about that. All I know is that she told me she wouldn't be gone long."

"How long ago was that?"

"Ten minutes, possibly." Charlotte glanced at her watch. "Maybe fifteen?"

"Did she tell you where she was going?"

"Outside, I think. She said there was someone she had to meet."

The spectator was growing impatient. "Nineteen seventy-nine," she prompted. "Who won that year?"

"Champion MacGillivray High Interest," Charlotte looked down and read. "Now that was a beautiful bitch. As I recall, she was handled by her owner and won the variety from the Bred by Exhibitor class . . ."

"Thanks!" Still clutching Tar's bowl, I hurried away.

At the equestrian center, "outside" was a big place. Edith Jean could have gone in any number of directions. I wondered why she'd felt the need to leave the building. Was she looking for privacy? Or, like Christian and Rosalind, meeting with someone she didn't want to be seen with?

The exits near the grooming area seemed the logical place to start. I was moving so fast, I didn't see Bertie until I'd almost plowed right into her.

She reached out a hand to steady me. I thrust the water bowl into it. "Here. Could you take Tar some water in the ring?"

"Sure, but where are you going?"

"I'm trying to find Edith Jean. I think something's wrong."

"What?"

"I don't know. That's the problem. She left the building for some reason."

"That's hardly suspicious behavior," said Bertie. "Lots of people go in and out."

"I know but . . ." I stopped and blew out a breath. "This just doesn't feel right."

"Okay." Bertie took the bowl. "Do what you have to do. I'll see to Sam and Tar. By the way, Edith Jean and I arrived around the same time this morning. We both parked in the lot just behind the building if that helps."

"It does, thanks." At least that gave me a direction in which to start.

As I pushed open the door that led outside to the lot Bertie had indicated, I was hit with a blast of hot air. Air-conditioning within the arena kept things at such a pleasant temperature it was easy to forget that it was summer outside. Temperatures had been in the eighties all week. I pulled off my cotton sweater and wrapped it around my waist. Just like the other lot earlier, this one was filled with cars, yet looked devoid of people.

Too late, I realized I should have asked Bertie what kind of car Edith Jean was driving. Bright hot sunlight reflected off the sea of shiny vehicles, blinding me momentarily. I let the door slam shut behind me, and squinted out over the lot. Unexpectedly, something behind me moved. I saw the motion out of the corner of my eye and spun around.

Damien Bradley stepped out of a shadowy recess. He didn't look pleased to see me. "Sorry," he said. "I thought you were someone else. I didn't mean to startle you."

"What are you doing out here?"

"Smoking."

Except that he wasn't. Maybe he had been, but he wasn't now. Nor did the acrid scent of tobacco smoke hang in the air. As Damien came toward me, I retreated a step. Then another. Since he stood between me and the building, I was moving out into the parking lot.

My response seemed to amuse him. Damien kept on walking. "What are you doing out here?" he asked.

"Looking for someone." I couldn't see the harm in telling him. "Edith Jean Boone. Have you seen her?"

"No. Though I wouldn't mind knowing where she was myself."

"Why is that?"

I was still backing up. Keeping a careful distance between us, I was heading down one of the rows now. The two of us were engaged in an awkward dance of advance and retreat.

"Edith Jean and I have some business to take care of," said Damien. "Nothing that would concern you."

"Don't be so sure," I said. Was this why Edith Jean had left the building? Had Damien lured her outside for some reason? I wondered what kind of business he thought they were going to transact.

Damien finally stopped advancing. He stared at me, perplexed. "You don't have to keep backing up. I know the kind of stories people spread about me. Your aunt and Sam Driver have probably given you an earful. But all I'm doing here is talking."

By now we'd reached the midpoint in the wide aisle between the parked cars. Damien was right, he hadn't threatened me in any way, but that didn't prevent me from being more comfortable with some distance between us. There was something menacing about his presence. And something unsettling about the fact that he'd been planning to meet Edith Jean out here. What did he have to say to her that couldn't be said inside, with the reassuring presence of other people all around?

"If you want to give me a message, I'll be sure Edith Jean gets it," I said.

"No, thanks." Damien smiled; it wasn't a pretty sight. "What I really want is for you to butt out."

I heard the van coming before I saw it. Even then, I was focused so completely on Damien that the sound didn't register at first. The rev of an engine was followed by the squeal of tires. Abruptly I realized that in the close confines of the parking lot, the vehicle was moving much too fast.

A dark-colored van skidded around the end of the row and headed straight at us. The van slid sideways; its tires threw up a spray of gravel. Damien had his back to the oncoming vehicle, but I was looking right at it. Sunlight glinted off the windshield; I couldn't see who was driving.

"Look out!" I cried.

Even as Damien's head snapped around it was already too late. The van picked up speed and kept coming. "What the hell—!"

I leaped toward Damien, reached for his shoulder, got his arm instead. I yanked hard to one side. Turning to look, off balance, he toppled toward me but it wasn't enough. The van was already on top of us. I felt the blow as it hit his lower body with crushing force.

The strength of the impact tossed us both through the air. I landed hard, coming down on the hood of a Mercedes-Benz. Pain shot through my shoulder, then down into my hip. A car alarm began to shriek.

Damien was on the ground below me; I couldn't see how badly he was hurt. Turning my head, I got a fleeting look at the departing van. The license plate had a picture of a peach on it. A Georgia peach.

Down on the blacktop, I heard Damien moan, then swear. At least he was alive, though he didn't sound too happy about it.

"Crazy bitch," he muttered.

"Damien?" Painfully, fingers scrambling for purchase on the shiny finish, I pulled myself over to the edge of the hood. My head was throbbing. I couldn't remember whether I'd hit it or not. Maybe the car alarm was making it ache. "Are you all right?"

"Hell, no. Something's broken, maybe my leg." He spoke slowly, and with obvious effort. "Plus I think I'm about to pass out. Either that or throw up."

I rolled slowly off the side of the car. As my feet touched down on the ground, I felt a sharp spear of protest in my hip, but everything held. I'd probably be covered with bruises in the morning, but otherwise I seemed okay. Gingerly, I knelt down beside Damien.

He was lying in the shadow of the big sedan. One leg was bent at an unnatural angle beneath him. Sweat beaded on his forehead and trickled down the sides of his face. He hauled himself painfully up on one elbow and glowered at me. "Can't you stop that infernal noise?"

"Sorry," I said. "Not my car." I stared down at him. "I heard what you said. You know who was driving the van, don't you?"

Damien gritted his teeth. His skin looked alarmingly pale. "She told me to meet her out here, said we had something to discuss. I thought . . ." He stopped abruptly. "Never mind what I thought."

"She who?" I had a pretty good idea myself, but I wanted to hear him say the name.

"You saw her. It was that damn Boone woman."

Damien expelled a harsh breath. His eyes rolled back in his head. I reached out and caught him as his upper body dropped like a stone onto the blacktop. His breathing was shallow and ragged. He'd passed out.

Quickly I stood and looked around. The van had vanished, taking Edith Jean with it. I'd hoped the car alarm might have brought a response from inside the building, but no such luck. Maybe with all the doors closed, they couldn't hear it.

I stood up and ran for help.

*   *   *

Inside the building, it only took a minute or two to rally the troops.

As soon as I threw open the heavy door, letting in the sound of the shrieking alarm, heads turned in my direction. Everybody who was anybody was sitting ringside, watching the judging. I found Nancy and Cliff and told them there'd been a hit-and-run accident.

Cliff pulled out his cell phone and called for an ambulance. Nancy rounded up several Poodle fanciers who were doctors. In no time at all, Damien was being attended to by much better hands than mine. That left me free to locate Edith Jean and find out what the hell was going on.

I'd been afraid that she was in danger from Damien. Now it looked as though I'd had things backward. But why? Had Edith Jean killed her own sister? Did Damien have information about the murder that he'd threatened to pass along to the police? Was that what had prompted her attack?

In the ring, Mr. Lamb was finishing with his bitch Specials. Within minutes, Sam and Tar would return to the ring for the culmination of the Best of Variety judging. Too bad I didn't have time to stop and watch.

I needed to tell Aunt Peg what was happening. Before I left the show ground, I wanted someone to know that I'd gone after Edith Jean, and why. Also, someone was going to have to step in and take charge of the raffle. Aunt Peg, with her flair for organizing people, would know what to do.

As I pushed my way through the spectators to where my aunt was sitting, the crowd shifted and I caught a glimpse of the raffle table. All at once I stopped running. Shock froze me in place.

Edith Jean was back in the building. She was manning the table, smiling and selling tickets, just as she'd done all week. As if nothing in the world was the matter.

How was that possible? I wondered. Could Damien and I both have been mistaken? I'd seen the van, but I'd never gotten a clear look at the driver. Could it have been someone else?

My head was pounding like a jackhammer. On top of that, the spectators began to applaud. The final cut for Standard Best of Variety had just entered the ring.

I closed my eyes and prayed for just one minute of peace, knowing full well that I wasn't going to get it. When I opened them again, Edith Jean was still there. She saw me staring and waved.

None of this made any sense. What the hell was going on?

27

"We have to talk," I said to Edith Jean.

"Certainly, dear. I'll be right with you. Just let me finish this sale."

While she did that, I enlisted Charlotte's aid in keeping an eye on our table. Yet again. I didn't let Edith Jean out of my sight for a second. As soon as she'd finished making change and filling out the ticket stubs, I closed my fingers around her frail wrist and pulled her away to a quiet spot beneath the stands.

"I saw you outside," I said. I was stretching the truth, but I didn't care. I was beginning to suspect that Edith Jean had been bending the truth every which way all week. "You were driving that van. Damien saw you too."

"I don't know what you're talking about. We really should get back to the table. It's almost time for the drawing—"

"Hang the drawing. I want to know what's going on. Why did you try to run over Damien? Were you hoping to kill him? Were you hoping to kill both of us?"

Uncertainty flashed across Edith Jean's face. Enough to let me know that I'd only been in the wrong place at the wrong time, not another intended victim. When she reached up and patted my shoulder guiltily, I pressed my advantage.

"Damien isn't dead. He's unconscious and he's badly injured, but an ambulance is on the way. Doctors are with him now. If you wanted to silence him, it didn't work."

Edith Jean looked annoyed. Clearly I hadn't told her what she wanted to hear.

"You weren't supposed to be out there," she said after a minute. "You were supposed to be watching the judging. Standard Poodles. They're *your* variety. You should have been at ringside. Isn't that where I told you to go?"

"I was worried about you."

"Did I *ask* you to worry about me?"

"I don't always do what people tell me to do." Aunt Peg could vouch for that.

"Apparently not." She was not amused by this deficiency in my character. "Damien and I had matters to discuss. You should have just stayed out of it."

If I had, Damien might be dead now.

"And those matters included running him over with a van?" I asked incredulously.

Her mouth set in a stubborn line. "He threatened me. I was acting in self-defense."

I wasn't discounting the possibility, but I wasn't accepting it without an explanation either. "Threatened you how?"

Edith Jean didn't answer.

"Fine," I said. "You don't have to talk to me. But you will have to talk to the police. Damien will wake up eventually. When he does, he'll tell the police you were the one who hit him. He'll tell them it wasn't an accident. Then you'll have to hope they believe what you have to say."

"He tried to blackmail me," Edith Jean spat out. "He thought because I was an old lady I wouldn't fight back. He thought I would just do whatever he said. I guess I showed him."

Now we were getting somewhere.

"What was Damien holding over you?" I asked. She didn't reply, but I hadn't really expected her to. I offered an answer of my own. "It had to do with Betty Jean's murder, didn't it? Is that how you hurt your hand? Shoving your sister down on the ground and making her hit her head?"

Edith Jean glared at me. "You don't know what you're talking about! I loved my sister. She was all I had in the world. I would never have done anything to hurt her."

The vehement declaration sounded like the truth. Not only that, but I wanted to believe it. Maybe I didn't know the Boone sisters well, but when I'd seen them together, they had seemed to share a genuine affection for one another. As I stood there, uncertain, tears welled in Edith Jean's eyes. One by one, they began to slip down her cheeks. Impulsively I reached out and gathered the older woman into my arms. Her slender body shook with the force of her sobs.

"Nobody knows how hard this has been for me," she said, sniffling loudly. "Maybe I went a little crazy when Damien came after me, but I had to protect myself. You see that, don't you? I wasn't able to protect Sister. When that bitch hurt her there wasn't a damn thing I could do . . ."

Edith Jean was mumbling into the folds of my sweater. For a moment, I thought I'd misheard. I grasped her shoulders and gently pushed her away.

"What bitch?" I asked. I'm a dog person. The invective rolled quite naturally off my tongue.

Edith Jean hiccupped twice, then swallowed hard. She struggled to compose herself. "I saw it happen," she said finally. "I was there. I saw the whole thing."

"You saw who killed Betty Jean?"

She ducked her head. I took that as a nod.

"Who was it? What happened? Why didn't you tell anyone?"

"What good would telling have done?" Edith Jean drew

in a deep, shuddering breath and answered my last question first. "I couldn't undo what happened. By the time I realized, it was too late. Sister was already dead."

"You could have seen her killer brought to justice," I said. "You still can."

"Not if no one believes me. It will just be my word against hers." Her tone was bitter. "Nobody even noticed I was out there. There's nothing as invisible as an old lady."

"Roger noticed you," I said gently. "He told me you were there. Why don't you tell me what you saw?"

"It was that flashy woman. Nina Gold. Sister and I were outside scooping. You know that, I told you all about it." I nodded.

"After a while, we went off in different directions. What's the point if you both clean up the same area? Anyway, it was getting late, I wanted to go back to the room. I went looking for Sister. That's when I saw her with Nina. It sounded like the two of them were arguing, so I went over to see what the fuss was about.

"Sister saw me coming, but Nina never even noticed. She just kept right on snapping and snarling. She was threatening Sister, telling her that she'd better not tell a soul about something she'd seen. Well you know how Sister was, nobody told her what to do. She said to that woman, 'I'll do whatever I damn well please. You can't push me around.' "

Fateful words, under the circumstances.

Edith Jean nodded, as if reading my thoughts. "And then that's exactly what Nina Gold did. She reached out with both hands and gave Sister a big old shove. I heard her head hit the planter as she fell. I knew right away something terrible had happened. That woman lit out of there like she had the devil on her tail. I started to go after her but I'm not as fast as I used to be. By the time I reached the corner, she'd left me behind.

"I went back to Sister, but by then people had begun to gather around. I stayed in the shadows, but I could hear what they were saying. Maybe it was wrong of me, but I just didn't want to talk to anybody right then. Maybe I was in shock. I went inside to think about what I wanted to do next."

"You talked to the police later," I said. "Why didn't you tell them what you'd seen?"

"So they could do what? Haul me down to their police station and ask more questions? Make me miss the show when I wanted to be here with Bubba? Do you honestly think they were going to arrest Christian Gold's wife on my say-so? And then what would happen? He'd go and hire some high-priced lawyer who would make me look like an idiot. How would any of that bring Sister back?"

"It wouldn't, but . . ."

Edith Jean planted her hands on her hips. She waited to hear my objections. To tell the truth, given the way she felt, I was having trouble mustering any.

"Everything's changed now, though," I said. "When Damien wakes up, the detectives will come and get you. You'll have to talk to them."

"I'll tell them I didn't have any choice," Edith Jean snapped. "That's what happened. Damien Bradley thought I was stupid, but it turned out I wasn't half as stupid as he was."

I thought about that, trying to fit the pieces together, seeing if I could make things work. "Did Damien set up a meeting with you? Is that why the two of you were out in the parking lot?"

"Meeting out there wasn't his idea. It was mine." Edith Jean sounded almost proud. "First I was going to do it while you were scattering Sister's ashes. I thought that would add a fitting touch of irony. Not to mention a nice distraction." She shot me an annoyed glance. "But then you refused to cooperate. How hard would it have been, really? Just for once it would have been nice if *somebody* could have helped me along."

Thank goodness that somebody hadn't been me, I thought. I'd been saved from unwittingly abetting an attempted murder by my own cowardice.

Edith Jean poked me in the chest with her finger. "As if it wasn't bad enough that you forced me to change my plans, then you ended up smack-dab in the middle of them. If you hadn't happened outside when you did, Damien wouldn't have been found until later and nobody would have been the wiser."

Like that would have been a *good* thing. Was it just me, I wondered, or was this conversation beginning to take on a surreal cast?

Behind us, the crowd at ringside erupted suddenly in a loud, sustained burst of applause. This wasn't the partisan clapping we'd been hearing all along, various factions signaling their support for one dog or another. This was a wild and joyous acknowledgment on the part of the spectators, indicating that the quality of the class they'd just witnessed was superb, the best that Poodledom had to offer.

That could only mean one thing. The Best of Variety judging was just about to end. Sam had finished showing Tar and I'd managed to miss almost every minute of it. I didn't even know how he'd done.

"Don't go anywhere," I said to Edith Jean. "I'll be back." I left her and sprinted to the ring. With luck, I'd catch the last go-round as Mr. Lamb pointed to his winners.

Luck wasn't with me. By the time I was able to push my way through the throngs, the spectacle was already over. A cream-colored dog with a handler from California was standing next to the Best of Variety marker. A black bitch from Texas was Best Opposite.

Sam and Tar were still in the ring, though. He and four other handlers were grouped behind the first two. Their

Standard Poodles had been chosen to receive Awards of Merit, meaning that the judge felt that their quality was nearly as high as that of his winners. The designation was both an honor and a distinction.

Sam looked delighted. Tar was cavorting at the end of his lead. Aunt Peg, when my gaze slid finally to her usual seat in the corner, looked ready to spit nails. Uh-oh.

There was no time to do anything about that now, however. The way my day was shaping up, dealing with Aunt Peg's mood was slipping lower and lower on my list of priorities. I saw Nancy Hanlon back at ringside. Presumably that meant the ambulance had come and gone and things were returning to normal.

If you didn't count the fact that Damien had nearly died and that a murderer and an attempted murderer were both running loose on the grounds. And as if that wasn't enough to worry about, once pictures had been taken it would be time to hold the drawing for the raffle.

One thing you had to say for PCA, there was never a dull moment.

I wondered if the police had been called to the arena to investigate Damien's accident. Were they there now? In these dense crowds could I possibly locate them and tell them what I knew before I had to go in the ring and pull tickets out of a barrel?

Stay tuned, I thought, and we'd all find out.

28

All week long there'd been police roaming around, both at the hotel and at the arena. Now when I needed one, I didn't see any. It figured.

Maybe they were outside, I thought hopefully. Drawing chalk outlines in the parking lot. Or doing whatever else it was they did at times like these. Surely an emergency call for an ambulance should have brought some sort of police response.

I was heading toward a side door to find out when somebody grabbed me from behind. I smelled Chanel No. 5. A long fingernail grazed my arm. "Let's go," said a terse voice.

Nina Gold. Assuming my compliance, she grasped my elbow and spun me around so that we were going the other way. Unless I missed my guess, I was heading once again to the relative privacy of the tunnels. I had to be the only exhibitor at the show for whom all the important stuff was taking place out of sight of the rings.

I should point out that it would have been easy enough to resist Nina's invitation. We were surrounded by people after all, many of whom I knew. All I needed to do was plant my feet and say no.

But now that I knew what she'd done, I was curious. I wanted to hear what Nina would have to say. And in the general scheme of things, whether I took my information to the police now or ten minutes from now wouldn't make much of a difference.

"All right," she said, stopping abruptly once we'd left the rings behind. "Tell me what it will take."

I stared at her blankly.

Nina looked impatient. She patted the slim purse that hung at her side. "How much?"

"How much what?"

"Let's not be coy, all right? I've got eyes, I've got ears, and I don't give a flying fig for Poodles. So while everyone here has been so infernally wrapped up in the show that they can't even begin to *think* of anything else, I've been paying attention to real life. I've been watching people."

"Me?"

"Among others. Don't bother being flattered. It's just something to do when Christian gets so busy talking about bloodlines and genetic anomalies that he doesn't even re- member that I exist."

"Is that why you got together with Dale? Because your husband wasn't paying enough attention to you?"

"I'm admitting nothing about that." Nina's eyes nar- rowed. "However, woman to woman, need you even ask?"

Well, no. Not really.

"I overheard what you and Edith Jean were talking about," Nina said. "Let's just say I was pretty surprised to find out that I was the topic of conversation. It's amazing the things one stumbles over on the way to the ladies' room."

Not in my experience, I thought. Not at this show.

"Edith Jean won't be a problem for me. I'll handle her little dilemma with Damien. By the time I'm done, he'll be happy to say that he threw himself in front of her van. That just leaves you. So I repeat, what's it going to take?"

"You must be kidding," I said.

"I'm not."

"You actually think I would agree to cover up a murder for *money*?"

"It wasn't murder," Nina said tersely.

"Betty Jean Boone is dead. What would you call it?"

"An unfortunate accident. All I did was give the woman a little push. Then she slipped and fell and hit her head. I had nothing to do with that."

"Why did you run away, then? Why didn't you try to help her?"

"I panicked. Anybody would have done the same. When I left I didn't even know how badly she was hurt. I thought she was unconscious; I knew someone would find her any second. What I didn't want . . . what I *couldn't have*, was for someone to see me there—"

"Standing over the body?"

Nina grimaced and lowered her voice. The words hissed out. "I couldn't be seen standing outside Dale's room. I wasn't supposed to be there, okay? I wasn't even supposed to be at the hotel. I'd told Christian that I was having dinner with an old friend from college who lived in the area.

"I knew my husband wouldn't be interested in something like *that*, not with this whole Poodle extravaganza going on. I never meant to end up in Dale's room. It just kind of . . . happened. You know what that's like."

If I thought I didn't, the fact that we were currently standing in an alcove would be a pretty potent reminder.

"Once I started thinking clearly again, I realized I had to get out of there without being seen. You have to understand." Nina's lower lip began to quiver. She caught it between the edges of her teeth. "Christian would kill me if he found out."

The damsel in distress act was a good one. I had no doubt that countless men had fallen for it. Women aren't so easily taken in.

"So to prevent that from happening, you killed Betty Jean Boone," I said. Just to make sure she knew I hadn't lost sight of the point of the conversation.

"I told you I never meant for that to happen. I looked around before slipping out of Dale's room; nobody seemed to be paying any attention to me. Then I ran into Betty Jean. Next thing I knew the woman was lecturing me about my behavior. As if she thought I gave a damn for her opinion. I didn't care what she had to say. I certainly didn't have time to listen. And I sure as hell didn't want to stand there arguing about it."

Talking and arguing had been two of Betty Jean's favorite things, I thought. She probably hadn't understood Nina's impatience at all.

"You have to believe me," Nina said. "I wasn't trying to hurt Betty Jean. I was just trying to shut her up."

The funny thing was, having spent the week with Edith Jean, I *could* believe that. It wasn't even a stretch. But unfortunately, there'd been nothing funny about what had happened next.

"Because Christian would kill you if Betty Jean told what she knew," I said. I didn't bother keeping the skepticism from my voice.

Nina's lips pursed in annoyance. I wasn't following her script. "All right, maybe I was being a little melodramatic. But that doesn't mean Christian wouldn't have gone ballistic. He'd have divorced me in a minute, and he had something put in our prenup called a "bad boy clause." If Christian had proof of adultery, I'd be left with nothing."

I guess I was supposed to be feeling sympathy. It wasn't happening. Somehow, being left with nothing did not, to me, constitute a valid reason for committing murder. Even accidental murder.

Nina's eyes searched my face. She frowned at what she saw. "You're going to tell the police, aren't you?"

"Yes."

"I have money," she said. "Lots of it. More than enough to make it worth your while not to."

I wondered—briefly—if there was such a sum. All week long, a surprising number of people had turned out to have a price. Did I have one, too?

Slowly, I shook my head. "It wouldn't be right."

Nina hadn't had time to argue with Betty Jean, but she was determined to argue with me. "What *is* right?" she demanded. "I'm not afraid of the police investigation. They'll find out what happened was an accident, just like I told you. But as soon as they start asking questions, my marriage will be over. Is that what you want?"

How much of a marriage could she and Christian have, I wondered, if Nina had been fooling around with Dale? "You made your choice," I said.

"No, I didn't. That's what I'm trying to tell you. I didn't choose anything about this. One minute, I was happy. Free as a bird. The next, some old lady was butting in where she didn't belong. *She* was the one who set the events that followed in motion, not me. Damn those nosy twins anyway."

The sisters hadn't been twins but I didn't bother to correct her. Instead I turned to go.

"Funny thing about that," Nina said. "I could have sworn I was arguing with Edith Jean that night. So how could I be in trouble for killing someone when she's still so clearly alive?"

And just like that, my focus shifted. I thought I'd uncovered everyone's lies, but I hadn't. Not quite yet. All at once I knew the real reason why Edith Jean hadn't turned in her sister's killer. I knew what Damien knew, the information Edith Jean had wanted so desperately to keep quiet.

Looking pale and troubled, Nina let me walk away. "You do what you have to do," she said.

Just watch me, I thought.

* * *

You would think at that point I'd have gone running straight to the police. Believe me, I'd have been happy to. I wanted nothing more than to locate Detective Mandahar and lay this whole sorry mess in his lap.

However, I was due in the ring to draw forty-two raffle tickets out of a big rubber tub. Forgot all about that, didn't you? I might have too, except that an announcement came over the loudspeaker, calling me to the gate.

Amazingly, I seemed to recall there'd been a time when I'd thought that taking a vacation without my seven-year-old son would prove to be relaxing. I'd anticipated having hours of leisure time to do exactly as I pleased. Yeah, right. If this week had contained one relaxing moment, I would like to have known when it was.

On my way to the ring, I ran into Aunt Peg. Actually it wasn't much of a coincidence. I got the impression she'd been looking for me.

"You missed the whole thing!" she cried. "How you could spend an entire week at PCA and still manage to miss the Standard Best of Variety judging is beyond me. What could you possibly have been doing that was more important than that?"

"Talking to Betty Jean's murderer," I said. The effect was somewhat spoiled by the fact that I was out of breath and didn't have time to slacken my pace.

"What?" Aunt Peg stopped in shock.

I kept right on walking and left her behind.

A moment later, Aunt Peg caught up again. That was the beauty of her long legs versus my shorter ones.

"I'm due in the ring," I said. We were almost at the gate.

"So I heard. So everybody heard. Do you actually know who killed Betty Jean?"

I leaned over and whispered the answer in her ear.

"You can't be serious. Why on earth would she have done something like that?"

"It's a long story. But it's true. Edith Jean saw the whole thing."

Aunt Peg was looking more astonished by the moment. I could totally empathize.

"Do the police know?" she asked.

"I don't think so."

"You have to tell them!"

As if that hadn't occurred to me.

"I'm planning to." The announcer was standing in the ring, thanking the raffle donors, holding up the barrel, and asking me to join him. "Just as soon as I get a free minute."

Trust Aunt Peg to take matters into her own hands. While I spent the next half hour drawing ticket stubs, listening to winners shriek with delight, and watching as they selected their prizes from the bounty on the table, Aunt Peg managed to locate Detective Mandahar and tell him enough of what he needed to know.

One minute Edith Jean was overseeing the prize selection at the raffle table. The next time I glanced over, the Boone sister had disappeared and Peg had taken her place. Fleetingly I wondered if Edith Jean had made a run for it. I needn't have worried; Aunt Peg, as always, had everything under control.

I drew the last ticket, heard the winner's name announced, and left the ring with relief. Sam met me at the gate. He looked worried.

"The police just took away Nina, Christian, and Edith Jean," he said. "Do you know anything about that?"

"Too much," I replied. I was just glad it was over.

Sam looped an arm around my shoulders. Still sore from earlier, I flinched at his touch. In the hours since I'd landed on top of the Mercedes, my body had probably bloomed with bruises.

His gaze narrowed even as he gently gathered me to his

side. "I heard there was some kind of car accident outside earlier. Anything you want to tell me about that?"

I thought for a minute, then shook my head. There'd be plenty of time for explanations later. Meanwhile, the day's three Best of Variety winners had just been called into the ring. There was only one PCA, and one chance to watch Best in Show. After all I'd missed earlier, I wasn't about to pass it up.

Three gorgeous Poodles, one Toy, one Mini, and one Standard paraded before the judge. I turned in Sam's arms and faced the ring. Even then, he didn't release me. My back braced against his chest. His chin brushed my hair. His arms cradled mine as he lifted his hands to clap. All around us, others did the same thing. Applause swelled and rose, filling the building with sound.

It was perfect. There was nowhere else I'd have rather been.

29

The Standard Poodle from California took Best of Breed.
Just in case you were wondering. Bubba won Best Puppy
in Show. I was surprised to see Edith Jean standing ringside when it happened. I left Sam and went to talk to her.

"You're back," I said.

"I never went anywhere." She moved over to make
room for me on the rail. Now that the show was mostly
over, the crowds were thinning fast. "You don't think I'd
have missed this, do you?"

"I thought you left with the police."

"No, Nina and Christian left with them. I just went outside and talked to the detective. He wanted me to go down
to the station and make out a statement. Of course I explained that I couldn't leave *now*. Best in Show was about
to happen."

Dog people. Aunt Peg would have done exactly the
same thing.

"I'm sure he was impressed," I said dryly.

"You got that right. He seemed to think he could bully
me into doing what he wanted. I asked him if I was under
arrest. He said no and I came back inside."

Steel magnolia, nothing. This southern woman was a
steel howitzer.

When Damien woke up, the police would be back. Then

Edith Jean wouldn't be a witness, she'd be a suspect. In the meantime, there was one last thing I needed to finish.

"I know," I said quietly.

"Know what?"

"About what happened to Edith Jean."

"I'm—" She stopped and looked at me for a long minute. "Oh."

"You didn't burn your hand, did you?"

"Not exactly."

"Edith Jean was right-handed. You're left-handed. I kept wondering how you managed to cope so well."

"Maybe I'm ambidextrous," she said brightly.

"You might be, but that won't make you Edith Jean. You had the locket all the time, didn't you? You never took it off your sister. It was always yours."

She lifted a hand to her throat. Her fingers toyed with the golden charm. "You must think you're pretty smart."

"No." I sighed. It occurred to me that I'd been half hoping for a denial. Now I knew I wasn't going to get one. "Actually, I must have been pretty slow to take this long to get it. That was why you went inside the hotel after your sister got hurt, why you didn't tell the police what you saw that night. Because you were afraid they'd discover the truth, that Betty Jean Boone was alive and well. And Edith Jean was the one lying dead outside."

I thought back, picturing the body I'd seen lying in the shadows. She'd been wearing the grooming smock and I'd assumed it was Betty Jean. Had I been the first to identify her? I wasn't sure.

Even so, the mistake would have been easy enough to fix. Betty Jean, by her own admission, had been there and hadn't corrected me. Instead she'd walked away and let the lie continue. Now I wanted to know why.

"I saw the two of you earlier in the grooming room," I said. "I could have sworn you were the one wearing the smock."

"I was. I'd put it on so I wouldn't mess up my clothes while we worked on Bubba. But later when we went outside, Sister was cold. You remember that night, it was chilly. Sister wanted to go inside and I told her to go ahead. I was busy scooping and I said I'd be along in a bit. But you know how Sister was, she could argue the hide right off a bear. Finally she said, 'If you're so warm, give me the damn smock.' So I did. I didn't think another thing about it until I heard that scream, saw her on the ground, and heard you say she was me."

So it *had* been my fault. That was hardly comforting news.

"Damien Bradley knew you both from way back," I said. "He used to show your Poodles for you. That was why he wanted you to pay. He could tell the two of you apart."

Betty Jean nodded briefly, acknowledging that I was right. It wasn't enough. I still wanted more answers.

"All week long I thought I was getting to know Edith Jean," I said. "Now it turns out I was wrong. Tell me about your sister."

"She was a good woman." Her voice caught for a moment. She cleared her throat and said softly, "One of the best."

"The two of you spent a lot of time arguing," I said. I wanted to understand what would make one sister walk away from the other's murder. In my experience, that wasn't something good women did.

"That was just our way. It didn't mean a thing."

"And yet you were willing to let her killer go free. Why?"

"Edith Jean was married when we were younger."

"Earl," I said. Just checking in case she'd been lying about that too.

Betty Jean looked surprised that I'd remembered the name. "I guess you were paying attention."

I always did, I thought. Which was how I kept ending up in conversations like this one.

"Earl had himself some money stashed away," she said. "It wasn't a huge amount but it was enough. When he died, Edith Jean inherited it. That's what's kept us going all these years. That and the fact that Edith Jean was tight as a tick with every penny she ever had."

"You resented the fact that she had money and you didn't."

Betty Jean's head snapped up. "I resented the fact that she had Earl and I didn't."

Oh.

"I saw him first, I was the one who brought him home. But Sister was the one he married."

"That must have been hard. Both of you being in love with the same man."

"Not for Earl," said Betty Jean. "That man had stamina like a bull."

Okay, now we were getting into the area of *more than I needed to know.*

"And then he died," I said. I hoped she'd been telling the truth about the tractor accident. I really didn't want to hear that he'd died of a heart attack in bed.

"Yup. And suddenly Sister was the one who held the purse strings. She was in control and she never let me forget it. That wasn't right. I was the older one; she should have had to listen to me."

Even after death, it seemed that the Boone sisters' bickering was destined to continue. "If you wanted your own money, why didn't you get a job?" I asked.

"Now how could I do that, when we had all our babies to take care of?"

"Babies?" I gulped.

"Our Poodles. Our puppies. Sister and I never had any children. The dogs meant everything to us. *They* were our children. I couldn't have left them alone all day to go to work somewhere else."

The problem—as every dog show exibitor knew full well—was that bredding dogs wasn't a money-making venture. Not if you did it right anyway.

"You were Edith Jean's closest relative," I said. "Wouldn't the money have come to you?"

Betty Jean shook her head. "The money Earl left was in a trust. Something he set up before he got married. It would support her—heck, it supported both of us—for as long as she was alive. After that it reverts back to some other member of his family, and the Poodles and I get thrown out on the street. It's not like I had any choice. Edith Jean had to stay alive and I made that happen. That's why I walked away on Monday night. Nina Gold kept my secret and I kept hers."

"Our last night," said Sam. "This week has really flown by."

It was later that evening and we were back at the hotel. Tar's Award of Merit rosette was prominently displayed on the dresser in Sam's room. Both our Poodles were sacked out on the floor. Sam and I had skipped out of the PCA banquet early. Now it was just the two of us.

Finally.

A proper bed, a door with a lock . . . I looked at Sam. He was looscning his tie. *And too damn many clothes on both of us*. We'd have to do something about that.

I lifted a hand over my shoulder, reaching for the zipper at the back of my dress. A knock sounded at the door.

"Don't answer it," I said quickly. "You know it's Aunt Peg. Or Bertie. Or some detective wanting another statement."

I'd told most of what I knew to the police. I'd related the end of the story to Aunt Peg. Then I'd put the whole thing out of my mind.

Damien was awake at the hospital. He wasn't talking

about his accident yet, but he would. When he did, justice of one sort or another would be served. For once, I intended to stay out of it.

Sam chuckled softly, moving past me. "They're all still at the banquet," he said. "I'll get that zipper in a second."

I reached out to stop him as the knock came again. "Room service," said a voice outside the door.

Sam opened up. He handed over a tip and accepted an ice bucket holding a bottle of champagne. The waiter handed him two tall flutes. Sam turned back to me. He pushed the door shut with his foot.

"Better than your meddling relatives?"

"Much better." I exhaled slowly. It seemed like I'd been waiting to do that for a while.

Sam's fingers were cold from the ice when he got to my zipper. I leaned back into him. Wondered if together we'd make steam. I heard the zipper hiss as the dress fell open. Sam nudged it from my shoulders, his hands sliding on bare skin. Maybe we'd just make sparks.

That would do.